MUMMY

MUMMY

DANIEL CURLEY

Houghton Mifflin Company
· B O S T O N ·
1987

Library of Congress Cataloging-in-Publication Data

Curley, Daniel.
Mummy.
I. Title.
PS3553.U65M86   1987   813'.54   86-20021
ISBN 0-395-42507-7

Printed in the United States of America

Q 10 9 8 7 6 5 4 3 2 1

To Audrey

MUMMY

I

MARC WILLIAMS passed through the blighted gate of the cemetery and turned right. Everything was much as he remembered it: a huddle of monuments, a rash of flowers, here and there a wooden cross crudely lettered, a few sunken, unmarked graves half full of rubbish, two or three pits small enough for a child. He stopped when he was almost face to face with the high wall marked off in squares where the dead were filed like letters in a sorting case. A sexton was climbing a rickety ladder with an armful of flowers for one of the top cubbyholes while a woman in black stood beside the ladder watching, her beads idle in her hand.

Williams now began to look seriously for his mother's grave. He remembered standing exactly so, facing the wall across the open grave while a priest said some words in Spanish that was almost as comforting as Latin. He looked farther and farther afield and at last had to admit himself baffled. Perhaps, however, he had forgotten. After all, it had been seven years. Perhaps he had turned left at the gate instead of right.

He began then to cross the cemetery, avoiding pits, stepping over tiny graves, and trying always to walk between the graves if there was any indication at all where he might respectfully set his foot. He passed the large tree he remembered and the monument to a group of men all strangely dead on the same date. The monument might no longer have been a mystery if he had thought to read the inscription, for his Spanish had improved remarkably after seven years in a Mexican prison. He was now assured, fluent, and thoroughly idiomatic. Unfortunately, the idiom was that of the underworld, and he found that he could now speak to Mexicans no more than when he had no Spanish at all. Desk clerks blanched at his first word and told him there were no rooms. At his second word they offered him the bridal suite free of charge. Waiters expected enormous tips but hid their disappointment behind many smiles. Taxi drivers drove him by beelines that would have terrified a bee. It was all very economical but far too tiring, so he quickly learned to pose as a tourist who could safely be lodged in a broom closet and charged any amount that happened to pop into a waiter's or a driver's head. And a tourist was basically what he was—one week as a tourist with a seven-year hiatus as a prisoner.

When at last he confronted the other wall, he began his search again. He was by no means so confident now, especially as he most certainly didn't recognize the two cubbyholes blocked with bricks laid without mortar. Possibly the nameplates had fallen off during his absence, but the bricks looked very old and dusty as if they had been there forever. Again his search was futile.

Now he retired to the gate of the cemetery and surveyed the scene once more. Everything was as it had been before except that the sexton was gone. He had taken down the ladder and propped it among the branches of the tree. Two dark wet streaks ran down the face of the wall where he had placed the flowers in bracket vases and watered them. The woman and her beads were as before. Williams now had no idea where to look for his mother. The cemetery office was closed. A large padlock convinced him that inquiry would be impossible.

It was disgraceful, he thought, to have forgotten his mother's grave. His most pious resolve in prison had been to make this very pilgrimage. He had not decided to amend his life because, as far as he knew, his life needed no amending, but he had felt it was fitting to make this visit, to say farewell to her whom he had planted in a foreign field as casually as he had sent her post cards from his wandering years in Europe, more casually than he had wired for money.

He was standing overcome by guilt and remorse when a man approached him and said one word, perhaps the only English word he knew, but it was the one word to which Williams could respond at the moment: "Mummy." It was obviously a miracle that the man could have read Williams's thoughts, but remorse and despair had paved the way for miracle, and Williams nodded silently.

The man made the gesture that seems to Americans to mean *go away* or *wait here* but in fact means *come ahead* or *follow me.* Surrendering himself to the mystery, Williams followed away from the gate, a few yards down the hill, around a corner into a narrow street, and finally into a plaza surrounded by souvenir shops, all garishly surreal like catchpenny booths at a nightmare fair. Now the man turned and gestured and said once more, "Mummy." He pointed across the plaza and smiled.

As they crossed the plaza, it became clear to Williams that they were approaching some kind of ticket booth. They made their way through a zigzag of pipe lanes, designed to control impatient crowds and prevent indiscriminate death by surging, although at the moment the plaza was deserted. Not even a tour bus was in sight.

At the ticket window, the man stopped and looked at Williams, who automatically pulled out money and presented it to the ticket seller. Williams couldn't think of the polite words needed to deny that he had a camera, so he bought a ticket for a camera as well as for his friend.

When they were inside the door and standing before the first of a long line of glass cases, it was clear that they were in the presence of the famous mummies of Guanajuato, and he at last understood the real nature of this absurd miracle.

The guide began at once to speak rapidly in Spanish, which would, of course, have been totally incomprehensible to the tourist he took Williams to be. As it was, Williams didn't listen anyway. He was too involved in the anguish of his loss and the hilarity of his error. Even so, he was held by the guide's insistence of language — and by a firm hand on his elbow. He couldn't help facing case after case of mummies, dry and leathery, their mouths gaping in a sort of universal howl. Nor could he help noticing sex where it was in any way apparent: shriveled penises, square, hard breasts. Sometimes there was just a wisp of dusty pubic hair. Then he tried to guess from the teeth whether the women were young.

He was not interested in the tallest mummy nor in the smallest mummy, perhaps a fetus, nor the soldier nor the man in dress clothes — not much clothing had survived. But he did feel a sort of sadness before the women with their imperishable nylons hanging grimy about their skinny ankles. If he had been asked in any language he could be expected to respond to, he might have said that he liked best the case in which a group leaning together seemed to be a church choir in full scream.

As they were about to pass out of the museum and into the light of day, the guide smiled and held out his hand. Williams peeled off a hundred-peso note and placed it in the hand. He was thanked but not warmly, so he added another hundred. Now he was warmly thanked with many embellishments concerning the improprieties of his parentage and the iniquities of his nation. The guide appeared now to choose to believe that Williams knew no Spanish whatever, just as previously he had chosen to believe he could understand everything. He smiled and took Williams's hand as he cursed him, but Williams was not particularly impressed. He could have burned the man down to the ground if he had chosen, but he did not choose. An idea had come to him, an idea he would need to go back into the museum to check out.

"Goodbye, goodbye," he said to the guide. "Thank you very much." And he turned and went to take another look at his church choir. He was drawn to it because as a child he had often gone with his mother to choir practice and had sat enchanted during her angelic solos.

He stood once more before the case. Yes, he was right. That did look like his mother. Horrified that he had noticed that shred of hair, he made a small frame of his fingers to check her stomach. He was able to make out a scar from a gall bladder operation, which he had never seen, and a scar from a resection of the bowel, which he had never even heard mentioned, although he had seen the medical report. He closed his fingers and turned his back. He sat on the floor and wept.

Now he remembered the guide's spiel, although he had not listened at the time. Bodies, it seemed, had only five years' tenancy in the grave. If the rent was not renewed at the end of five years, the body was dug up and examined. If a mummy had been formed, it was put on display. If not, the wreckage was burned. Not all graves created mummies. There was some sort of mystery to it. He saw her poor, dear stockings, her vanquished pride.

He sat with his back against the wall and his eyes piously lowered until a tide of tourists began to wash about his feet. Then he fled to his hotel, a luxurious and ancient inn just where the road to Dolores Hidalgo begins its steep climb out of the city. He sat in the courtyard and drank a beer and considered ways and means. Above him in the tree, a colony of boat-tailed grackles shrieked and squawked in their many voices and brought a touch of the jungle into even that sleepy corner.

The obvious thing to do was to go to the museum, demand his mother, and take her home for proper and eternal burial. But there was a difficulty. He couldn't bring himself to go in and give a name to that poor woman in her wretchedness, for she was a woman who had decreed in her will that she was to have a closed-casket service because she could allow no one to stare at her when she couldn't stare back. And there she was, worse than naked, reduced to a hank of hair, a patch of badly cured leather, and the filthy rags of her stockings. The only mercy was that she was nameless.

His mother's lawyer had made her estate available to him on his release, and it was an amazing estate, far beyond his wildest dreams of what might be the fruit of her long and modest life. So there was plenty of money to carry out any scheme if only he could hit on one. He could, for example, pretend to be a private collector and offer to buy that particular mummy at a high price with complete anonymity all around—for him, for the museum officials, and for her. It could work. On the other hand, he could wind up back in jail with the key thrown away this time. At the very least, they could get him for violating his parole. When they let him out of prison, they gave him twenty-four hours to leave the country. They could get him for using a false passport—actually he was using two. He had dropped off the train for the border and doubled back to Guadalajara to a shop his instructors had told him of where anything could be forged at reasonable rates. There would also be such legal niceties as attempting to corrupt public officials, attempting to deprive the Mexican people of a national treasure, and God knows what else piled on top of his old conviction for dope running.

It would do him no good to protest his innocence. It never had when he could speak no Spanish at all, and now with his new fluency in the argot he would only condemn himself as a hardened criminal with each word he spoke. He could now explain himself in his own words, those fatal words. He could explain that he had no idea how the car he was driving at the time turned out to be loaded with cocaine in all its crevices, spare tire and seat cushions, ceiling liner and floor mats, false gas tank and fender wells. Even the steering wheel was hollow, and the head of the tutelary Saint Christopher unscrewed. He had simply come down to bury his mother and had then begun to drive her car back home. The customs officials told him they had stopped him only because he was the most innocent-looking tourist they had ever seen, exactly the one they themselves would have chosen to run a cargo of dope across the border.

Williams guessed that someone had loaded the cocaine into his mother's chaste old Buick while it was in the garage waiting for him to pick it up and drive it north. What he did not guess was that Someone had enemies and that there had been an anonymous tip to the police. Not that any of it mattered. There went seven years of his life down the drain. But he would start fresh now with the aid of his mother's amazing fortune, the gradual accumulation from her little shop of Mexican art and artifacts. She must have bought very shrewdly on her frequent trips to scour the Mexican markets. But first . . .

And here he bogged down. His filial duty was more or less clear, although he still had no idea how he was to carry out the details of the rituals for which he longed. But given the irregularities of his position, there seemed no possibility of an open and direct approach to the officials in charge. He thought of setting fire to the museum and escaping in the confusion with his mother on his back, for all the world like the pious Aeneas. But he walked around the building and surveyed its blank stone façade, and he saw that there was nothing to burn. He himself refused to subject his mother to the further indignity of another visit, and he squirmed with anguish as he saw the tour buses disgorging their multitudes, cameras flashing, and as he saw the holiday hordes of Mexicans swarming up the hill to stand patiently in long lines, eating ices, while they waited for their great holiday treat. Clearly he would have to do something and at once.

He saw now that stealing his mother was all very well — if he could accomplish even that — but what was he going to do with her then? There was still the problem of getting her from Guanajuato, Guanajuato, to Alpha, Illinois. Transport, top priority, he thought, and felt that he had at last made a start on a plan. For days he wandered the city and in his imagination fit his mother into all sorts of crates and barrels and sent her home by air, by sea, by bus, and even by parcel post. It was really through this vision that he first discovered how deeply he was already committed to taking her back to Alpha for decent burial in the bosom of her family, in the heart of her country. For a moment he wondered if this might be poetry but wisely decided against it. Somehow, though, he had no confidence in these schemes. He circled the museum by day as much as he dared, prowled the streets of the city, and in the evening sat in his courtyard and listened to the cursing of the grackles.

"Transport?" he said to the grackles, but they were not interested in his problems, having to get ready for the night and the raids of owls drifting down from the mountain. Transport? he said to himself and got a reply scarcely better. With his margarita in hand, he strolled across the courtyard to inspect the ancient ox cart in the corner. Ancient? He had seen carts like it still in use deep in the country. He could load his mother in that and go along home. He checked the great wooden wheels and the plank bed of the cart. He shook the uprights and rattled the horizontal bars. Sound. All sound. He could see himself standing in this very cart and being taken back to prison, his head bare and proud. It is a far, far finer thing, etc. He could throw in a load of hay on top of her. Or oranges. Then he'd have something to eat on the way. Hay and oranges. Then the oxen could eat too. One mile an hour, eight hours a day for two thousand miles—make it easy on himself. Make it easier, say ten hours a day. Ten miles a day. Two hundred days. Not even a year. He was amazed. He despaired.

On his way back to his table, he consulted the misshapen stone saint at the angle of the wall. The saint was clearly up for anything—that's why he was a saint. His large head would hold any plan and know nothing of amazement or despair. His large feet would take his child's body anywhere the plan required. Two thousand miles was no more to him than to a jet. Williams was humbled but he knew he was no saint and he refused to regret it.

Now he was making progress. He had got as far as transport. He was going to need a car, a large car, a very large car. He looked at the largest cars he could find but no car was large enough, so he had to consider crossing the border—to say nothing of a large part of Mexico—with a coffin strapped to the top of the car. His mother's modesty seemed to demand at least a coffin. Mexico posed no problem, he thought. Almost anything can be explained in Mexico. But when he imagined himself being scrutinized by the first pair of cold blue eyes at the border, his courage failed him.

He could dress her, of course, in an old-lady dress, old-lady high laced boots, and say she was his grandmother, 150 years old, and sound asleep. A passport proving all this would be no more problem than his own had been. He had learned much in prison besides filthy Spanish.

Once he thought he had solved his problem when he saw a Rolls Royce station wagon parked near the butcher shops in the market. A Rolls Royce station wagon? he said to himself, and he wandered around it accompanied by small boys, the guardians of the car, armed with fierce sticks and lethal stones.

"Beat it, gringo," the smallest boy said.

"Beat your mother," Williams said out of the corner of his mouth. It might have been a mixture of genres but the boys backed off.

"A Rolls Royce station wagon?" Williams said to the owner, the quintessential British squire of some earlier century. He even wore a tweed jacket with a leather patch where the butt of his gun nestled. Perhaps he was a specimen kept on tap for period English movies, like a czarist general in Soviet films.

"Ah, yes," the squire said.

"But why?" Williams said.

"Very practical idea," the squire said. "It's the only car in the world that will hold a whole stag."

"I see," Williams said. "I see. Are they hard to come by?"

"Had to wait three years for this," the squire said. He lavished minimal coins on his retainers and received smiling curses that made even Williams blanch. He drove off like a man who has just bagged yet another stag.

"Psst, señor," someone said. Williams turned and found himself face to face with the head of a pig, enormous, pink, and shaven. Ropes of sausages dangled over it. Piles of feet and tails lay beside it. It was all there, although in somewhat disordered form. "Señor," it said again.

"Me?" Williams said.

"You want to buy a car?" the pig said.

"Why not?" Williams said. He had had no luck so far. Possibly a pig might know something hidden from him.

"Have I got a car for you," the pig said. "Just step into the shop and we'll talk."

Stepping into the shop was easy. There was no practical division between the shop and the street. Everything that wasn't street was shop and everything that wasn't shop was street. He brushed aside a beaded curtain of small sausages and was in the shop almost without changing position. He turned toward the head, expecting it to turn to him for more private talk. However, what he saw was a lean little old man dressed like a member of a mariachi band: tight black pants and jacket highly ornamented with silver and silver braid, and an enormous hat that made him look like a dyspeptic mushroom.

"Señor," he said, "the car is new."

"Is it stolen?" Williams said.

"Señor," the man said. He drew himself up until he seemed about to launch and disappear into the upper reaches of his hat. "Señor, we have all the correct papers."

"Of course," Williams said. He had all the correct papers himself, two sets of them, one in the name of John Doe and one in the name of Richard Roe.

"This car," the man said, "has never been driven. My grandmother won it in a lottery."

"Your grandmother?" Williams said.

"She couldn't even drive it on Sunday because, pobrecita, she lives next to the cathedral."

"What a pity," Williams said. He felt he might have been better off dealing with the pig.

"Sí, qué lástima," the little old man said in English.

"May we look at the car?" Williams said.

"Of course," the man said. "Let me tell you, it is a Buick Electra—"

"A Buick Electra," Williams said as if really impressed, although to tell the truth he didn't know a Buick Electra from a Toyota Orestes.

"To be sure," the man said. "And it's loaded: PS, PB, PW, A/C, AM/FM 8 tr cass, mint cond, 40 mpg—"

"40 mpg?" Williams said.

"Hwy," the man said. "Blk/blk lthr int, mag wheels—"

"Your grandmother is some kind of dude," Williams said. "How much?"

"It has to be seen," the man said. "Come with me." He took Williams's arm and tried to draw him under the shadow of his hat.

"Tomorrow," Williams said. "I'll look at it tomorrow. How about noon?"

"Eleven o'clock?" the man said.

"Here?" Williams said. He had an idea that a man who would be at the same place on consecutive days might be more legitimate.

"Here at eleven o'clock," the man said.

Williams went back to his hotel and took another look at the ox cart. Two hundred days with the ox cart might in the long run be quicker than trying to cross the border with a stolen car. He consulted the stunted saint, and he consulted hummingbirds busy at the great wave of bougainvillea cresting over the wall. There were three different kinds of hummingbirds — and none was the ruby-throated kind he had always thought unique — but the consensus was that if he didn't like the man's papers he could always refer to his own forger, a thoroughly reliable man endorsed by the best convicts, who, whatever their mistakes, never got caught because of inferior documents.

On the way up to his room so he could come down properly to dinner, he stopped on the stairs to elicit an opinion from the bronze figure on guard there. This was a knight in armor, taller than life and thinner than life, a figure complete with lance and shield. "Don Q, Don Q, what shall I do?" he said in his most poetic vein. The Don looked calmly at whatever the future had in store for Williams. He was at this moment being the man of ultimate wisdom rather than the man of ultimate folly. "I see," Williams said, "I see. Take it as it comes, eh? Roll with the punches. Nil admirari and all that. I thank you, Don Quixote." So he turned and went down without ever having properly gone up.

At eleven o'clock the next morning, Williams stepped into the butcher shop. The little old man was not to be seen. There was one customer and the butcher, who was whaling away with a heavy cleaver at his block. *Thwack*, and the whole shop shook. The festoons of sausages swayed overhead. The ears of the pig trembled. The floor cringed. "Señor," the customer said in the voice of the old man. "Señor, you are punctual." *Thwack.* Williams looked at him. He was twice the size of the old man and half the age. *Thwack.* He was wearing a T-shirt from South Dakota State University, black pants like a waiter's, and truck-tire sandals. *Thwack.*

"And so are you," Williams said. *Thwack.*

"Shall we go?" the man said, now in the voice of the man whose clothes he was wearing. *Thwack.* He led off and Williams followed. Don Q be with me, he said to himself.

They went through the market. Williams was hard put not to get lost in the crush. Everywhere sellers were selling, buyers were buying, weavers were weaving, cooks were cooking, sweepers were sweeping, as if there would never be another market in all the history of the world. Sellers clutched at his arm. Sellers called down to him from seats at the high end of their long sloping bins, "Hey, señor, you want oranges, avocados, bananas, shoes, pots, embroidery, leather, tomatoes? You want a nice dress for the lady? You got no lady? Wear it yourself. You'll be so pretty. You want a wrist watch, alarm clock, machete, nice melon?" Williams smiled at all of them and pretended not to understand. It was better for everyone that way. "How about papayas, pineapples, guavas? Dried herbs? Crucifix, Madonna, Sacred Heart, ham sandwich? Wicker and straw and woven grasses? Tin hands and feet to your favorite saint. Ex-votos for sale. Breasts and bellies, nose, ear, what ails you? Rugs, masks, genuine reproductions of Mayan flutes? Buy, señor, buy. You want roses?"

As he passed among the beggars outside the market, Williams scattered alms from the pocket he kept filled with the appropriate coins, five- and ten-peso pieces. He surfed into the open on a swell of blessings. Still the man did not look back. Fortunately, the big 77 on his T-shirt distinguished him from the Dallas quarterbacks, who were 12, and the Los Angeles pitchers, who were 34. He led the way through alleys and side streets and arrived at last, not at the cathedral as promised, but at another church Williams could have reached by himself in half the time. And there in an alley beside the church they found the car.

It was in a shed originally intended, perhaps, for burros. At least there were still mangers built against the wall of the church. The shed was dim, but Williams displayed his expertise as a buyer by reading the word *Buick* and the word *Electra* on the body. He kicked the tires for good measure.

"Hey, cut that out. Jesus, Joseph, and Mary, what do you think you're doing?" The voice was shrill and truly pained and seemed to come from the car itself. Perhaps this was one of the new computerized cars that can talk to you and tell you what ails them.

"It's all right, abuela," the man said. "This gentleman wants to buy your car, so naturally he has to kick the tires."

Williams looked into the car and saw the future, something like the opposite of déjà vu. There was an old lady sitting in the middle of the back seat just as he imagined his mother would sit, wizened, dusty, and motionless, although his mother would certainly never again tell him to cut out whatever he was doing.

"And he'll have to open and close the doors to see if they squeak and try out the horn and the lights." Williams resolved to look under the hood as well to make sure there was an engine.

"Oh, to be sure," Williams said, "the horn at the very least."

"Now," the man said, "I must bring the papers." And he filtered through the dusty light and vanished, leaving Williams alone with the car and its indwelling spirit.

"With permission," Williams said. The old woman gave an idol's nod. He opened the driver's door. It was profoundly squeakless, but the car reeked of incense and candles. He thought he could even smell stagnant holy water. The front seat was more a shrine than a seat. A red light burned before an icon that looked like Quetzalcoatl Vanquishing the Powers of Darkness. A spray of palm draped over the icon, and a sunburst of straw lurked behind it like a monstrance.

He turned on the lights and walked around the car. All in order, front, rear, and sides, with the side lights green to starboard and red to port. He touched the horn and ran for cover — it had been programmed to blare the opening of the Notre Dame fight song.

When it seemed safe, he continued his inspection. He reached in and popped the hood. The old woman was upon him before he got around to the front of the car. She slashed at him with her rosary and ran to the wall of the church. She pounded on the wall. "Señor, señor," she shouted. "Send angels with flaming swords. He's wrecking my car all to pieces. Help me, señor." Williams put his hand to his cheek and it came away bloody. He was glad he didn't have to get this little old lady all the way to Alpha, Illinois.

With the hood open, he found the engine. He even found the dipstick. He pulled it out. "Señor," the old woman shrieked. "Señor, for the love of God, help me before there is nothing left." Williams checked his escape routes. The old woman pounded on the wall, and the dust of ages rose slowly in the sun-streaked air. Williams touched his finger to the dipstick as he had seen a man do in a movie. He rubbed the oil between his thumb and forefinger and looked wise. He smelled his finger. Oil beyond a doubt.

"Betrayer," the old woman screamed at the wall. "Always betrayer. Always for the man. Blessed Mother," she said softly, "help a defenseless woman."

Williams looked over his shoulder, but retribution did not appear to be forthcoming. He found the trunk lock and opened the trunk. Everything seemed to be in order.

"Monster," the old woman shouted as she abandoned all hope of succor and took matters into her own hands. She

tottered toward him, rosary whirring and knitting needle poised
for the coup de grâce. He easily kept the car between them.
She easily kept herself between him and the door. He wondered if a sharp rap on the church wall would get him anywhere and how strong male bonding really was.

This might have gone on until one of them dropped — and
Williams had an idea who it would be. He saw himself on the
ground trying to fend off with his last strength the inevitable
descent of the abhorred knitting needle. There seemed no
other end to it, but finally the little old man with the big hat
appeared with the papers in his hand. "Abuela," he said quietly. The old woman stopped on a centavo. The rosary coiled
gently around her wrist. The needle lay down like a fang.
"He's ruining the car," she said. "By all the saints . . ." She
began to name them.

"He must inspect the car," the old man said. "Proceed,
señor, proceed. I see you know what you are about." He gestured toward the open hood, the trunk. "I heard the horn
myself. Very pretty. Your national anthem, perhaps."

"Thank you," Williams said. Now he began his serious
inspection in his own area of expertise. He lay under the car
and inspected the fender wells. He had the old man drain the
gas tank and refill it to its rated capacity. So far no snares and
no delusions. He probed the seat cushions and the ceiling
liner with the second fang, which he found on the back seat.
The old woman screamed as if her own bowels were being
pierced, but he was merciless. They were not going to catch
him twice the same way. The steering wheel seemed solid,
and there was no Saint Christopher, although God knows he
was going to need one — of his own choice — perhaps a Saint
Jude as well.

Then, profiting by his hard-earned instruction, he dropped
the tire wrench onto the cobblestones. The old woman groaned
and fell to her knees. "Señor," the man said, "is this truly
necessary?"

"In the United States," Williams said, dropping the jack handle, "this is known as state-of-the-art inspection."

"Truly?" the old man said.

The old woman was whipping her beads through her fingers and mumbling a litany that had got as far as impotent saints abandoned by the church and powerful gods never recognized.

"Truly," Williams said. He dropped the jack and listened complacently to its good steel clang. He knew all about tools cast in gold and silver—platinum even, embedded diamonds—and he wanted none of that. He stepped back for the total effect. The car was a sober black so much like a gangster's car that no one could suspect the driver of having designs. "How much?" he said.

The old man named a price that staggered Williams until he translated it into dollars. In dollars, it was probably not much more than the price paid by the Notre Dame alumnus who first bought it. Williams got it for something less than the asking price, being given a trade discount because of his command of the argot.

Having secured his car, he felt he had made progress, but he also knew he had gone nowhere. He circled the museum as before and prowled the city, considering ways and inventing means. The prevision of his mother enthroned in the back seat proved at once to be fraudulent: she could never be bent into a sejant posture. He crawled into the trunk and found that even a little old lady would never be able to stretch out at her ease. Besides, he had been taught that it was a bad idea under any circumstances to be found with a body in your trunk.

Jumping all the way from concealment to display—the old "Purloined Letter" trick—he envisioned his mother as a hood ornament, a figurehead. But he didn't want to spend his life looking at and around her, a constant reproach and a judgment. He thought briefly of mounting her on the roof, but good Lord, the police would have him at the first stop light once the mummy was reported missing. He might disguise the car as an elephant and put her in a howdah on top. To what end? He could say he was advertising some such movie as *A Passage to India*. She could play Mrs. Moore. However, he suspected that howdahs would be hard to come by in Guanajuato, although an elephant's head had been reported seen at the roadside out in the country somewhere. Of course, one might at need substitute a balloon basket for a howdah, but balloons were scarce too. One night he thought he saw a vast, brilliant balloon blotting out much of the sky, but it was only a paper balloon with a candle in it, sailing past his window.

Then one day as he happened to be straggling through a narrow cobblestone street, he was stopped by a sound that awakened ancient memories. It was the sound of a hammer beating on iron. At once he was taken back to his earliest childhood as he stood with his father in the blacksmith's shop. The smith, an ancient, hearty man, hammered the glowing iron and sang as he worked. He plunged the iron hissing into a tub of water. The noise and the steam and his father's strong hand made up almost his only memory involving his father.

Now he turned from the glaring street into the dim cavern of a shop. There was the smith hammering iron on an anvil. There glowed the forge. There stood the tub ready. The smith looked at him crossways and went on hammering, singing an obscene song the while. On a radio, a priest intoned ritual prayers with responses. When the smith looked at him directly, Williams pointed to his own eye and swept an arm around the dusky shop. The smith nodded and remarked to the hissing tub that all gringos are crazy.

It was immediately clear, once Williams's eyes were accustomed to the gloom, that in addition to welding tractor hitches, which seemed to be the work in hand, the smith did a business in ornamental ironwork. There were tables and chairs and grilles hanging from all the walls and stacked to the ceiling in all the corners but one. In that one corner stood

a crude suit of armor to which Williams immediately responded.

He examined the armor. The breastplate was etched with
the design of a head, perhaps a classical allusion he didn't
catch, although it looked to him more like a Smiley Face with
the mouth drawn in upside down and a lot of hair flying about.
Or perhaps it was supposed to be Medusa—unless it was
simply the traditional Moor's head cut off and held up by the
hair for all to see. Over all the armor was burnished bright
and protected by a coat of something like shellac. He walked
in a narrow arc before it, studied it from the left, studied it
from the right. He peeked under its arms and between its legs
and stood on tiptoe to look over its shoulders. He checked
buckles and laces to see how it came apart. He thumped it
thoroughly as if he had really finished the medical degree he
started. He caught the smith's eye and made a lifting gesture
with his hands, the gesture usually reserved for the admiration
of breasts. The smith rolled his eyes as if he expected to learn
some despicable perversion just invented north of the border.

The armor was not as heavy as Williams had expected. He
lifted it easily. It seemed to be made of something not much
heavier than sheet metal, but it was carefully done with proper
joints at elbows and knees and heavy straps and buckles where
the limbs met the trunk. The breastplate, he saw, was hinged
and opened to reveal a neat set of shelves as if for a liquor
cabinet. The headpiece latched front and back, and the visor
swung up like something in a boy's book of knights.

It was clear that his brittle old mother could be fitted into
it without more damage and outrage than she had already
suffered. When he was satisfied, he approached the smith
directly and in full flood of his prison rhetoric. The smith
visibly shifted gears and named a price half of what he had
intended to ask. The deal was quickly settled for half of that,
although Williams was in no mood to haggle and would have
given something near the smith's top price and deprived both

of them of the real pleasure of the occasion. The smith, for his part, was pleased to get anything at all. He would have been willing to give the armor away just to rid his shop of involvement with such an obvious underworld figure. When Williams demurred about the shelves, the smith removed them with a blow of his hammer.

Later, in the courtyard of his inn, Williams encountered a new problem and found a brilliant solution. "Qué pasa, Doc?" the doorman said in the voice of Bugs Bunny. He glanced at the armor.

"I'll use it in my business," Williams said. "I have a liquor store in Salt Lake City, and I'll use it to advertise Don Q rum."

"Of course," the doorman said. "Good luck."

From the window of his room, Williams saw the doorman climbing on the car and inspecting the armor. Williams opened his mouth for a proprietary shout but thought better of it. Let him look, he said to himself. Let them all look. And they all did look. Waiters left their loaded trays on the hood and scaled the car, over the bumpers and up the sides. Gardeners laid their trowels and their secateurs on the roof and went up after them. The night manager brought out a chair at 2 A.M. American tourists left the sign of Adidas on the hood even when Williams was in plain sight at his table under the tree. They clanged open the visor. They screeched open the little door in the chest. They felt into the arms and legs and found exactly what it suited Williams for them to find—nothing. They stared at their hands and went away muttering. And lost interest. Nothing could be better.

And so Williams became a familiar figure in the city, an identified eccentric with a suit of armor flaunted on top of his car. The armor was known to many as Don Q, the car as Rosinante, and Williams himself as Sancho Panza. He was doing good to others and no harm to himself, although he seemed actually no closer to his goal than ever. But finally he recognized the hard fact that only a desperate plan had any hope of success. And his desperate plan was no plan at all. It was simply straight-ahead action, taking things as they came.

Fortunately, while he was in prison he had been well prepared for life on the outside. Overpowering guards, picking locks, and smashing display cases were among the most elementary of his lessons, so when at last he decided to act, he could set out for his evening's work with the uneasy confidence that he was as well prepared as anyone for what he had to do.

He parked his car around the corner, near the cemetery where he had parked his rented car that first day when he tried to find his mother's grave. He prowled out of the narrow cobbled street into the moonlit square. Everything was pale and still and slashed here and there with dense moon shadows. The souvenir shops were all closed down, their rags and shards for once decently hidden. A watchman sat on a stool beside the museum door. Williams and the watchman contemplated each other. They were all there was to look at, not even a dog, not even an ice cream vendor with his little cart. He knew he looked like the rankest of American tourists, wearing an enormous poncho with a business suit and highly polished shoes. For days he had had little to do but have his shoes shined.

Williams lit a cigarette and approached the watchman. "Nice night," he said.

The watchman agreed that it was a nice night.

"Cigarette?" Williams said.

The watchman accepted a cigarette and they smoked together in silence.

"How do you feel about living a long time?" Williams said.

"The idea has always appealed to me," the watchman said and handed over his keys. "Would you mind binding me hand and foot," he said, "and placing a gag in my mouth? It will give a better impression."

"Unfortunately," Williams said, "I did not come prepared for that. I intended to hit you over the head or throttle you."

"What a pity," the watchman said, "but never mind. There is some rope inside. With your permission?" He took back the keys, went inside the museum, and came out with precisely the rope called for.

"I'll be gentle," Williams said.

"But not too gentle," the watchman said. He was clearly a master realist, a man Williams would have been glad to have along with him for facing the unforeseen but certainly all too real future.

When the watchman was adjusted to their mutual satisfaction, Williams entered the museum and counted the cases with the aid of a flashlight. When he got to the proper one, he stopped and, keeping the beam of his flashlight low, identified his mother by her feet. He had come properly equipped with glass-cutting tools and tape for the broken glass, but when he was face to face with the work, he said, "To hell with it," and went out and found a large stone with which to smash the glass without finesse or subtlety. His prison mentors might have demurred — or again they might not. They were always willing to allow a man his feelings, provided the feelings didn't cause him to botch the job in hand. They were, after all, professionals and had their professional standards.

While he was outside getting the stone, he took the gag out of the watchman's mouth and put a cigarette in, promising to replace the gag and clean up generally when he came out again.

"American cigarette butts," the watchman said.

Williams felt foolish, unworthy of his expensive education, but he said, "Of course."

Now he made his way back into the museum and, without reflecting further, smashed the glass in the very face of the large, appalled gentleman singing next to his mother. He worked the glass fragments loose until he had an opening large enough to allow him to operate without damage to himself or to her.

Then he turned off his light and in total darkness wrapped his mother in his poncho before he tried to lift her at all. She was very light, with the surprising lightness of birds. She was also very long and stiff and awkward. He slung her over his shoulder like a rifle or a piece of lumber and went out again into the moonlight. For a moment he leaned her against the wall while he picked up four cigarette butts and adjusted the gag.

"Good luck," the watchman said, "although I can't pretend to understand or approve. I only hope it's nothing too nasty. You must have your reasons, of course."

"Of course," Williams said. He fixed the gag in place. "Tight enough?" he said. The watchman nodded. "Too tight?" Williams said. The watchman shook his head.

The square was as pale as a dream, and he went through it like a dreamer, successful against all probabilities, until he was almost back in the dark and cobbled street. At that point he had to pass very close to the last of the shuttered shops. A dog barked. A little boy rolled out from under the shutter and confronted Williams.

"Mummy?" the boy said.

Williams's heart raced. He felt that the jig was up. The boy would scream with indignation. The dog would bark. The neighborhood would turn out. The police would arrive. And he would go back for a postgraduate degree in criminal techniques with emphasis on evasive action.

"Mummy?" the boy said again and held up a plastic model of a mummy. It looked to Williams as if it might even have been modeled after the very one he had over his shoulder.

"One hundred pesos," the boy said.

Williams shook his head and plodded on. His mother was at last beginning to assume her weight. It would have been so much simpler in the beginning to buy the model if only he had known about it.

"Fifty pesos," the boy said.

"No," Williams said.

"Twenty-five," the boy said.

Williams stopped and fixed the boy with his eye and delivered a "no" of the most spectacular and baroque quality.

The boy dived for the partly lifted shutter. "Five pesos," he called as he rolled out of sight.

And Williams was home free — or at least as free as he could be, speeding through the night with his mother cater-corner in the back seat like a long stick and the Don couchant on the roof.

He drove past his own hotel and up into the mountains, where he effected the merger of mother and Don on a cement table in a picnic area near the crest of the range. His only difficulty was that when he tried to remove her pitiful stockings, her toes tended to drop off, so he gave up and left well enough alone. Then he drove back to his hotel, where he intended to lie low for at least a month.

He was not displeased the next day to find himself described in the press as a fiend, a ghoul, a hardened master criminal, the scum of the worst gutters of a suffering nation — his language had clearly impressed the watchman. He read all the accounts several times and listened complacently to pronouncements by the very federal government itself. A special mass was broadcast for the repose of the poor wandering body, untimely snatched from its rest. All was as it should be. He had had the satisfaction of exploring his basest fantasies without any danger to his moral nature.

The police were baffled but not so the press, although reporters had to be content with fanciful speculations about why anyone would steal a mummy. One erudite journalist supposed that there was a sudden revival of interest among medical men in ancient formulas, one of which involved the use of mummy dust. But the majority created splendid underworld plots in which a woman was buried with a great jewel in her belly, or in which a woman had a treasure map tattooed on her back, revealing the hiding place of the loot of a great holdup and/or of the key to a legendary cache of dope.

Or yet this marvelous woman might have a tooth full of microfilm containing God knows what international secrets. One paper even went so far as to publish halfheartedly a list of notorious criminals recently released from prison. Only a long prison term for the master criminal would account for the delay in searching for the mysterious woman. The list even included a mangled version of Williams's name, but there was no follow-up, although he suffered some days of acute anxiety.

The pièce de résistance of journalism, however, was an interview with a boy who on the night in question had met the Devil, three meters tall, breathing fire, and dressed like a gringo. The Devil talked as if he had come straight from hell—even the dog had been unable to bark—and he staggered under the weight of the True Cross, his eternal burden. The story was treated with mock solemnity, but it was picked up by the international papers and spread around the world.

Williams was astonished—and gratified—to read about himself in *Time* and the *Times* of London. He was also bemused to learn that a cult had begun to spring up on the spot, just there by the last souvenir stand. Mysterious markings appeared on the pavement, daily erased by traffic and daily renewed. Propitiatory offerings were left against the wall in spite of editorials, sermons, and even police surveillance when the matter seemed to be getting serious. Why, there was even a deflection of tourist traffic, a change in the patter of the guides, and a whole new line of infernal figures in the shops, based, of course, on ancient Mayan-Christian models. The boy himself was sent off, at government expense, to school in the United States. "To the land of the Devil," he said as he was taken away. A flood of new offerings appeared, and a funeral mass was said, just in case.

By the end of the week, the story had become so prominent in the consciousness of the world that Williams felt perfectly safe in resuming his own legend. He could, he knew, have appeared naked in public in broad daylight, have robbed banks with impunity, have corrupted a thousand virgins. No one was prepared to recognize anything other than the Devil in his true form, the very Cross itself, and a miraculous mummy.

When he checked out of the hotel and drove off, he was accompanied by the sincere blessings of the staff, and not only because he had tipped them well. He and Don Q and Rosinante had added to their lives an interest they were genuinely sorry to lose. The porter even reached up and rapped the Don on his head for good luck. Nor was the staff alone in wishing Williams well in all his endeavors. The watchman at the museum would remember him in his prayers for many nights to come, not only because Williams had tucked a glorious tip into his jacket pocket as recompense for any inconvenience but also because he had proved himself a man sympathetic to certain interesting ideas about a long life. Naturally the tip was not mentioned to the police or the press, and the very professional nature of the knots and the gag discounted from the outset any theory of an inside job.

As Williams left his inn and prepared to pull into traffic, he had to stop for three burros loaded with firewood—and the driver, a certified Indian with big hat, poncho, sandals, and enormous machete. As the man passed, beating his burros all the way, he tossed a note into Williams's lap. *Don't go north*, it said. *They're watching the road.* Unfortunately, Williams was turned into the northbound pattern and roared off up the hill, made a U-turn around the back of the inn, and came down the southbound lane.

His first reaction when he read the note was absolute terror, but by the time he made his U-turn, he had realized that he was being looked after, that the old-boy network of his late prison was going to see him through. When he had made the circuit of the inn, however, and was back where he started, he had also returned to terror. It occurred to him that there must be some reason all those thieves and murderers had their eyes on him.

II

BECAUSE HE couldn't go north, he went south. He went all the way south as if to get a running start when he did decide to go north again. He nuzzled along the border of Guatemala like a blind kitten groping for the tit. But there was no tit. He wandered into the Yucatán because he had heard of a ferry to Florida that had just been started or was about to start. Everybody knew about the ferry. Oh, *sí, sí.* It was at Campeche. It was at Cancun. It was at Mérida. Everybody knew about the ferry but no one had done anything about starting it. He went up the peninsula through Quintana Roo, and he came back through Campeche and Tabasco, where he thought always of Graham Greene's whiskey priest and his dying perception that the one thing worth doing was to become a saint. Perhaps becoming a saint was indeed the one thing, and perhaps Williams himself might qualify by wandering up and down the land with his mother on his roof—unless he would sooner qualify as the Wandering Jew. The fact that he was neither Catholic nor Jew failed to daunt him. Faith faded to nothing before the enormity of his works.

At night when he slept in the car, he saw the car as an altar tomb with the armored Don recumbent on the top and he himself the decomposing body inside. He thought at such times of finding some local painter—an Indian, of course, some mute, inglorious Rivera—to paint a hopeful image on the ceiling of the car, just where he could begin to make it out as the night faded. A dove perhaps. Or an angel. A rising sun. A small Resurrection. He had seen just the thing in an English country church. The tomb was a sort of three-decker affair with the idealized knight stretched out on top, legs crossed, and below that the tomb itself containing bones or whatever, and below that a memento mori, the decomposed body carefully done in marble. He had got down on his stomach for a better look and had worked his head through one of the low arches that supported the tomb. His left hand with a flashlight went in through another arch. There, face to face with Death, he caught, out of the corner of his eye, a flash of color on the bottom of the tomb. It was a small Resurrection with saints and angels, and God in his glory, placed just over the face of the stone body to be a comfort through the endless centuries of waiting. He did fancy a Resurrection.

In his going to and fro in the land and up and down in it, he touched most of the important archaeological sites and came to believe that every patch of jungle held a city yet undreamed of, that every hill was the outline of some fortress temple of still unknown civilizations. He vowed that if he was ever able to bury his mother properly, he would go back to school for a new degree, in Mexican archaeology. By then, taking into account his travels, his seven years in prison, his mental anguish, he might finally be ready to learn something. His earlier bout with the university had been largely inconclusive. It had probably been good enough for a first education but just barely.

Naturally the Don attracted a certain amount of attention.

"I got him in the Gulf Stream," he would say. "I was after marlin, but this is what I got." He knew that anyone who bothered to ask would rather hear a good lie than the boring truth. "He was hitchhiking near Guadalajara," he would say, "and now I can't get rid of him." He listened hopefully to his own inventions. Perhaps someday he might invent the truth. "We were both staying at an old monastery in Taxco," he would say. "His car had crapped out or maybe his horse had died. Anyway, he had been waiting a long time for someone going his way. I said, 'But I don't know which way I'm going.' 'Neither do I,' he said. 'That's why I chose you.' And being chosen," Williams said, "I had no choice." That at least was very close to the truth. Sainthood or eternal exile could not be very far away.

At one moment in a suburb of Mexico City, he thought he had discovered a solution, a place where he could hole up until it was safe to go home. He was wandering, lost after missing a turn on the Periférico when he saw a watchtower complete with gun slits and a commanding view of the approaches. He drove slowly around the block, admiring the high blank walls of that corner house and locating only with difficulty the large steel gate. He could drive through that gate and be safe forever. The place was a fortress.

There was no indication that the house was for rent, but if necessary he could buy it out from under the present tenant. Money was no problem, thanks to his mother's patient industry. He directed a thankful glance aloft without interrupting his plans. He stopped the car, got out, and approached the gate.

The omens were good. A small sign said in Spanish and English, Ring Bell and Wait. He rang or perhaps he didn't, for the bell was so far away or so small or so broken that no sound came from inside. He waited. Now the omens were not so good. He noticed at last a small ceramic plaque that said in faded script, Museo Leon Trotsky. However, he did not stop planning but incorporated into his plans his own road to Damascus and an instant conversion to Communism. The thing to do was to become curator of the museum or if necessary buy the whole thing from the Trotskyites, who couldn't be a very well endowed group even by the modest standards of lost causes.

He rang again. When he was about to recant his his conversion, a small door opened in the big one, and a young man beckoned him in. The door was barely wide enough for him and was open barely long enough to let him in. The good old customs were clearly being kept up, and Williams expected to be asked at once to produce his already tattered new credentials. But the young man only led him through a conventional patio—in full view of the gun slits—to an entrance to the house where a massive steel door stood open. He explained in perfectly good school English that this was the door and that Williams should enter. Then he teetered between his obligation to induct Williams into the mysteries and his need to unlock the gate for a party just coming out another door of the house. Of course, there might be a tip as well— a contribution to the museum. "Go," he said to Williams. "See," he said. "I come," he said. And he went.

Williams was just as well pleased to be left to his own devices. There was a good deal he was not interested in. He was not interested in Trotsky's desk or his books. He was not interested in his bed or his breakfast. But he was interested in the thickness of the walls: delightfully thick. And in the shutters on the windows, which were serious and stout. And in the doors between the rooms, which were like the doors of submarines, all metal and locks. The place should do very nicely. He hummed a bit of the "Internationale."

"These marks—" the guide said. He had come in silently and was invisible until he spoke. He waited for Williams's attention. He did not look like a man who had been well tipped. "These marks were made by bullets during the first assassination attempt. They fired through the window." Williams nodded thoughtfully and stuck his finger into the holes to measure their depth. The walls were very good indeed.

"And this is where they killed him with the ice ax."

"Ice ax?" Williams said. His university had somehow skipped over the death of Trotsky.

The guide made a sweeping chop in the air. "Ice ax," he said and lightly touched Williams on the left temple. Williams felt the blow on both temples at once and quickly ran his fingers into all the bullet holes for reassurance, but when he turned toward the window, he found he was looking across the garden at the guard tower and the lowering gun slits. Two men were staring at him through the slits.

"Who are they?" he said.

"Oh, people," the guide said evasively. "People like you."

Williams knew he had to be lying, because there were no people like him, no people cursed with a suit of armor and a mother and a car hounded from one end of Mexico to the other. No people traveling with two passports, both forged. No people protected on the one hand by thieves and murderers, and hunted on the other by whatever was worse.

"What are they doing up there?" he said.

"Admiring the view," the guide said, although Williams could plainly see that he himself was the view. Pierced by axes, pinned against bullet holes, he could feel stigmata breaking out all over him. Next they would be running their fingers into holes in him, tracking his blood around the house. No, thank you.

"I think I'd like to leave now," he said.

"This way," the guide said. "Wait for me at the gate while I get the keys." Williams knew this was the guide's way of getting himself out of the line of fire, so as soon as the guide had disappeared, Williams stepped into the bottom of the tower and removed the long rickety ladder that led up to the guard room. And while the men up there were kneeling at the trap door, shouting down at him in what he took to be Bulgarian, he made a break for the gate.

He saw that no place was safe enough and that his only hope lay in constant motion. He renounced forever his allegiance to the Party, although he did not forget a magnificent tip for the guide, who tucked it away quickly before his supposed tourist could change his mind or, more likely, discover his mistake in converting pesos into dollars.

Rejecting forever the vanity of taking thought for the morrow, Williams abandoned himself to the endless flow of Mexico City traffic and drove continuously for three days before he chanced to find himself in open country. He seemed to be following signs for Cuernavaca, which was as good a place as any, but he never got there. "Oh, yes, yes," everyone said whenever he stopped to ask, "this road will take you to Cuernavaca." They neglected to mention, however, the right turns and the left turns and the fact that he was headed in the wrong direction.

He stopped once to make inquiries at a store on the last fringes of the city, which reappeared from time to time, now on the right, now on the left, now dead ahead on a sure collision course, but he never got there any more than he got to Cuernavaca. When he walked into the store, the the storekeeper began to dump oranges into the pan of a scale. "Oh, yes," the storekeeper said, "oranges. Five kilos of oranges. We had an American once. I know all about Americans. Five kilos of oranges every day." Williams paid for the oranges and left without saying a word. After all, he would have to eat something, although five kilos of oranges every day seemed unlikely. However, he considered that in his long absence he might have lost touch with American folkways.

He veered off from the city and wandered long in a treeless plain. He was glad for the oranges. They relieved his thirst and gave him something to do. The only relief from the monotony of the landscape was a group of stylized mountains that sprang directly from the plain like enormous monoliths. They lacked only a hanging wood, a wisp of cloud, and a tiny Buddhist monk to be perfectly suited to an old Chinese painting. He passed these mountains three times before he shot off in some new direction and once more faced the everyday Mexican mountains that were always springing up around him, blocking his way or eluding his approach indifferently. He also faced across a great distance a single tree as accidental as the Chinese mountains.

For a long time he didn't seem to get any nearer to the tree, and he grew impatient to rest in its shade. But as he got nearer he saw that the shade was already spoken for. Men, women, and children were strewn about in picturesque attitudes. The men hunkered in a circle. The women were seated in the pools of their skirts. And the children splashed in a great sea of shadow. Williams felt he might at least steal a few moments of shade on the pretext of asking directions.

"Is this the way to Cuernavaca?" he said. The women smoothed the edges of their skirts and drew their rebozos around them. The children froze as if they had changed their game to Statues. The men passed the word *Cuernavaca* around the circle, testing and tasting it. It came back, having gathered a snowball of wisdom.

One man got up and approached Williams, who stood just outside the limit of the shade. "Hola," he said.

Williams addressed the top of the man's straw sombrero. "Ola," he said. He had never seen it written and didn't know about the *h*.

"Please come in," the man said. He seemed to open a door and step aside for Williams to enter. Williams gauged the door and stepped in. "This is my saint's day," the man said. "You must have a drink with us."

"Congratulations," Williams said, "and thank you." He had to abandon his guess that they were all waiting for a bus. Not only was the ceremonial tequila with salt and lime produced out of the air, but one of the women tended a tiny portable stove on which she was making tortillas. A hot tortilla found its way to Williams's hand. He hunkered—an art he had learned in prison. In spite of having grown up in the Midwest, he had been deficient in country manners until he attended the big P.

He saw at once that he might be in for a long squat of it. He couldn't bring up the subject of Cuernavaca without being guilty of seeming to want to rush away, and they couldn't bring it up without seeming to want to get rid of him. This could go on for hours. He excused himself and brought a fresh bottle of tequila from his car.

When the bottle held only one small swallow that everyone looked at but no one drank, the man across from Williams said to no one in particular, "Cuernavaca? Cuernavaca? Juan Hernandez has a cow with very large horns."

"I think," another man said, "Juan Hernandez should cut the horns of his cow."

"Juan Hernandez is a very stubborn man," another said. There was a general murmur of assent.

"And where might I find this Juan Hernandez," Williams said, "and his wonderful vaca—cow?"

"Straight on the way you are going," the saint's day man said.

"Is it far?" Williams said.

"Five kilometers," a man said.

"Two," another said.

"Seven," another said.

"Not far." To this everyone agreed.

Williams said, "And where else does this road go besides to this horned cow?"

"It goes all the way to Tenancingo," a man said.

"Or to Villa Guerrero in the other direction." Much of the time Williams couldn't tell who was speaking. The tops of all the sombreros looked very much alike.

"And where else?" he said.

A murmur ran around the circle, which Williams interpreted as a shrug.

"It goes to my Uncle Ramon's," a child shouted, "where the pig has a thousand babies."

"A million," another child corrected.

Williams stood up. All the men stood. He worked his way around the circle, giving and receiving high fives and embraces. He left fully refreshed, half drunk, and not at all informed.

He hadn't gone five miles before a truck passed him with a rush of speed and a long blast of the horn. The whole party was in the back, down to the little stove smoking near the tailgate and turning out tortillas.

He no longer cared where he was going. He certainly had no commitment to Cuernavaca. If Cuernavaca was as good as anywhere, anywhere was as good as Cuernavaca. He had only to keep moving and hide his tracks. In fact, if Cuernavaca was the one place he couldn't possibly find, it was the best of all possible ideas that the entire countryside should report to his pursuers that he was headed for Cuernavaca.

West was the only way he hadn't tried, so he tried it. But he didn't like it. Now the mountains were continuous. He was either going up or going down and always going around sharp curves. He was always behind a truck with an ear shattering exhaust and a vicious aura of diesel fumes. One day he spent twelve hours going a hundred miles. And when he got to the sea, there was no tide. The surf was O.K. but he couldn't bring himself to trust a sea with no tide, so he immediately turned around and started back for the central plateau, where there was nothing to trust or distrust.

Again he took twelve hours to cover the same hundred miles. This time he sat for four hours behind a bus that had passed him on a blind curve while he was groping his way around and trying to see through solid rock. The bus then settled into its lowest gear—it had a deafening exhaust and a suffocating aura—and he was rid of it only when it broke down on the sharpest, blindest curve in all that impossible road. Even then Williams didn't dare creep around the bus until he was waved on by the driver, who didn't bother to check for oncoming traffic. Of course, he got behind a truck almost at once, but at least the pitch of the exhaust was different and the color changed from blue to brown and the bumper slogan he read every minute changed from The Force of Destiny to King of the Road. From time to time an orange would roll off the load, and Williams would stop, pick it up, and suck the juice. In this way he relieved the boredom, which he might otherwise have ended—together with his life—by overtaking his roaring, stinking Atalanta at some narrow crest or some impossible turning.

When he was at last back on the central plateau, he felt more at ease. The road ran straight all day, and he could see for miles around that there was nothing to see. When he was lonely, he pulled over to the side and put up the hood of his car. Many people stopped and did unspeakable things to the motor so that sometimes he really did need help. Then he would wait for a Green Angel if he was on the main road or, if he was in the wilderness, a lift to the nearest shack with *Mecánico* scrawled on it. They took out his thermostat. "Oh, señor, in Mexico we don't use thermostats." They talked to his distributor. They casually rearranged his wiring so that the motor worked but the air conditioner ran backward. They charged him a dollar and he tipped them five. And the Green Angels even spoke English. It was part of their qualification for the government job, that lovely free service for tourists in distress.

"Anyone can be a mechanic," one told him, "but not everyone can speak English."

"It is very difficult," Williams said. And the conversation switched to Spanish. The Angel spoke English very well, but he was not at ease with the idioms. He had never been out of Mexico and hadn't had the advantage of an American prison.

Once, when Williams had raised the hood in the midst of a desolate plain, an area apparently abandoned by man and certainly cursed by God, a woman stepped out of the brush and offered him an iguana.

"What do I want with an iguana?" he said politely in English.

She smiled. Her face was like a jaguar mask on the wall of a Mayan temple.

He tried it in Spanish. To his relief he discovered that she didn't speak Spanish either. His Spanish wasn't fit for the ears of a jaguar.

He looked at the iguana. The iguana grinned at him. The woman pantomimed cutting the iguana's throat. Then she passed it before her mouth like someone eating an ear of corn. Her eyes studied him. Her cheekbones rose among the lizard's legs like twin moons among pines.

He was startled, he was aghast, which she took for assent and at once dispatched the iguana and began to cook it. While it cooked, she prepared Mickey Mouse cactus, pulling out the thorns and slicing the ears thin.

From then on, he stopped and raised his hood when he was hungry as well as when he was lonely. He was in no hurry. He tried stopping in the most desolate spots he could find. No place near a village would do. No place where there was a house in sight. He even avoided the small palmetto shelters beside the road, where people came out of the brush to sell something. But wherever he stopped, a woman appeared almost at once. She brought him chickens. She brought him kids. In the middle of the desert she brought him fresh-caught fish. For her fire she had her choice of acres of litter along the roadside. Even in the most deserted areas, paper blew along the highway, plastic slowly tattered on the bushes. There were always a few twigs, a dead branch of mesquite.

The problem of keeping clean, however, forced him to seek less baroque solutions: he simply stopped at a hotel and turned in his laundry and had a bath. He would have preferred something more elegant, but he was in no position to be finicky. He had indeed contrived something very like the ancient manna that fed the Israelites, but he was unable to invent a modern shower in the wilderness. He would certainly have been happier in some easygoing antiquity of more manageable needs and wants.

However, since he had certain intractable twentieth-century ideas about cleanliness and order, he was forced to settle for what there was at hand, so he checked into a hotel at Pátzcuaro one winter morning, gave up every stitch of clothing to his name, and went to bed until evening when his clothes were returned, cleaned and pressed down to the last pleat of his boxer shorts. He dressed then and went out to look for some mundane food.

The tables were set in the patio of the hotel, and since the night was cool, four great braziers blazed at the four corners of the central fountain. At one end of the patio a buffet was laid out. A swan carved in ice floated on a mirror lake as if its folded wings were the very Cornucopia itself, out of which all good things flowed: piles of fruit, oranges, papayas, mangoes, apples, bananas, pineapples, vast trays of pâté, aspic in the shape of a fish with an olive eye, compote by the gallon, cakes and pastries in mounds, huge joints of meat, and chef-hatted servers standing by with sabers drawn.

Williams was overcome. He wanted it all, and he gagged at the thought of a single mouthful. He drew away and was led to a table near one of the braziers, where the fire scorched his face and seared his eyeballs while his toes congealed on the flagstone floor. Smoke blew in his face, and ashes fell on his clothes and hair. "The fish," he coughed. "I'll have the fish. Only the fish."

"May I suggest the fish?" the waiter said, not to be done

out of his patter. "The lake of Pátzcuaro is famous for its whitefish."

"The fish sounds good," Williams said. He coughed and hacked and wiped his eyes and knew his place.

Actually the fish was very good, lightly sautéed and delicately seasoned, and he was able to enjoy it once he thought of covering it with his napkin and operating on it as under a gynecologist's sheet. No one else seemed to be having his problem.

When he was finished and escape seemed near, he sensed a stir among the diners. People were drawing back from the table, turning their chairs, and settling down to watch — him. He straightened up and dropped his napkin over the fish as if to say, "Show's over. I'm done." But they kept on staring. He knew he was as well and carefully dressed as anyone, but he felt for his fly, deeply hidden under the Niagara of the tablecloth. O.K. He ran his hand casually over his face to check for crumbs, smears, and stray drops of wine, and still they stared. He tried to outstare them but could catch no eye at all. They all pretended to be staring at something behind him, but he was on to that trick. He surely wasn't going to turn around and let them see whatever it was they had written on his back. They kept moving their chairs to adjust their sight lines.

This was getting on his nerves, although he knew very well that they couldn't possibly all be detectives and agents and hired killers. He looked around for the waiter, and as he turned his head he saw, directly behind him, four men standing motionless. Four could easily be assassins. His instinct was to dive under the table, but he froze.

They were dressed in the common white shirts and white pants. Their hair was long and thick. They were the very people he dealt with every day, except that their faces were pale and pink, their eyes fixed and blazing blue. He only wished he knew just what it was that had caught up with him.

Two of the men stepped forward. They had guns. No, canes. But that was little consolation, because canes would be sword canes. He looked toward the servers, who had put down their weapons and were standing with folded arms. One of the men stamped his foot. Now it would begin.

And it did begin. The men who had not moved now produced from somewhere about their persons an ordinary guitar and a sort of flute, fashioned in clay in the shape of a cock and balls. They then evoked a music so strange, so Chinese, so Moorish, that there was no placing it. And the others began a kind of clog dance on three legs. Williams knew the answer to the riddle of the sphinx, so this was an easy one: an old man goes on three legs. And, yes, they were getting older all the time, slowing gradually to a standstill. But then they just as gradually built up to a frenzy, leading each other around the floor like a proverb. Williams also knew the proverb and couldn't see how it applied to him.

This insight led to the conclusion that the men were, after all, entertainers brought in to demonstrate this ancient Michoacán dance, which was gay and noisy but somehow not at all friendly—present company excepted, of course. He understood that they were masked as Spaniards and that the dance might have been called the Hidalgo, Go Home dance.

None of this was at all difficult for Williams once he was assured that the sword-gun and the satire were not aimed at him. He knew, as any boy knows if he has read the proper adventure books, that Cortez had blue eyes and was therefore confused with the god Quetzalcoatl. More important, however, Williams knew that the face he had seen was the face of Don Q, a man of immense dignity, misunderstood and derided but persevering in his quest to a point far beyond hopelessness. He ran after the dancers and bought a mask with no difficulty. Then he went out into the yard of the inn and reverently placed the mask inside the Don's visor. It covered his mother's face, to be sure, but it covered it like a coffin mask, an Egyptian image of immortality. Certainly he owed them both that much.

In the morning he set out again, and when he stopped beside the road and raised his hood, the woman brought him a kid. She stepped out of the brush where a horseman would show only his hat, and she offered him the kid. She held it to her bosom like a darling. She and the kid gazed at or around or through him with identical eyes, large, quiet, and soft. When he smiled and nodded, she smiled and slit the kid's throat. There must be, he supposed, a lesson in there somewhere, but he failed to grasp it, so he followed her into the brush when she suggested a little stroll while the kid cooked. She was an expert at pantomime.

They had just completed the essential pantomime and lay together on her enormous skirt, quiet eye to soft eye, melting and running into a common gaze, when, around the corner of her ear, he became aware of a pair of hard-used feet in indestructible sandals and of something he took to be the last ten inches or so of a machete blade. Against his better judgment, he rolled over to verify his impression. There were four of them, each with the largest, shiniest, sharpest machete in the world. They looked like a classic painting of the revolution or the end of things in general.

"Buenas tardes," one said.

From this, Williams deduced that it was already past noon and that the last meal he wasn't going to eat was lunch. There seemed to him nothing more sad than to die in the afternoon and without lunch. He could smell the kid cooking.

"Buenas goddamn fucking tardes," Williams said, groping through his prison argot for some reasonably polite greeting.

"Claro," the man said.

Clearly what? Williams thought. But the man had already exhausted his Spanish, and pantomime took over once more. The woman sprang up and ran to the man and flung herself on his bosom. Williams was pleased to see a woman actually throw herself on someone's bosom, but it didn't make up for dying without lunch.

The man and woman belabored each other in a language that might have been excavated from Tzintzuntzan or erupted from Iztaccíhuatl. The other three stood at attention and presented machetes nearly as long as themselves and far more shining. When the conference was ended, the man brandished his machete and sprang at Williams. The other three closed in. The arc of the machete swung far behind Williams's ear, and he had time to note that death had the smell of garlic, an observation he regretted not being able to share with the world. But the touch on his shoulder was the touch not of steel but of flesh, and the kisses on his cheeks were the kisses not of angels but of men.

They all crowded around him and embraced him. Their machetes towered over everyone, threatening not only his neck and ears but all necks and ears that were not precisely where they had better be. They shouted and cheered, and the smell of garlic was now the smell of life, but it was a life that remembered death.

The tight knot they all made began to surge toward the woman, who had stood modestly to one side, waiting to be served her lover's hand or her lover's head. Either would have been acceptable. Williams was carried along toward her like a football caught in a scrum, and when he came out she took possession of him as coolly as a fly half who knew all along that he could seize the ball and run forever.

The man—now that Williams was reasonably sure he was alive, he felt obliged to take up once more the dreary process of trying to account to himself for things—the man, who appeared to be the woman's father, joined Williams's hand and the hand of the woman. The gesture was unmistakable. The other three cheered and set up a depressing clatter by knocking their machetes together. They were clearly the traditional brothers. Williams tried to think of the Spanish for "old badger game," but that had not been in the curriculum of his Spanish course. The kid was now ready, so they ate. It was very good, like the first breakfast after the last supper.

Father led off into the brush. Daughter motioned Williams to follow and entered into full possession of him by humbly following in his footsteps. The brothers, he supposed, came on behind. At least no one seemed to suppose for a moment that he would try to escape. Immediately, the road, the litter, and all other hopeful signs of civilization disappeared, and they were well on their way back to wherever their language came from. But as they went on, it was clear they were following a path and not only a path but a track much used by wheeled vehicles and dotted with mounds of manure. Williams discovered that he had only to look at the brush just right in order to see tracks branching and crossing. It was like looking at a cornfield: one minute a mass of undisciplined foliage and the next minute impeccable rows of well-trained plants, and, if he moved only slightly, chaos again.

At last they entered a clearing and stopped. There were half a dozen huts. Adobe, Williams supposed. An old woman was boiling up a pot of something under the general supervision of a pig, a hen, and a yellow dog. A young girl led three burros into the clearing from the other side. Each burro carried two drums, probably water. From another direction, three women and three girls brought home the family wash in bright plastic washtubs, red and yellow, balanced on their heads. Babies slung in rebozos, of course. Williams looked into the distance but couldn't imagine where they could have found water to wash in, what irrigation ditch ran through this desolation to what more savable desert, what muddy pond held back the last of the summer's rain to what end besides laundry.

The women lowered their tubs to the ground and closed in on Williams's bride with shrieks and squeals suitable to the occasion. They hurried her away with pats and caresses to one of the huts for the great female mysteries of preparation.

Williams and the men looked at each other sheepishly until the women were out of sight, and then they all grinned, although Williams wasn't sure what he had to grin about. He wasn't cheered much when he saw one of the brothers drive a yoke of oxen out of the brush, dragging the car behind them. The hood was still up and another brother sat at the wheel, blindly steering left and steering right but making no impression on the irresistible plod of the oxen.

The male mysteries consisted largely of a clay jug that was passed from hand to hand. They drank. Williams pretended to drink. He felt he would need his entire presence of mind as the day wore on. The men patted and caressed him and knocked him about jovially. They sang to him and taught him a dance and gave him the best of all possible advice, that spoken in a totally unknown tongue. They even produced skyrockets and aerial bombs for him and set them off as if he were a saint's day or a famous victory. When they were done with him, they shoved him into the hut and settled down to the serious business of life: singing and dancing and sleeping it off.

She was waiting for him. She did not look particularly prepared, but she had her wordly goods spread out as if for a garage sale. Item: two rebozos, one good and one not so good. Item: skirts and blouses of many colors to gladden a man's heart or at least a woman's. Item: a yellow plastic washtub, undistinguished but serviceable. Item: a stone quern complete with stone grinder. Williams began to feel he had moved into one of the mock-up rooms in the Museo de Antropología in Mexico City, and he had not yet even begun to contemplate all that was to be his, including his very own machete and half a bottle of tequila.

He had as well a wedding shirt that had already been to a good many weddings, a large straw sombrero that might have been new or at least was as good as, and a pair of sandals with soles cut from the living rock of a Uniroyal steel-belted radial tire. He also had a neatly woven hammock, so he lay down. She brought him the tequila and awaited his pleasure. She would not, he believed, be truly happy until he began to beat her.

The smell of tortillas woke him. He turned in his hammock and rolled to the floor. She was just bringing in a plate of tortillas she must have made for his breakfast. She gave him beans and watched him eat. There was even a shred of yesterday's kid. She watched him with the limpid eyes of the kid. His shirt had been washed overnight, but she dressed him in the wedding shirt instead, which seemed to him ominous. She was wearing a white dress and the better of her rebozos. She seemed well pleased with herself, although he could not remember beating her.

When they went outside, he politely turned his head aside from whatever the brothers were doing to his car. They seemed to be trying to jack it up but were still at the stage of shouting at each other and kicking the tires. The old woman, little more than a heap of rags, still crouched beside her boiling pot. At the edge of the clearing a small boy was giving instruction to a still smaller boy in man's duty to the environment. The teacher took down his pants and squatted and directed his pupil to a spot directly behind him and to an identical position so that the finer points could be closely observed. A yellow dog watched benignly. Again Williams chose to look elsewhere and saw . . . a priest, robed and ready, standing with his back to the car as if it were the altar of his own church, with Don Q, a particularly military saint, stretched out on the retable. It seemed that nothing bore close inspection this morning.

The brothers had by now succeeded in placing the jack but did not appear to be able to agree on how high to lift the car, so they reverted to shouts and kicks. The kicks now included a light donkey cart, which they had drawn up beside the car. It occurred to Williams that they intended to take his wheels for their cart, a stylish sort of arrangement that he had more than once noted in his travels, although he had never before this wondered where the wheels came from.

The priest motioned for Williams to approach. Behind him, the car shuddered and rose and tipped toward him, then sank back to rest. The Don muttered and clanked. No one seemed particularly interested in the ceremony, although they were all witnesses. It might be a necessary ritual but it required no one's attention. The old woman went on boiling her pot. A boy tried to urge a flock of goats off in some uncongenial direction. A girl prepared three burros with water drums. At the edge of the brush the ecology lesson went on. The car shuddered again. The brothers shouted. The dull thud of their kicks punctuated the priest's opening remarks, which seemed to be in Latin. Perhaps out of a confused sense of priestly fairness, he was going to conduct the ceremony in a neutral language that would give no one the disadvantage of understanding what he said.

He looked at the bride and spoke. She did not look like a woman being spoken to. She said nothing, so when the priest spoke to Williams he felt it unnecessary to commit himself to anything. The priest was now clearly winding himself up to the climax of his mystery. As his fervor rose, so too rose the car behind him. As he lifted his hand to pronounce a blessing or hurl a curse, the car gave a further lurch, reached new heights. The Don groaned and rolled over. His outflung arm descended in a fierce arc and smote the priest to the ground.

Instantly the clearing was deserted. The old woman's fire smoked. Her pot bubbled. Williams was now alone except for the black heap of the priest, except for the Don — and except for his mother. He let the car down and stored the jack properly. He composed the Don once more and saw to his lashings. There was clearly no hurry. Even Williams himself was impressed by the speed and accuracy of justice. He went into the hut and changed into his own shirt. The wedding shirt he left neatly folded and only slighted stained in the armpits with terror. "I would not," he said, as if engraving his words on the air of the woman's hut, "have been much good with a machete."

Then there was nothing to do but drive back to the highway, guided by the tracks of his own tires and the providential cairns of manure.

III

WILLIAMS SUSPECTED after his miraculous escape that he was being watched over, and not only by thieves and murderers. At the same time, he felt it would be foolish to press his luck. In fact, he thought he might just about have run out of luck in Mexico, so he braced himself to try the border and headed cautiously north, hiding his tracks and eating only at first-class hotels and having his car serviced only by certified dealers. Still, luck or no luck, the crossing did not look easy.

He probed the border from coast to coast. He was afraid in Brownsville, and he was afraid at Laredo, El Paso, and Nogales. He despaired at Mexicali and Tijuana. He considered sneaking through on a slow day and slipping across in a crush. He wondered where he could find an impresario who could get him and the Don in as a couple of wetbacks. In the end, he decided to try Reynosa, largely because he had never heard of it. He decided to try a slow day, a Sunday.

So at four o'clock on a Sunday afternoon, he followed signs

that said To the Bridge and stopped behind a few cars obviously waiting to cross, although the bridge was nowhere in sight. The line crept forward toward the corner. More cars piled up behind him. He was pleased to see Texas number plates all around him. He could already see in his mind's eye the welcoming golden arches of McDonald's.

He turned the corner. Still no bridge. The line stretched ahead of him around another distant corner. It reminded him of Sunday nights coming down from Wisconsin when he was a child, the lines piled up at toll booths, the heartbreaking lines for road construction. Some nights in the fog it was as if they had gone adrift on Lake Michigan with ghostly boats on all sides of them being towed home for the season.

He bought a taco from a vendor with a little cart. Half an hour later and ten yards along, he bought an ice cream. He imagined that his first Howard Johnson's ice cream cone would give him terminal la turista. He declined an incredible bargain in Mexican wooden chairs, rush seated, highly decorated, stacked on the back of a burro. He declined a scarf that was really a veronica. He declined a Day-Glo *Last Supper*. He ate another taco. Things were not going forward very fast. He no longer took much comfort in the Texas number plates. The cars, he now saw, were all filled with Mexicans, no doubt coming back from a day of mother's home cooking or just from buying a tankful of cheap gas, which they would surely burn up waiting in the line.

"Hola, amigo," the motorcycle cop said as he rested his hand on Williams's door. He was doubtless relieved to see a Mexican number plate.

"Buenas tardes, sir," Williams said. He might be at a loss for the polite forms of ordinary conversation, but he knew how to address a guard.

"Many people," the cop said.

"Very many," Williams said.

"You picked a bad day to cross."

"Clearly," Williams said. "But I'm in no hurry," he said, choking down a strong, hot taste of vomit.

"Lucky for you," the cop said. "Nice armor you've got there." He raised his eyebrows toward the Don without taking his eyes from Williams's face.

"Very old," Williams said.

"You better have papers on it," the cop said.

"Something of the family," Williams said.

"Perhaps they'll let you through. It isn't as if you claimed to be a descendant of Montezuma and were carrying out the family jewels."

"Oh, I have those too," Williams said. That pleased the cop, who had apparently decided that the problem of the armor would soon be taken care of by more appropriate authorities. Probably he was going off duty at five anyway and wanted no complications at the last minute.

The cop laughed and waved and gunned his engine. He did a U-turn and roared off without looking, secure in the knowledge that no one would dare—well, anything.

Williams, now left with nothing to do but think and move his car forward a few inches now and then, thought of a new worry. He had traveled so freely up and down Mexico that he assumed crossing the border, on the Mexican side at least, would call only for another of his many explanations of the Don. He had been sure that anyone with any claim to expertise would recognize at once that the armor was of very recent, and very inferior, workmanship and that it was, at best, Mexican folk art, exactly what he had intended to pass it off as on the American side.

Someone was trying to sell him a tablecloth that was also the Shroud of Turin. He waved it away.

"What?" the salesman said. "You don't want a genuine replica of the Shroud of Turin?" He was dressed up as a Mexican, no doubt to please American tourists, with a big sombrero, a wedding shirt, a poncho, dazzling charro pants, truck-tire sandals—the works.

"Thank you, no," Williams said.

"Ah, but think of your mother," the salesman said. "Women love the Shroud of Turin. They love the little Savior."

"I do think of my mother," Williams said. "God rest her soul."

"Well, then," the salesman said, "your wife. A man with an important car must have a wife. You do have a wife?"

"No wife," Williams said. This was getting nowhere, but it was passing the time.

"Your sweetheart, then," the salesman said. "It will show her how much you think of her. She'll think it's almost a promise, under the very eye of the Sacrificial Lamb. She'll go wild. You'll see. Of course, you and I know — "

"No sweetheart," Williams said. He found it curious that until this catechism he had lost track of the fact that his life was so thoroughly lacking in women.

"How about a sister? Sisters can do much good if they wish, and they are often pious."

Williams shook his head.

The salesman looked stern, as if he had finally discovered the true depths of Williams's depravity, his despicable faggotry.

"The life I lead," Williams said, "doesn't give much time. Moving all the time."

"Ah," the salesman said, "a different woman in every town. Perhaps we should talk wholesale. Buy by the dozen — "

The line of cars moved forward suddenly for a hundred yards, and the salesman found himself with his head in someone else's window, and Williams found himself alone again with all the feminine company he could handle. "I'm doing my best," he said to the roof, although at the same time he was painfully aware that throughout his previous life, his best was just what he had failed to do, a post card here, a snapshot there, here a little bill, there a monstrous debt. He tried to steel himself for the crossing, but he knew it was no longer a question of his best. Now it was a question of luck, of miracle even. "At least wish me luck," he said. Silence was the loud reply.

Once the cop had raised the matter of documentation, Williams thought of things he should have thought of before. He ran through in his mind the location of the forgers he had known in prison and came to the reluctant conclusion that the best was as far away as Guadalajara. He was by now within sight of the customs barrier, but he could still pull out of line, make a U-turn, and head for Guadalajara or somewhere else, perhaps back to the gates of the prison to give himself up. He eased forward another few inches.

"Day visitors, left lane," a guard said, walking down the line. "Tourists, right lane." Williams started to pull into the right lane. "Left lane for Mexican cars," the guard said.

"American passport," Williams said. He was stuck now. He could only go on.

"Good afternoon," the customs officer said. "Your tourist papers, please." Fortunately, Williams had thought to have those forged. They were in perfect order. "Have you enjoyed your stay in Mexico?" the officer said.

"It has been very educational," Williams said. He preferred to add as few lies as possible to the weight already on his soul.

"And this object?" the officer said, glancing at the Don.

"A statue of my father," Williams said. "I had it made in Guanajuato."

"Very distinguished looking," the officer said. "I think I see a slight family resemblance."

"I really take after my mother," Williams said and wondered what the officer would find to say if he opened the Don's visor and had a look inside.

"May she thrive and prosper," the officer said.

"Alas," Williams said.

"Qué lástima," the officer said, knowing full well that only Spanish could express a true concern.

"Pity indeed," Williams said. "I came to Mexico to bury

her," which was true enough even if a good seven years out of date.

"The land of Mexico is specially blessed," the officer said. "It is good for burying."

"How true," Williams said.

"Your car," the officer said. He began to pace around the car like a monk meditating in a cloister. Williams fell in beside him as if for a quick Ave or two. "I know a man," the officer said. "You must think of import duties."

Williams had not thought of import duties.

"You must think of the cost — hundreds of dollars — of having the car fixed to meet United States standards of emission control and God knows what else. Very expensive." He shook his fingers as if he had burned them.

There was plenty of money in the bank. He had only to write a check, but there was the slight difficulty that his forged passport was not in in the name of Williams, persona non grata in Mexico after that misunderstanding about the cocaine.

They continued to pace around the car, appreciating its finer points. "This man I know . . ." the officer said.

"To be sure," Williams said.

"He can take the car off your hands and save you much worry and much much money. No problem."

"No problema, indeed," Williams said. If he was going to have to deal with some man, he would prefer to deal with a man he himself knew, even if it meant going back to Guanajuato or even to Taxco. A man at the border would count on your desperation. But to be polite, he said, "Tell me where to find him."

"I will tell you where to meet me, and I will take you to him myself," the officer said.

"I'll have to think about it," Williams said.

"You can get rid of the car here and walk across the bridge," the officer said.

Williams gestured minimally toward the Don.

"You can take him across in a cab," the officer said.

"That's so," Williams said.

"I do it for the memory of your mother," the officer said.

"Many thanks," Williams said.

"Sincerely," the officer said.

"Of course," Williams said. But each knew that the other was quietly estimating the size of the officer's commission on the deal.

At that moment, a man wearing the uniform of the American customs came out of the Mexican custom house. God knows what he was doing there. Probably some international technicality. He looked at Williams. He looked at the car. He looked at the Don. His eyes were intense blue. Williams knew the eyes of a machine gunner when he saw them.

"I'd have that off of there if I were you," he said, shooting the Don full of holes. "There's no telling what's inside it."

"It's a statue of his father," the Mexican said.

"So he says," the American said. "I've seen statues of the Virgin Mary stuffed with dope and with a jewel in her belly button."

At the mention of the Blessed Mother, the Mexican blessed himself.

"And so have you," the American said. "Not that it's any business of mine — yet." The *yet* was very gentle, just the way he would touch off a burst of machine-gun fire.

"Would you mind?" the Mexican said.

"Not in the least," Williams said. He fumbled with the lashings of the Don, tightening the knots, cursing, laughing, wondering what he would invent this time.

The American stood aloof. The Mexican began to work at the knots.

"To tell the truth," Williams said — the knots slipped apart under his hands — "to tell the truth, my grandmother is asleep inside the statue. She is very old. And very stiff. And it's the only place she can stretch out. So be careful."

The Don was now freed of his bonds and was attempting to slide off the roof.

"Gently," the Mexican said. He helped Williams lower the Don to the ground. "A very sound sleeper," he said.

"I filled her with tranquilizers to see her through the trip," Williams said. "Nothing will wake her."

"Let's have a look," the American said. He opened the Don's visor and lifted the mask. "That is one old lady," he said.

"Poor soul," the Mexican said. "Let us respect her sleep."

"I'd take a look around inside," the American said. "There's plenty of room inside for anything. I'd take a look."

And Williams knew he would take his look when his turn came. "She doesn't have any clothes on," he said. "She can't stand clothes in there."

"Call the matron," the American said. "I've seen coffins come through here full of dope. I've seen corpses stuffed with diamonds."

While they waited for the matron, Williams eased off the Don's headpiece and undid his buckles. "That looks like more than tranquilizers," the American said. "You must have really shot her up. Don't worry. If you've got it, we'll find it."

"Prescription stuff," Williams said.

"Sure," the American said. "I've seen prescriptions for a ton of cocaine."

"Wow," Williams said, covering a multitude.

The matron efficiently covered his mother—grand-mother—with a blanket, and the Mexican officer examined the Don in all his cavities. The American watched professionally. Clearly he knew he could have done better. Williams also watched, with great anxiety. He knew there was nothing to be found, but he had also known there was nothing to be found seven years ago when the customs officers began to search his mother's car. The world was certainly full of surprises.

"You should be ashamed of yourself," the matron said. "You

aren't taking care of that old lady at all. Her skin is as dry as an iguana, and she is very stiff. You must rub her with baby oil and massage her gently. See that you do it."

"That's no way to treat your grandmother," the American said. "At least not on the other side. We have laws." He glanced across the bridge at the Land of Laws.

"I do my best," Williams said.

"You'll have to do better," the matron said.

"It's a lot of trouble to be in charge of an old lady like that," the Mexican said.

The American frowned.

"You can't imagine the trouble she's caused me," Williams said. He reviewed vast distances, years in prison, dangers, hardships, hiding, panic, and endless flight. He saw much. He feared more. He began to cry.

"Ah," the matron said, "if you are truly sorry — "

"He is truly sorry," the Mexican said. "He is clearly the best of grandsons, but even the best of grandsons may not know — why, even I do not know — the care of such an old lady."

"A little baby oil," the matron said. "It would not hurt to have it blessed by the priest. Don't cry."

"He's got plenty to cry about," the American said. "He shouldn't have taken on the care of such an old lady if he didn't know what to do about her. We'll know what to do about him."

The enormity of his crimes was at last bearing down on Williams. He longed for punishment and atonement, but he knew there was no atonement for such as he. He longed to throw himself at the feet of the Mexican officer and beg for punishment, dire and unending. He thought of the comforting rigors of the old prison almost with ecstasy. But then he wondered what would await him on the other side of the river. He had never experienced an American prison. It might be worse. It might be beautifully worse where they had laws.

And in this moment of hesitation, he was lost. Some other word was said. Some other thing was done.

"We can't stand here all day," the American said. "Maybe you'd better just tell him to pack up his traveling junk yard and leave him to us."

Williams could think of no words to express his indignation. Inwardly he apologized to the Don. He tried to explain to his mother.

"Speak for your own side of the river," the Mexican said. "Here we can stand all day in respect for a man's decent tears. Once he is at your end of the bridge, you can harass him as much as your conscience permits, but here" — he turned to Williams — "do you feel able to make an effort?"

It seemed to Williams that since he had found his mother he had done nothing but make an effort, an effort piled upon a struggle, piled upon a convulsion, piled upon an agony. Of course, he knew there had been better moments, but he couldn't remember any of them just then. Without any effort, however, he went along with events just as if his mother had reared up on her hind legs and was calmly irradiating him with the Right Way.

"Is it all right to put her back in the statue?" he said.

"Naturally," the Mexican said.

"I wash my hands of it," the matron said. The setting sun poured light over her hands like Pilate's water. "If you put her back in there without oiling her, I wash my hands of it."

"It's only until I can get to a motel and a drug store," Williams said.

"See that it is," the matron said, hanging out her hands to dry.

"I'll be waiting for you," the American said and started back across the bridge.

"I'll meet you at the bandstand in the zócalo," the Mexican said. "Nine o'clock."

"I'll be there," Williams said.

"That will give you time to take care of the old lady," the matron said. "Would you like me to come and help you?" She smiled a most un-Pilate-ish smile.

"No, thanks," Williams said. "I'll manage." He fully intended to manage. He would manage first of all by setting out for Oaxaca, the farthest place he could think of that didn't involve crossing a border.

IV

WILLIAMS WAS not one, no matter how terrified, to approach Oaxaca directly, so he traveled across Mexico in disguise and as unobtrusively as possible. Sometimes he traveled up and down Mexico. Sometimes he was John Doe and sometimes he was Richard Roe. He had passports to prove either, both forged. His evasions were fully justified. There were people interested in him — and not only the Mexican Mafia. The federal police thought he was carrying cocaine, and lots of it. And the CIA was betting military secrets. They were wrong, of course, but that wasn't their fault. Informers, anxious to be helpful, had guessed there was something about the armor and couldn't imagine that it was purely a local matter and of interest only to the implacable Jouverts of the Guanajuato cops. In any case, finding or keeping an eye on Williams had become a major industry south of the border.

Devious as he was, however, he couldn't avoid at last arriving in Oaxaca, although he did contrive to approach it from the south, from the general direction of Guatemala, Belize, and Quintana Roo. And approaching like this with his face to the north, he felt suddenly hopeful, as if he had at last begun his true journey through the endless mountains, across the high plateau, through Southland and Heartland, to end finally where he had to go, Alpha, Illinois, home for both of them.

It was Christmas when he got to Oaxaca. He knew it was Christmas because even in the poorest sections snowmen were pasted to windows, spavined trees flaunted gay streamers, family shrines blinked red and green like anywhere in the world. Even the cathedral winked LOVE, PEACE, JOY in colored lights. Fireworks and aerial bombs told the good news.

In the main square there was a confused crèche, the inspiration of many pieties, ranging from baroque Magi to a pre-Raphaelite Madonna, all life size, to tiny Toltec shepherds in the far hills being sung to by tinier angels of no known persuasion. The presence of the familiar figures made Williams feel happy and safe until he observed that there were only two Magi. Disappointed, he turned away. The afterimage told that the two kings present were both clearly Aryan, so the missing one had to be Gaspar, the Ethiopian.

He sat on a bench in the square to consider his position. He had set out for Oaxaca, and he had got to Oaxaca. Good. Except that he had now run out of plan. He had also exhausted the momentary euphoria he felt when he turned north for Oaxaca. Crossing the border was not going to be any easier than the last time he tried. He was going to have to keep moving and by no means necessarily to the north. For the moment, however, he was safe. He was impeccably disguised as a tourist: straw sombrero, poncho, white pants with drawstrings at the ankles, truck-tire sandals complete with dirty feet and broken toenails. Everyone spoke to him in English. The band played Sousa marches. Santa Claus strolled past in a velvet suit the color of dried blood. Santa's attendant photographer pointed his camera at Roe, who shied behind his sombrero like a guerrilla about to be captured. "Nice picture?" the photographer said. "Nice picture with Santa Claus?"

"Fuck off," Doe said in flawless Spanish. He was so rattled that he blew his cover, but fortunately, the photographer was only a photographer, and Santa, whoever he was, was out of hearing.

All along the north side of the square, people were celebrating Christmas by breaking dishes. At first Roe couldn't see the dishes actually breaking. He would hear a crash on the cobblestones and turn in time to see children scramble for the larger pieces, hurl them into the air to crash again. At a dead run they crunched the smaller pieces underfoot. Finally he concentrated on one booth in the middle of the row of booths. Crashes to left and right did not distract him, and he was rewarded by seeing the eaters begin to come alone and in families to the edge of the sidewalk and hurl their earthen bowls into the street. Once he had seen it, it was easy to see again. A child took a family bowl to the street and tossed it high—not quite so high as a man's head but very high—and turned back to get another bowl, always waiting for the proper deployment of tourist cameras.

Williams left the square and drove in circles—actually rectangles—in mazes of one-way streets until he found a hotel with a proper drive-in patio for parking. The patio was long and narrow and poisonous green, walls and flagstones. There was an aluminum tree suffering from something that looked like Dutch elm disease or perhaps mange. The inevitable yellow dog was named Sultan. His diseases and infirmities had no names.

In the morning he looked out into the puke-green courtyard to contemplate the problems of the day, the first of which, he believed, was to find a garage to paint his car and provide the final service under the 50,000-mile warranty. But he was mistaken. The first problem was quite another. Even before he could begin his contemplation, he saw men dressed as tourists walking around his car and taking notes, photographing the armor from all angles, standing on the bumpers to reach the armor and rap it thoughtfully, tap it, cock their heads as if sounding wine barrels.

The men had obviously got their ideas of tourists from an assortment of comic strips, for their shirts were mumus and their shorts lederhosen. Only their sombreros showed a genuine Mexican touch, being large, embroidered with silver thread, and hung about the brim with tiny balls, rather like a grape arbor. Their running shoes, however, would have given them away even if the looseness of their shirts hadn't allowed him glimpses of the harnesses of shoulder holsters. He knew he was in trouble.

He felt that the best thing to do under the circumstances was to eat a hearty breakfast, so he went into the dining room and seated himself at a table where he could watch the door and his car at the same time. The men had by now disappeared. He hoped they had gone off to report finding a green car with red armor when what they had been looking for was a blue car with black armor. The next time they saw it, it was going to be a yellow car with green armor. He was gaining time all the time.

He ate his *huevos rancheros* surrounded by a geriatric tour group, all discussing in raw midwestern voices, loudly and in great detail, the history of their bowels for the past twenty-four hours. It was not the conversation he would have chosen at matins, and for the first time he left his refried beans untouched. Even the steaming chocolate was not to his taste. He wondered if he was coming down with something. But the sight of the dog Sultan pissing on the wheels of his car brought him back to a sense of his danger, and he began to mature his plan for the day.

The first stage of his plan was to take the car to a garage for tuning and painting. *No problema*. The second step was to separate car and armor for a time, to present not only different colors but a different outline to confuse pursuit. Changing colors was all very well during the day, but at night there was always the danger that the silhouette of the car and armor might be mistaken for what it really was.

With appropriate encouragement (in dollars, *por favor*) he got the armor painted green at once. He took the precaution of spreading his handkerchief over his mother's face so it wouldn't be sprayed green through the slots in the visor. Her face was already silver from the first painting—and it was not unbecoming—but green was another matter, particularly for a mummy.

However, what to do with the armor now that he had it away from the car was indeed a *problema*. He hadn't a clue, but he borrowed a pushcart and set out into the streets. Thoroughly disillusioned by now with the effectiveness of his disguise—the sombrero, the poncho, the sandals—he hoped, with the pushcart, to be taken for an expatriate American who hoped to be taken for a poet or a painter or at least an alcoholic novelist. This disguise was entirely successful. The police spotted him at once and radioed in for any reports of stolen green armor. Of course there were none, but this fresh scrutiny did nothing to ease Doe's raging paranoia.

As he went on vaguely in the direction of the square, he fell in behind a priest and two altar boys. One of the boys was swinging a censer, and the smell was worth following. It wasn't long before people along the route realized that this was a religious procession in the best tradition. Some blessed themselves. Some dropped to their knees. Some trailed along behind the pushcart. And some stuffed flowers in all the joints in the armor, in the vents in the visor, in the iron clutch of the hands. They also kissed it. Touched it. Planted candles around the edge of the cart. And hung the armor with medals, rosaries, and ex-votos of all kinds: tin hands on the hands, legs on the legs, hearts on the clanging breast, and breasts on the hearts. It was perfectly clear to everyone that this was some particularly holy and powerful relic come from a church so far away that it was days too late for the procession of images, which made it only the more powerful, therefore, the more efficacious. Roe plodded on, muttering Aves, chanting Glorias. Now even he didn't know who he was. The police blessed themselves and cleared a way, held up traffic at cross streets, opened sight lines for tourist cameras. The tourists took their photographs and bought hastily adapted relics of the Green Knight. It was good business for everyone.

Roe had a vague idea that he would follow the priest to his church and store the armor in the sanctuary along with the other graven images, the perfect place to hide a purloined mummy. But as the procession was skirting the square, he had a better idea. The priest stopped and everyone stopped behind him. Officious women straightened the flowers around the armor and relighted candles that had gone out. The priest urged the thurifer to fresh heights of diligence. A heavy cloud of incense reeked from the censer. But the priest, still dissatisfied, snatched it from the boy and with his longer, more powerful arms created arcs of titanic proportions. He seemed overcome by the vision and the incense.

Doe saw his chance. He stepped from the line of march and approached the nearest guard at the crèche. "Buenas," he said.

"Buenas," the guard said in the safe and comfortable Mexican way—it is always *días* or *tardes* or *noches* without the trouble of looking at a clock.

"We have come from the village of Santiago de Guerrero," Roe or Doe or somebody said.

"Never heard of it," the guard said.

"It's in the mountains," Roe said. "Very far." He waved vaguely in no particular direction. Fortunately Oaxaca is in a valley, so there are mountains everywhere and perhaps even Santiagos. "This is a very holy priest of Santiago—"

"He looks like Father Guillermo from the church of Santo Domingo—"

"His brother," Doe said. "A very holy man."

"Indeed," the guard said. He refused to commit himself and used none of the two dozen, more or less, inflections that allowed the word to mean almost anything.

"And he had a vision that told him to bring the sacred image of his church here to Oaxaca, to take its place in the Nativity." The guard and Roe both blessed themselves.

"You talk more like a gangster than a pilgrim," the guard said.

"Oh, I was, I was," Roe-Doe-X said. "But I am now doing penance in the mountains." He wondered if this was true. As disguise piled on disguise, he was no longer certain exactly who he was.

"The king who is missing from the Nativity is Gaspar, the Ethiopian," Roe said, "and he can go right there." He pointed to the spot where Gaspar should obviously have been standing. He began to slide the armor off the cart.

"Hold on," the guard said. "Not so fast."

"This armor *is* Gaspar," Roe said, inspired. "It is a reliquary containing a sliver of the left thighbone of that very king."

"God preserve us," the guard said. "The saints protect us. And the Holy Mother guide our steps."

"Amen," Doe said. "Help me prop him up. He's been lying down for three hundred years and is pretty unsteady on his legs." While the guard steadied the armor, Doe — or Roe — took candle after candle from the cart and dripped wax around the armored feet, binding them fast to the pavement. Someone was being very resourceful, but it was hard to tell who — Roe or Doe or the gangster or the pilgrim or the tourist or the expatriate or even the drunken American novelist.

The priest wandered off. Some of the crowd followed him, for he was obviously a very holy old man much given to dreaming dreams and, like as not, unseasonably seeing visions. The others completed their devotions, stood up briskly, and went about their business: sold a few flowers or oranges, posed for photographs, ate an ice, picked a pocket or two, sold the odd souvenir, offered their services as guides, told many lies, and in general carried on the day.

Doe retired to a park bench and watched Gaspar fade into his surroundings, become part of the scene, the inevitable third king. When he was satisfied with his handiwork, he bought himself a new outfit—alligator shirt, Levi's, Adidas shoes, a Canon T-50—and moved into Hotel El Presidente, *ex convento* Santa Catalina.

He spent a lot of time photographing El Presidente's doorman, a downy youth dressed as a sixteenth-century cavalier, complete with plume, sword, and buckled shoes. Roe made a note of the costume for future use and snapped another picture. Inside the hotel he avoided the corridor of pictures of the convent before its restoration. It had been for a time a prison and after that was in ruins. He preferred his private dream of the convent, the gentle, contemplative life of the nuns. He preferred above all not to reflect that every place that had walls strong enough to hold prisoners had at one time or another been a prison—that, in Mexico at least, stone walls do indeed a prison make—so he paced other cloisters, thought other thoughts.

At lunch he avoided the dining room—the trick wall of emergent pots made him uneasy. From a distance the pots looked like a cresting wave of breasts about to engulf him. Closer, they were eyes staring at him or mouths ready to suck him down. "None of the above," he said under his breath, and went out into a cloister to share his sandwich with a pigeon, which ate from his plate in spite of the efforts of the waiter, the head waiter, and a gardener to shoo it off. "Suffer little pigeons," he said three times. He was already well into the spirit of the place and was disappointed when the pigeon refused beer. He would have sat there all afternoon and drunk beer after beer while the pigeon, a very slow eater, finished its share of the sandwich, but he wearied of the four people at the table next to him. It was impossible to sort them into couples because they were all inventing such lies about historic sites and bargains, about hotels and restaurants, about lost luggage, pickpockets, and la turista that he had to conclude that none of them had ever before laid eyes on the others.

He went off to the desk to ask for mail, although no one knew where he was. He was astonished, therefore, when the clerk said, "Oh, Señor Doe, we have been expecting you," and handed him a thick packet of letters. He sank into an easy chair near the desk and began to go through his mail. There were six invitations to buy additional health insurance and four to accept credit cards with ruinous lines of credit. There were three letters from women suggesting another meeting at El Presidente and one letter from a lawyer involving a paternity suit. There was also one from his own family lawyer asking what the hell he was up to.

As he sat there marveling that all these people knew where to find him and coming to realize he had better vanish from that hotel, from that very chair, without a trace and at once, a man stepped up to the desk and asked if there was any record of a guest driving a 1985 Buick Electra, black, with armor, white. No, sir, there was not. The man was disguised as an American dentist, complete with American dental assistant, but Roe knew his type, so he got up and went out to take another picture of the cavalier doorman.

"Buddy, old pal," Doe said to the youth, "how would you like to make a hundred dollars?"

"Peso $ or dollar $?" the boy said reasonably enough.

"Like pesos, fifteen thousand," Roe said.

"Done," the boy said.

"That's what I like to hear," Doe said. "Greed," he added in English. So they changed clothes in Roe's room, and Doe became a doorman.

It was not hard work once he mastered the art of not tripping on his sword while he was lifting bags out of the backs of taxis and airport buses. He didn't have to say much, for he was allowed only two phrases in English: There are no vacancies and Are these all your bags? He learned these very quickly. He was not allowed to say thank you for tips, because *gracias* is the one word all Americans know, and therefore they like to hear it. The job was as simple as that, except for the obvious English professor from UCLA, who asked about a green Buick Electra with red armor.

The doorman—his name was Rodrigo—smiled and said "Sí, sí" in his most ingratiating manner. He could just as well have said *no, no*, but *sí, sí* is always more agreeable.

"Green," the professor said. "Verdigris," he said. "Mesa Verde. Verde!" He rapped his knuckles on the nearest taxi.

"There are no green taxis," Rodrigo said. He had not been selected for the job because of his brains but only because of his slender duelist's figure. Of course, he spoke filthy Spanish, so the translation is only approximate.

"Rouge," the professor said. "Oh, shit," he said. "French." But he couldn't get any closer than Colorado and gave it up. He touched his eye and glanced around. He shaded his eye with his hand like an Indian scout or a statue of Admiral Dewey.

"Oh, sí, sí," Rodrigo said.

"Gracias," the professor said, and with a lordly gesture passed over a fistful of coins, almost all of the smallest denominations. Doubtless everyone had been cheating him since the minute he landed.

It was very late when the doorman finished work, let in the last reveler, let out the first adventuress. He was almost at his room when he realized he had no room. John Doe—Richard Roe—was long since asleep in his bed, and where Rodrigo would sleep, God only knew. As he paused to process this new data, he observed a tray abandoned on a bench outside what should have been his door. What should have been two empty glasses held virtually untouched margaritas. The salt rims were barely disturbed. One glass showed a trace of lipstick. It was clear that some people were better at being Roe—Doe—than others. He wished he had been around to pick up some pointers. He drank both drinks without thinking further, shuddering at the salt kiss left as if for him alone.

Then he abandoned the hotel and went out into the street. The margaritas quickly took hold. He, Roe, considered one lethal—and so apparently did Rodrigo. The square was the only place he could think of, so he went there. No dishes were being broken. No shoes were being shined. No photographs were being taken. There was only one guard at the crèche, and he was on his hands and knees scrabbling up coins that had been flung about the feet of the Green Knight, Gaspar, Williams's secret mother.

The scene was so much like a familiar dream that Rodrigo was reluctant to interfere. He saw himself in the posture of the guard snatching up coins with both hands, more and more coins, more than he could ever garner. However, he did finally say "Hola." Enough was enough. Even dreams can go too far.

"Hola," the guard said. He turned his head slowly, took in Rodrigo's shoes, his hose, his sword, his velvet pants, his lace collar, his doublet, his plume. "Who the hell are you?" he said.

Rodrigo wished they could do it twice, because he wanted to say "Don Rodrigo" and he wanted to say "A trash sticker." But since he had to choose, he chose "trash sticker." He wasn't sure he was up to the swordplay demanded of Don Rodrigo, especially since the guard's hand had gravitated to the butt of his gun.

Rodrigo retreated to a noncommittal distance and drew his sword. "A trash sticker," he said and speared an errant McDonald's wrapper, which would have seemed odd to him if, in his capacity of doorman, he hadn't seen people checking into the hotel with suitcases full of Big Macs.

"Pardon me, Comrade Trash Sticker," the guard said. "I didn't recognize the uniform."

"It's the new issue," Rodrigo said. "You'll get yours in a few days." He was impressed by the guard's reply and even learned a few new words in an Indian dialect not taught in the northern prison where he had matriculated. "It's not so bad once you get the trick of the sword." He learned some more words.

"Comrade Trash Sticker," the guard said. "I've got to take a crap so bad I can taste it."

"Go up into the hills with the shepherds," Rodrigo said. "They do it all the time." He gestured toward the tiny Toltec shepherds awestruck on knee-high hills in the remote reaches of the crèche.

"Better not," the guard said. "They'd think it was an ava- lanche. "You" — and he took off running — "keep an eye on things." He was gone in the direction of the market before Rodrigo could say anything more than "Comrade Guard — "

He couldn't decide whether or not his new duties called for a drawn sword, but he drew it anyway and tried to look alert. He found alertness tiring, however, and dropped to his knees to look for coins. Not a one. He rested a moment on his knees but froze when two pairs of very large sandals and the hems of two very long brown robes came into focus. Fortunately, he was just behind Gaspar and in the posture of adoration.

"The turkey got away," one man said.

"Vanished into thin air," another man said. "What a tur- key."

Rodrigo recognized the men who had been photographing his car and armor. They were now disguised as Franciscan monks, but there was something about their speech that was unconvincing.

"A regular bunch of turkeys," one said. "Angels out of paint- ings, Indian shepherds, King Arthur–type armor, and some Don Zorro just over from the old country." He gave Rodrigo a kick and toppled him over. "Gobble, gobble, gobble," he said.

"Hey," the other said, "monks don't act like that." He tried to set Rodrigo on his knees again, but Rodrigo was too scared and stiff to balance well at all.

"I'll put some lead in him for ballast," the first thug said. Rodrigo heard the slither of the gun from its holster, heard the click of the hammer.

"Cut the shit," the second thug said, "and give me a hand." Together they managed to get Rodrigo onto his knees and balanced him, propped him with stones around his feet and knees, placed his sword in his hand.

"There now," the second thug said. "Pax vobiscum, Don Zorro."

"What a crummy statue," the first thug said. "I could do better with a pumpkin head. Dominus vobiscum." They went off twirling their rosaries like zoot suit key chains and very decidedly swishing in their robes.

Rodrigo got to his feet, counted all his arms and legs, checked their machinery. He had got as far as four when he saw a figure glimmering toward him through the square. Since it appeared to be a ghost, he suspected that the gangsters had indeed ballasted him with lead, but he could find no evidence to support that hypothesis. The figure came on, ever more like a ghost as it became clearer. It was a lady of the sixteenth century. She was wearing a long white dress and a high-draped mantilla. She might have had legs or, like the queen of Spain, she might not. She seemed to roll toward him like some surrealist invention. When she was close to him, she stopped. He thought he could hear the squeak of brakes. He braced himself for some high-flown conversation in the manner of court as imagined in a provincial capital.

"Hola," she said.

He took a look at her. "Hola," he said ceremoniously, to be on the safe side—the sixteenth century was a long way back.

"What company you with, motherfucker?" she said with elaborate fan and eye play.

He took a good look at her. She wasn't that black. "Company C, Royal Dragoons," he said. Perhaps after four hundred years even ghosts forget the details.

"I mean what dance company, asshole," she said. She achieved an even more graceful fall to her mantilla.

Dance? Dance? Dance? he said to himself. "Folklórico Oaxaqueño," he said.

"Liar," she said. "Oh, what a liar. I've been dancing my ass off all night with them at Hotel Monte Alban. You were never there."

"The road company," Rodrigo said. "I'm with the road company." He might not have been bright, but he was very fast. "We just got into town tonight. We were doing a special for the military at El Presidente."

"Good house?" she said.

"Wall to wall," he said.

"Good tips?" she said.

"Modesty forbids," he said.

"Buy me a drink," she said.

He didn't think that was a very good idea on top of the margaritas, but her eyes, her fan, the fall of her mantilla, her little dancing shoes that peeped. There was also a decided odor of sweat and musty costumes, so he agreed.

"Comrade Trash Sticker," the guard said when he returned, much pleased with himself, "some people have all the luck. Here I scramble around on my knees all night and come up with centavos. I leave you for five minutes"—actually it had been nearly an hour—"and you find a queen."

She validated him with her fan, her eyes, her mantilla, and she even managed a whiff of perfume like crying on demand. She curtsied with delicate hints of bosom. Rodrigo made a leg. The guard saluted.

"But just to show there's no hard feelings," the guard said, "I'll sell you that armor there. The mayor says to get that pile of shit out of there and it's yours. Like new. What's it worth? A thousand pesos?"

Rodrigo hesitated.

"Eight hundred," the guard said.

Rodrigo hesitated again. He was wondering what kind of price could be put on the sacred mummy of Richard Roe's mother.

"Seven-fifty. That's the lowest I can go — and I'm losing money."

"Done," Rodrigo said before the price could become any more humiliating.

The rest was simple. Roderigo arranged to pick up the armor at the southwest corner of the square at eight-thirty. In the voice of John Doe he telephoned the garage and arranged to pick up his car at eight — two members of his colonial household would pay in cash — dollars, *naturalmente*. He even persuaded the girl to run off with him and have fun, unlimited travel, unbridled lust, and machine-gun bullets for breakfast. He didn't tell her about the Mafia or the federal police or the CIA because he didn't know about them, or about the Guanajuato cops because he did.

"I really want that armor," she said.

"We'll see," he said, liar that he was.

"I can just see it in my room," she said. "I'll stand it in the corner and put a plant in its head. The leaves will grow out of those holes and hang down like a beard. Crazy."

"Crazy," he said.

They picked up the car and they picked up the armor. She directed him out of town by secret routes, but when they got to her house, she had him stop and she got out. Her husband was leaning against the gate, smoking an evil morning cigar. He charged Rodrigo for the whole night. "And the armor," he said, brandishing the cigar.

"Not on your life," Doe said. He laid down rubber and found his own way out of town.

He drove fast and he drove far, and he never learned what

an uproar there was in Oaxaca over the outrageous theft of a sacred image from the city crèche. He didn't realize that he was now being pursued by the Oaxaca police as well as the Guanajuato cops—and the Mafia and the feds and the CIA. All it meant to him was that he was just where he was before. He had lost no ground and had pulled off one more dull and stupid evasion in one more dull and stupid town he would never have to visit again.

V

NOW THAT Williams had gone up and down in Mexico and from side to side across it and had gained for his trouble only continued hardships and a wretched life, he decided that he had run out of possibilities and would have to try new dimensions. The central plateau had exhausted length and breadth, and the mountains had taught him all he wanted to know of up and down. Unmoved, he watched silent jets drag their webs across the highest skies. Trains, buses, and the fishing boats of smugglers were only chimeras. He turned then in the only direction left to him and disappeared into the blank spaces of the map, driving only where no roads showed, stopping at hotels only where there were no towns. His life was still hard and his condition wretched, but he took comfort in the thought that no mere murderer was going to find the hole he had slipped through and track him where there were no tracks.

He had no idea where he was or where he was going or where he had been. Each night he checked the Pole Star and resolved to go north, but each morning he set out at random down a path through the fields of trash that opened before him like the Red Sea.

So there he was one day when he stopped to consider his position, which was no worse than it had ever been. He despaired. All day he had seen no one and eaten nothing. No matter how suavely he raised his hood, no one appeared. There was no manna in the wilderness, not even a mess of stewed cactus. He was having a protein fit and needed a bite of something to cheer him up.

His ears were ringing. He felt his forehead and took his pulse. All O.K. But his ears were still ringing—no, it was the sound of church bells coming to him across the stony, trash-ridden fields. He located the church in a clump of trees off to his right and a little farther along. The bells continued to ring—one was cracked—calling the faithful to evening services. It seemed to him that *faithful* was exactly the word for him, so he allowed himself to be called.

Accordingly, he turned onto a cart path, which had all the disadvantages of improvement. It was deeply rutted, and the ruts were set with large embedded rocks. Cows and goats lay in the middle of the way and moved aside only when he eased his car over one last boulder and nudged them with his bumper. There were also craters that threatened both his car and the lining of his stomach. The sour taste of dilemmas rose in his throat, and he wished for lower gears, for stronger guts.

He glanced ahead and was reassured to see that the church tower was something like a hundred yards away. But almost at once the cart path dropped into the bed of a stream and seemed destined never to climb out. Then the hundred yards became a mile, two miles, something mythically endless, as the stream bed wound and twisted over rock ledges and among boulders with constant threats of annihilation to anything that could possibly be scraped off the bottom of the car: muffler, tail pipe, gas tank, yea, the very floorboards under his feet. Over his head, the Don complained in every joint and clanked and moaned most piteously. Williams didn't dare even think of his mother, racked and tossed and battered in the bosom of her iron protector.

He went north and he went south. He went east and west, those old, abandoned directions. He seemed to have circled the village at least three times when at last he rose out of the ravine where ruts showed that cars — or at least ox carts — had gone before him. He would not have chosen the spot himself, for it was no less steep and rocky and improbable than any other place, but he felt this was no time to question the wisdom of the ancient inhabitants.

He found himself at the beginning of the village street, broad, dusty, and pitted with holes that looked like dry hog wallows. A hag crouched over a cauldron not quite in the middle of the street, cooking up some mess that was indescribable and probably unpronounceable, certainly inedible. She looked like Hardy's old furmity woman arrived at some further stage of disintegration that even Hardy had not been able to imagine. Williams steered very wide of her and managed to avoid the deepest of the wallows at the same time. Pigs — there were plenty of pigs even if they were reduced to taking dust baths — pigs moved reluctantly out of his path, staring over their shoulders contemptuously like teen-agers moved along by the police. Hens squawked and fluttered. Burros with their pack saddles still in place stared at the wall to which they were tied. They were no more interested in Williams than was the old woman with the cauldron.

Hoping for better things in a town where perhaps no car had ever been seen, he turned the right angle in the street and came into what he supposed was the main square. The street here was suddenly broader, dustier, and more deeply pitted. The church he had seen from across the fields dominated the scene or tried to, for it had formidable competition from a battered, many-colored bus, composite survivor of innumerable wrecks. The bus was asserting its claim by drowning out the church bells with the roar of its exhaust and by casting a black cloud of stinking incense over everything: the church, the pigs, the hens, half a dozen hags crouched over their cauldrons, the long line of men seated against the wall across from the church — knees up, heads down, eyes hidden by sombreros in various states of dilapidation, their only marks of identity — and, needless to say, over Williams himself.

He parked the car in front of the church and got out. As he approached the wide open doors, he heard the chanting of the priest, he smelled the incense, and a great feeling of content fell over him in a cool shower. Before he could enter the church, however, he had to pick his way among various bundles of rags abandoned just in his path. Suddenly each bundle shot out a gnarled and scaly claw. But he was prepared. He reached into the special pocket he kept filled with the smallest of small change and scattered his alms freely. Each coin was clutched and kissed — or bitten — and then waved in the sign of the cross before being withdrawn forever into the heart of the rags. Williams imagined that octopuses must eat like this.

Then he stepped into the church and stopped. His mouth was open. He had never seen anything like it. On all sides dull gold struggled to gleam. Every inch that was not gold was covered with paintings and inscriptions. Clearly it would have been the Sistine Chapel if it could, but failing that, it was itself and splendid. He forgot the service and stared about him. He could find on the ceiling and walls all the Bible scenes he ever knew, Nativity jostling Passion, Adam and Eve trending eastward and meeting themselves in glory at the Judgment. Virtue Rewarded and sinners in Hell Fire. All was as it should be. There was even, he thought, Don Q in armor with one foot on the neck of the vanquished Dragon.

He was trying to decipher an inscription that seemed to bear on his case, but it was just too far away to be seen clearly.

He realized at that moment that everything had stopped. The worshipers — five or six old women — were filing down upon him. The priest had paused before leaving the altar, perhaps with a view to an ironic bow to the backs of his admirers. And the priest and Williams were eye to eye.

Williams slowly advanced the length of the church and met the priest at the rail. "Father," he began and hoped one word would pave the way for another. He had no idea why he was there or what he was going to say. "Father, I'd like you to say a mass for my mother." Of course he didn't say it like that, but he hoped that it sounded better to the priest than it did to him.

"My son," the priest said in perfectly intelligible Spanish, "I do not understand your dialect. I speak only Spanish, Otomi, and some Mazahua, together with Inglésh, which I have never had a chance to speak to anyone."

"English?" Williams said, scarcely believing that he might be freed from the curse of his prison argot.

"Yes," the priest said, "Inglésh. BBC. CBS. Radio. Eye estudiar las programas and escribir listas de sentencias igual in Español and Inglésh."

Williams's brain reeled. He had never before realized the awful responsibility of speaking English. In fact, he barely recognized it now, he was so busy adding *e* to esimple English words beginning with *s* to get a glimpse of the Spanish words and then discarding the *e* and throwing infinitive endings to the winds to arrive back at the light of reason. "Oh," he said, "lists of cognates."

"Veraciously," the priest said, smiling and nodding. "U R correcto. Oh, sir," he said and clasped Williams's hand, "U no imaginar mi felicidad at the apprehension of Et tu, Brute — divino Shakespeare pronunciar en Latin — en Inglésh, U two Bruto. A-O.K. La solution total de mi problemas, la Piedra de Rosetta de mi labores."

Williams suddenly wanted to lie down, but he clung desperately to his original question. "Will you say a mass for my mother?"

"Para el reposo de la alma de la mater?" the priest said. "Naturalmente. Mañana por la mañana."

"Tomorrow morning?" Williams said. He had hoped to have the mass said at once and be on his way, wherever that was. "But," he said, "it is not so much the repose of her soul —"

The priest held up his hand. "Mi enfante," he said, "las almas, totalmente, requerir los oficios eclesiásticos."

"Truly," Williams said. He felt as if he were sinking helplessly into a morass. "But" — and he struggled — "it is her body —"

"Las almas in purgatorio —"

" — stolen by grave robbers —"

"Miseria!"

" — and wandering God knows where —"

"Dios preservar."

"The mass?"

"Absolutamente mañana, but en presente to mi residencia for comestibles and potables." And he took Williams by the arm and led him, unprotesting, out of the church.

In his delight with meeting Williams and having an opportunity to practice his long-hoarded English, the priest had neglected to change out of his vestments. But only Williams seemed to notice that. At the door of the church, the bundles of rags that had shot out claws for Williams's coins now shot out the same claws for the priest's hand, which they kissed or bit with the same avidity. It was a blessed relief to Williams to listen disinterestedly to the babble of Latin and — he supposed — Otomi. It was better even than silence.

At dinner Williams met the priest's housekeeper and was informed, perhaps needlessly, that she did not speak English. In fact, she was not an *orador* even of Spanish. She and the priest exchanged few words in any language, and Williams wondered what the old woman made of the priest's Otomi.

She was a very old woman indeed, distinguished from the bundles of rags at the church door only in being upright. Williams thanked his stars that seven years in a Mexican prison had prepared his stomach for whatever food might come out of her kitchen, but the food was delicious, however fatal it might have been to lesser men. The priest's wine was of the communion variety, perhaps not yet blessed in the church or cursed in the kitchen, for one of the bits of information he had decoded from the priest's rambling cognates was that the housekeeper was a witch.

"Oh, yes," the priest said, "a bruja formidable. Eye retener the bruja en mi residencia para guardarse de brujería." Each time the priest said *I* he pointed to his eye and smiled and nodded as if congratulating himself on achieving at least a bilingual pun.

Having survived — or so he supposed — the worst the witch could do in her kitchen and the best the priest could do in his cellar, Williams went to his car and brought in a bottle of brandy he had been saving for some occasion that seemed likely never to materialize. It was a great relief to him that *brandy* is a universal word and the shape of the bottle an even more universal sign.

"Primero," the priest said, "ceremonia to the mater, alma reposada and cuerpo vagabundo." He lifted his glass and paused, conscious of having proposed a gracious toast in flawless English.

Williams's graciousness was able to rise only to the response, "The mater, alma and cuerpo wherever." But it seemed to be acceptable and they touched glasses and drank.

"Es necesario," the priest said. It suddenly occurred to Williams that the priest, creating English out of the air in his earnest isolation, had in fact created a simple dialect of tourist Spanish.

"Es necesario that la bruja considerar total that the primera ceremonia es to la Mater, la Virgen."

"The first toast to the Virgin?" Williams said.

"Yes," the priest said. "And the second ceremonia to la bruja." He filled both glasses and raised his toward the witch, who had all the while stood impassive beside the door to the kitchen. Williams hastily raised his glass in her direction and drank, even more bemused than usual by this unexpected elevation of his mother to a state of confusion. When the priest had drained his glass and set it upside down on the table — and Williams had followed that good example — the witch abruptly turned and disappeared, still impassive but perhaps appeased, into the kitchen.

"The bruja primera with excepción of la Virgen," the priest said, "and la Virgen primera unicamente because en el loco cerebro of la bruja la Virgen and Coatlicue are unidas."

"Curlicue?" Williams said apprehensively as he saw a formidable third going to make up a new trinity with his mother and the Virgin.

"Coatlicue," the priest said, "terrible mater diosa of the aztecas." He quickly blessed himself and reached for the bottle while an affirming crash of pots echoed in the kitchen.

"Really terrible?" Williams said. Like any good son he was worried about the company his mother kept.

"Terrible, terrible, terrible," the priest said and blessed himself three times. "Two cabezas tremendas."

"Two heads?" Williams said. He didn't think he was going to approve at all.

"Two cabezas of — "

"Jaguars?" Williams offered. He had a rudimentary sense of the iconography. After all, he hadn't entirely wasted his seven days as a tourist.

"Serpientes," the priest said and pantomimed enormous fangs to leave no doubt. "Collar," he said and passed a heavy necklace over his head, preened, "collar of manos humanos" — he hacked off his hands at the wrists — "and corazónes humanos." He disemboweled himself, missing his heart by a wide margin in his frenzy. "And uno cráneo." He carefully lifted off his skull and placed it, grinning, in the loop of his necklace. "Terrible." He was now too spent to bless himself.

"Es necesario dormir," he said, and indeed he looked exhausted. "La bruja es conductor to Urr dormitorio. Es infernal heretica. Eye disembark." And he went. But he stuck his head through the door and made small circles around his ear with his forefinger. "Loca," he said and rolled his eyes toward the kitchen. "La Virgen, Coatlicue, la bruja — una." He meshed his fingers to show unity. He spun his finger around his ear once more and pointed to the kitchen, pointed to himself, pointed to Williams, and disappeared for good.

Williams had no trouble finding the witch. He opened the door and there she was, sitting upright in the dark, staring directly at him. He knew there was no use talking to her, so he folded his hands as if in prayer and laid his head on them to pantomime sleep. She came past him, took a candle from the table, and led off into a dark corridor without once glancing at him. He followed.

The corridor seemed to have as many twists and turns as the river bed that had circled the town three times before it finally released him to his fate. At last she opened a door that looked exactly like any of the doors they had passed. She stood aside and allowed him to enter first. She had, he thought, very good manners for a witch.

The room was small, almost a cube. There were no windows, but an arch led to a smaller room, which he at first took for a bathroom but which turned out to be a kitchen, apparently unused for a very long time. In this room too there were no windows, but an open door led out into a tiny garden, walled about by high whitewashed walls and dominated by a single large tree shading the entire area. Radiating from the tree were wedge-shaped beds, edged with tile and containing nothing but hard-packed earth. Not even a weed had been able to grow there.

Williams realized at last that he was in a monastic cell,

doubtless one in a long series of such cells, and the ancient silence of the place seemed to promise a long night of dreamless sleep. Tomorrow would doubtless be the better for this blessed rest.

Then he turned and saw that the witch had come into the room. She had closed the door and was standing with her back against it. When she saw that she had his attention, she laid a finger across her lips and with the other hand motioned him to stay where he was.

"Do not try to say a word," she said, and he understood her perfectly. "I put a magic powder in your food, and now you can understand me perfectly. But you must not try to speak, or the spell will fail and the consequences will be most unpleasant." She paused as if expecting him to speak and the unpleasant consequences to descend at once.

But Williams was so astonished that he could say nothing. It was indeed magic that he could understand her as easily as if she had been speaking Spanish. In fact, the terms of the spell seemed to be that her Otomi should come through to him as perfectly fluent Spanish, easy, idiomatic, and far more filthy than his own. Already he felt he had learned enough to be accepted as a revered master of the language if by any misfortune he was ever sent back to prison. He was beginning to look for consolations in anticipation of that end, which seemed more and more probable.

The reason that the witch was as understandable as if she had been speaking Spanish was that she was speaking Spanish. She had mixed no potion with Williams's food, although the sleeping pill she gave the priest was real enough. On the other hand, she really was a certified witch, but as Williams was later to hear her remark on various occasions, a good lie takes less out of you than magic and often serves as well. The lie that she spoke no Spanish had served her well for many years with the priest and had enabled her to gain a cheap respect as a reader of his secret thoughts. In fact, the priest spoke of her with the same awe he would have shown for a clairvoyant dog. And now the same lie, brushed up and refurbished, was keeping Williams quiet just when she didn't want to be bothered with irrelevant questions and chatter. She could save her strength for better things.

She crossed to the bed and demonstrated its firmness with just the tips of her fingers, although the springs groaned and the headboard trembled. She turned back the covers and released an icy blast that burned Williams with fear. "To bed," she said. "Undress," she said. "Not a word," she said. Racked with fear as he was, stifling with protests, Williams was not about to say a word. Words had long since failed him, and even if he had not already been convinced that she was a past mistress of unpleasant consequences, he would have been speechless.

The consequences that immediately developed, however, were of such an unpleasantness that he was forced to wonder what worse could have happened if he had violated the taboo and spoken his thoughts. He modestly undressed with his back turned and slipped into the icy bed. Then, up to his eyes in bedclothes, he turned to her, half expecting her to soften, to bend tenderly and give him a good night kiss.

She was approaching the bed, unwinding her rebozo, unbuttoning her blouse. The furrows of her face stood out like a contour map in the harsh light of the bedside candle, her sunken cheeks, the crests of her cheek bones, her eyes blazing like pools catching the brightest sun. With her thumb and forefinger she snuffed out the flame. "Move over," she said.

He scurried to the far edge of the bed, abandoning one cold spot for a spot even colder. "Hold me," she said. He didn't think of refusing, for this was his oldest dream, embracing the impossible. The dog-faced girl with the harelip was the least of it, although the first, the obese girl with the dead babies, the deformed, the diseased, the ferocious. This was his lot, his only lot.

He turned cautiously toward her. Felt the leather of her skin. Trailed his fingers over the contour ridges of her ribs, bump, bump, bump. And got his arm around her. It was like holding a tepid bag not overfull of bones, no worse, although the smell was unbearable: old sweat, old flesh, the stifling odor of his grandmother's house.

"Kiss me," she said. It was no more than he expected — it was always in the dream. He felt for her head, her pitiful thin hair, smelling of dust and the pungent odor of mesquite smoke. Her breath stank of rotting teeth and abominations.

But just as he was about to touch her lips, there was perfume. He felt her hair writhe slowly under his hand, thicken, twine about his arm. Her body moved against his, twisting slowly, filling out. It seemed to him that she was a balloon luxuriously inflating. Her skin was soft and smooth as if just bathed and oiled. He gasped.

"If a woman can't do a thing or two for herself," she said, "what's the use of being a witch?"

He was terrified — but not too.

VI

WILLIAMS'S FIRST thought when he opened his eyes in the morning was escape, but he had slept late. A cup of chocolate was steaming beside his bed, and the witch was just coming into the room from the little garden. In the light of morning she seemed even more dry and furrowed than before. She spoke to him in Otomi, which he no longer understood. He took that as a sign that magic was suspended for the day and that he might speak, although there was nothing in particular he wanted to say. He had much to think about, however, and to cover his thoughts he ventured on "Good morning" in Spanish and English. She covered her ears and shook her head and motioned for him to get up.

He eased to the edge of the bed and sat up, modestly draped. He looked for his clothes and saw them neatly folded on a chair across the room. "Please," he said and gestured for her to leave. Instead, she brought his underpants from the pile— they were washed and ironed—*ironed*—and she knelt and slid them up his legs under the sheet. Her hands were like sandpaper. He didn't know whether to be amused or embarrassed, so he was both, and deeply disturbed into the bargain. She dressed him garment by garment, and when he was ready, she led him back to the dining room, where the priest was waiting for breakfast.

"Good morning," the priest said in Spanish. "What a good night's sleep I had. Your visit is good for me. Speaking English is good for me — but not before breakfast. English before breakfast is bad for the stomach. I slept so well I would have missed mass if my good angel hadn't waked me." He spoke here in Otomi to the witch, who just then was bringing in great beakers of orange juice. Possibly he was repeating *good angel*, for he smiled and drew a halo in the air over her head. There was no indication she was listening to him in any language.

"Perhaps tomorrow morning you will come to mass," he said and knocked back the orange juice.

"Tomorrow I will be gone," Williams said in English, thinking that the least of evils.

"It would have been nice," the priest said, "to have seven in the congregation for once rather than the usual six. Sometimes I think of killing one — this is a joke, my son — just to change the number.

"Of course," Williams said. "But perhaps a new person will come."

"No hope of that," the priest said, slipping a whole egg yolk into his mouth as if he were giving himself communion. "They only come to borrow the sacred images for a procession, and they have a procession only as an excuse for shooting off fireworks. They are so bored."

"At least you have six," Williams said. He was finding the eggs extremely *picante* and was glad for a chance to air-cool his mouth.

"Alas," the priest said, "they are all witches and come only to defy Blanca." He rolled his eyes toward the kitchen and his own resident witch.

"Alas, indeed," Williams said, but he thought, Alas for them — unless, of course, they were witches far out of the ordinary. He hurried through the rest of the meal in order to be on his way as soon as possible.

The priest wiped his mouth with a much-darned but very clean napkin. He burped or perhaps murmured a blessing and rose from his chair and led the way out into the street. Giving himself a shake and plumping himself up like a pillow, he said, "Mi lástima Inglésh. U R abandoner mi. Eye M desconsolado. But ambular U with dios. The mater is with U. Eye have sensibilidad que — that — the mater is proxima vigilar U."

"That is very comforting," Williams said, although it wasn't.

They were now approaching Williams's car. "Mi bendición on Urr automóvil," the priest said and stopped with his hand half raised for the blessing. Williams also stopped. His car was up on blocks. All four wheels were missing. The hood was up, and it was clear at a glance that the battery had been taken out. Williams walked slowly around the car, kicking each block to assure himself by the pain in his foot of the reality of the situation. Gently he lowered the hood to conceal, as far as possible, his shame.

"I guess I'm not going anywhere today," he said.

"We retornar to mi domicilio and Urr brandy for conversación in Inglésh," the priest said.

And Williams said, "Eye subordinar to U."

And so they continued — as the old song has it — both day and night. By day Williams talked Inglésh, and by night he understood Otomi but not much else. By day the priest was linguistical and historical, by night he was heavily drugged. He would start each morning by remarking how well he had slept since Williams's arrival. Up to then he had been troubled, he said, by evil dreams, clearly sent by the Devil to tempt him as if he were a new Saint Anthony. Delicious young Indian girls came to his bed, and he wrestled the night long with temptation and with them. He had taken voluminous notes, which he expected Williams to help him prepare for the press as the first step in the documentation of his claims to sainthood. He further explained the wonders of his church and read tearfully the poetry of the inscriptions on the walls and ceiling. To Williams's relief he forgot to translate them from the sixteenth-century Spanish of his predecessor, a man he called a second Saint John of the Cruz. "Cross," he emended, flinging his arms wide but failing always to collect the precious stigmata.

Peculiar as all this was before breakfast, Williams preferred it to talking Inglésh after breakfast, so he prolonged their morning walks more and more until sometimes they did not return to the rectory until noon, their feet dusty from walking on the bottom of the river or their hair covered with cobwebs from climbing stepladders in the church and butting their heads into particularly obscure corners to admire some special lines of the Mexican Saint John of the Cross, a man who seemed in his own time to have had as much claim to be a Mexican Saint Anthony, on the basis of his hag-ridden dreams, as Williams's friend and mentor.

Four hundred years before, he wrote:

> Protect, Thou wilt, my trembling soul from sin,
> And all the works Thou let'st the Fiend
> Encompass me about. His imps and succubi
> Disturb my sleep and make my dreams
> The very test of grace in me, Thy delight.

Williams knew little or nothing about Saint John, but he had serious doubts about Saint John II's claims as a poet, although at the same time his claims as a Saint Anthony had to be taken more seriously. There were witches abroad, leading men — saints — to destruction. By day and by night the witch was the witch, attempting by none too subtle means to win the souls of men for Evil.

During his solitary hours while the priest visited the sick, helped the needy, and supported the fainting, Williams speculated on the danger the witch posed for him, although when he examined himself he could find little in the way of soul to be lost. Still, there were other assets, less weighty perhaps, that he preferred not to be without: his sanity for one thing, his physical strength for another. Already he began to long for the quiet of prison, where he could now tell stories no one would believe, but everyone would love, of his feats of prowess, of his eroding flesh.

"Now," the priest said one morning as they paced among the boulders of the stream at great risk to their arms and legs and the solemnity of their meditations. "Now you have been here a month."

"A month," Williams said as he surmounted the worst of the boulders in his path. He had been observing the moon in all its changes, just as he had done in prison, and he was well aware that the moon was once again full.

"And you are looking well and fit — as fit as I feel — and ready for your journey."

In fact, Williams felt anything but fit. He felt as if he had been strained through a very fine sieve indeed. His head was dull. His stomach was weak. His bowels were lax. He reeled when he stood up from bed in the morning and reeled into it again at night. But still the witch's power enabled him to get through another night and stagger more weakly through another day.

A little research in the priest's library reassured him. He found that Coatlicue, no matter how terrible her form and her power, was not known for killing men by excess. He did ponder, however, the sentence that ascribed to her the ability to turn herself into the most beautiful of women in order to lure men to their deaths. Perhaps this was, after all, only a polite sixteenth-century way of saying the same thing.

"Tonight, my son," the priest said, "I will pray for the return of your wheels and your acumulador — your battery. You will see."

"But," Williams said, "couldn't you have prayed for their recovery before this?" He banged his shin on a boulder he had thought it safe to ignore. The priest, for his part, seemed to drift around boulders without seeing them. His perils were not of the visible world.

"Prayers," the priest said, "must be prayed in the fullness of their time."

"And the time is now full for my wheels and my battery —acumulador?"

"Why not?" the priest said.

"Don't forget to pray for air in the tires and a charge on the battery," Williams said.

"Prayer can do all things," the priest said.

In the morning Williams sprang out of bed as if it were Christmas, and fell back into bed from dizziness and weakness. More cautiously he eased himself over the edge into the attitude of prayer. Gradually he straightened, and rearing himself slowly, he balanced his head into the fully erect position. It was just possible today but might not be possible tomorrow if anything went wrong with the priest's prayers. He refused to think of what the witch might be praying—and to whom.

He had thought before this of making his escape on foot, but he had never been able to find any path out of the river except the one he and the priest used on their morning walks. The way he had come into town seemed to have vanished completely. He had walked for miles in both directions without ever losing contact with the church spire.

"The car is ready," the priest said before breakfast. "It is a miracle, another bit of evidence in support of my claim to sainthood—there must be miracles, you know. And another sign is your own present state of grace, which shines in your face with the translucence of fine porcelain." This poetic flight impressed Williams as more rare than anything he had read in the mural works of the second Saint John.

"I shall write in support of your claim," Williams said.

But the priest was slurping in his eggs and said next, "U R simpático. Eye"—since his hands were full with his knife and fork, he wisely winked his pun — "eye necesitar to voyage with U to the próxima village. Eye [wink] guidar U."

"Than-Q," Williams said, and he would have been glad to kiss the priest's hand if it had stood still long enough for him to grasp it.

At that rate breakfast was soon over. Now the priest did not try to restrain Williams, who ran into the street. Not only had the wheels been restored, but the car had been washed and polished, and bunches of flowers were tied to the door handles and the outside mirrors. Great indeed was the power of prayer. His enthusiasm was checked, however, when he saw that the witch was sitting in the back seat, looking more like a mummy than ever.

"The bruja acompañar us," the priest said.

Williams managed a grunt that was accepted as assent.

The priest directed Williams to the end of the village street opposite the one he had first driven in on. This was their usual way down into the river, a path best suited to an exceptionally agile goat. But when Williams stopped at the brink, the priest said, "Necesitar fai-th." Of course, the *th* came out as *t*, but he was especially proud of his attempt, little reassuring as it sounded.

The priest made the sign of the cross. The witch spoke a few words, which Williams didn't understand because it was only 9 A.M. And Williams eased the car into the path. The descent was smooth and easy. "U R fácil," the priest said when the car stood on the bottom of the river. He gestured toward the opposite bank where a good track, cut into solid rock, rose in easy switchbacks to the top. In all the mornings he had walked with the priest and in all the afternoons he had walked by himself, he had never noticed this path.

"Secreto," the priest said, smiling modestly as if he himself had just hacked the road out of the rock.

From the top of the bank, an arid plain stretched into the distance. The surface of the ground was thickly covered with stones, all about the size of a man's fist, very much as if this were the local crop, turned up like potatoes and waiting to be gathered. There was some cactus, less mesquite, and nothing else growing as far as he could see. The priest directed him to follow a faint track. A jack rabbit bounded before them. A cloud of ravens hovered over them. This was indeed one of the blank spaces on the map, but Williams did not feel comfortable here.

After two hours of picking his way across the plain and getting off the track time after time, Williams noted that the land was beginning to rise, perhaps toward an imposing butte that he had long since made his landmark when all else failed, as it often did, for the track, faint at best, could sometimes not be made out at all and sometimes only when the light fell on it just exactly right. It seemed to him possible that a village was hidden by the butte and that there might be a real road leading away from the village to some place less blank.

However, the track not only approached the butte but climbed it in beautifully engineered sweeps. Williams hastily looked a question at the priest, who simply smiled and waved him on. In the rearview mirror, the witch also smiled and showed her fangs. At the crest of the rise, the road at once dropped into a deep depression that Williams could only suppose to be an old volcanic crater. And in the middle of the crater was just about the last thing he had expected to see, an automobile graveyard.

The cars were drawn up in a circle, facing inward. Their hoods were all up as if signaling distress, as well they might have been, for they were all up on blocks, not a wheel among them. The priest directed Williams with great precision to a spot in the circle and had him stop there. "Es necesario," he said, "a momentito." He measured the smallest possible moment with his thumb and forefinger almost touching. He got out and opened the trunk. Williams supposed that locked trunks posed no problem for the witch—or what was the good of being a witch at all?

Williams now began to look about him. Directly in front of him was a mound made up of all the wheels of all the cars, laid carefully one on top of another like masonry. The mound was rectangular and low, very even except for one place where the wheels were set back to form steps. On the top of the mound was an isolated stack of wheels. The cars about him, he now noticed, were by no means as forlorn as he had at first thought. To be sure, they were up on blocks and their hoods were up, but the engine wells were full of greenery, cactus in full blossom, red and yellow, with sprays of mesquite. On each radiator cap a lighted candle flickered in a breeze Williams had not until then noticed.

"Señor," the priest called from behind the car, "es necesario— " But whatever was necessary was drowned out by a flood of rhetoric from the witch. Williams had never heard her speak like that, day or night, but he reasoned that he was wanted for something, so he got out and went to the back of the car.

The others were waiting for him, but to his astonishment they were dressed in elaborate costumes, capes and head-dresses of brilliant feathers, undoubtedly worth a fortune and countless years in prison for poaching endangered species. He saw at once, however, that the costume of the priest was less ornate than that of the witch, whose plumes towered and waved and thoroughly dominated the entire scene.

"Una ceremonia of bruja," the priest said, looking not in the least abashed.

"But you—a priest," Williams said in whatever language came to him. It might have been Otomi.

"Oh," the priest said, "sometimes she helps me and sometimes I help her. We get on." Williams supposed the priest had lapsed into Spanish or that the witch had laid another spell on him to allow him to understand Inglésh. She had certainly laid her usual spell, for he began at once to understand everything she said.

"We want to show you our temple and our altar," she said,

"in this place where the old tongues are spoken and all understand them."

"We will all wear masks," the priest said. "Yours is black."

"Of course," Williams said. "Naturally."

They ushered him up the steps to the top of the mound.
"Put on your mask," the priest said. "Play your part. Even if
you don't understand it, the sun will."

Williams wondered if he didn't mean Son, but thought that
the pun might not hold in Spanish — or Otomi — or ancient
Nahuatl, which, to be sure, they must have been speaking
under the circumstances.

"Please, honored sir," the witch said with a formality she
had never showed by day or by night, "all you need to do is
lie on your back on the pile of wheels while we pray over you."

"Only pray?" Williams said, for he had seen the obsidian
knife in her belt and had a sense of what was coming.

"And one or two other little ceremonies," the priest said.

"We must be sure that the sun shines," the witch said.

"Oh, yes," Williams said. "Of course." He took a last look
at the ring of cars about him, at the sun glinting on their tops,
at their flowers and candles, and he lay down. He knew the
witch could have broken him over her knee like kindling. All
he could see now was the sky, and that was too bright to look
at. It seemed to him that the sun needed none of his help. He
closed his eyes.

He felt his shirt being gently unbuttoned. He opened his
eyes. The witch, in the double rattlesnake mask of Coatlicue,
was bending over him. The priest, in a jaguar mask, purred
beside him. He sighed and closed his eyes — he thought for
good.

"Look," the priest shouted.

Even Williams looked, straight up into a cloud of ravens.
But he was undoubtedly still alive. He felt his chest and found
it good. He sat up.

With their backs toward him, the witch and the priest were
looking down at the cars, at his car. "Idiot," the witch said.

The priest crossed himself. "Quetzalcoatl," he said. "He was to come again, the blue-eyed one. It is a sign."

"It's stout Cortez all over again," the witch said bitterly. In her long life as a witch, she had had time to read many things and absorb many cultures.

"Quetzalcortezle," the priest said, and his feathers rattled about him. This was far too curious for Williams to resist, no matter what the demands of good manners, so he got up and joined them, buttoning his shirt as he went.

When he came to the edge of the platform, he could look down on the top of his own car. It seemed much as usual with the good Don in his place and, he supposed, his mother in hers. This wasn't exactly what he had planned for his mother's second entombment, but at least it had a certain dignity.

Then he observed that the jolting and jerking of the stones of the plain and the rocks of the river must have flung open the Don's visor, and he looked, not into the gaping eyes of his mother, but into the bright blue eyes of the old-man mask he had placed there at Pátzcuaro and since forgotten.

"It's no good," the priest said. "Anyone who travels under that sign is protected."

"That is true," the witch said, "but we know of one who is not protected by any sign. And we know that the sun must be made to shine." And she made a lunge at the priest, who began to dodge about the platform.

Williams saw this as the perfect time to withdraw gracefully. He ran down the steps, jumped into his car, and began to back out of the circle. Up on the mound, the witch was bending the priest back over the altar. The obsidian knife gleamed in her hand.

Well, Williams thought, martyrdom is surely one of the roads to sainthood. He would be sure to report it—if he ever reported anything.

VII

THE BLANK spaces on the map were all very well for a time.
He was hidden. He was safe. But he wasn't getting anywhere.
Moreover, he began to perceive that the blank spaces were
only the meshes of a net and that his security was only an
illusion. Marked roads began to press in on him from all sides,
rivers, mountains, and the names of towns. He had used up
all his options, and at times there seemed to be nothing to
do but drive directly north as far as he could go, as far as they
would let him, driving, walking, crawling in the direction of
Alpha, Illinois, until the end.

At other times, however, he still tried to find new ways. He
felt there had to be something he hadn't tried, a new direction,
a whole new dimension. He explored caves and canyons and
the sources of springs. And he passed from one blank spot to
the next in the dead of night, crossing highways in the dark of
the moon and when no cars gleamed within the wide horizon,
entering into new obscurities and passing on.

And when he was safe once more, he stopped and drank

the cheap brandy he needed to help him sleep, upright, his hands clutching the wheel. He hoped that, at some moment of sleep or drunkenness, the automatic gyroscope his mother had so long ago set spinning in his gut would take over and lead him by ways he couldn't have imagined to safety and success and home.

This was his hope but not his expectation, and instead of finding his way to the north, he kept finding a way down to the west coast. Sometimes the whole country seemed to slope in that direction, and he just rolled down to the sea. He skulked past Acapulco and Puerto Vallarta because he knew those were precisely the places anybody would look for a gringo. He avoided even Puerto Escondido and Barra de Navidad because he guessed that a really devious gringacho might be expected to hang out there. He was at the edge of despair, which even a bad Catholic knows is the one unforgivable sin.

So he wasn't surprised that the morning came when he woke up in one of the lesser circles of hell. He wasn't sure which one. The smell of burning filled the car, and when he opened his eyes, he saw flames in all directions, very small flames creeping through the dried grass. The car sat in the middle of a burned path. Brilliant dots of color pulsated in the black grass, and he feared for his eyesight, his sanity, and his immortal soul. He shook his head and rubbed his eyes and determined to live a better life. The dots persisted. A horrid sound filled his ears. Demonic laughter and something like music, perhaps half a mariachi band, the wrong half. There was also a basic roaring in his ears that would not go away. A new life was definitely in order.

The dots of color vibrated more violently. He wanted very badly to adjust them. They were pale blue and yellow and orange and bright blue and red and green. A bit of yellow exploded in his face. He felt that his real torments were about to begin. But as he resigned himself to eternal horror, the color resolved itself into a tiny bird clinging to the aerial of his car. It was a highly improbable bird, containing in itself most of the colors that tormented him. But it was a bird. Perhaps it could be handled. He would have been relieved except that the laughter went on and the music and the eternal roar rolling around and around in his head. And the flames everywhere, hemming him in.

Since his eyes were apparently not about to degenerate into a TV color storm, he decided to try them further. And a very little way off there was a beach and an ocean and rolling surf. The waves broke along the beach with a prolonged crash and passed on, the sound dwindling into the distance until over-whelmed by the uproar of the next wave. Still, a bird and an ocean were better than the torments of the damned or perhaps a ghostly conversation in Inglésh. The fire was only a fire in the grass — probably he had forgotten his campfire again. Even the demonic laughter now seemed capable of less than fatal explanation, perhaps nothing worse than bandits and mur-derers, and indeed came from a group of men lounging near, against, and on a sort of oversized rowboat drawn up on the beach. He began to count them but realized at two that he was outnumbered — if not, in fact, at one. There were fifteen of them. The two actually sitting in the boat were making the music on an untuned violin and a cracked cornet. Possibly the result would have been more pleasing if they had been playing the same song or if the men singing had been singing either of the two or even any recognizable tune.

Of course, Williams could have started his car and driven away, but he flattered himself that he knew fate when he saw it, so he got out and waited for some sign of recognition from the men on the beach. As soon as he stood clear of the car, they began to come toward him, still singing. He hesitated a moment and added a hoarse version of "Streets of Laredo" to the uproar. There was no particular reason for his choice. He just wanted to make sure he wasn't intruding on the musical territory staked out by any of the other singers, each of whom seemed to be going his own way quite as if alone.

He began to walk and met them just where the sparse grass gave way to beach sand. He stopped. They stopped. He waited for some revelation and meanwhile toured Laredo once more. One by one they fell silent as if arriving independently at the moment of recognition.

When the tumult and the yowling died, he addressed the group in general with a polite "Good morning." The response was not reassuring. He got a bark here and a grunt there and something that might or might not have been a word. After several attempts, he gave up and fell back on a stupid grin, a shrug, and a gesture with his hands that even to him meant nothing. The reply was in kind, and one of the men stepped forward and gave him a high five, spoke a few words. Williams longed for a dose of the witch's potion that had allowed him to understand Otomi and Nahuatl, although he was reasonably sure that what he was hearing now was no language he had ever heard before.

Pleased that things were going so well, Williams made the universal gesture of smoking and waved his hand in the general direction of his car. He intended to suggest that he would go and get cigarettes and bring them back so that everyone could smoke, stand about, and perhaps think of a song they could all sing. However, the message was received as an invitation to accompany him, so they all began cautiously to approach his car as if they were about to turn its flanks and encircle it.

It was a small misunderstanding but it opened the way for better things. No sooner had the men stepped inside the still-flickering ring of fire than they began to cross themselves and fall on their knees. They knelt in an arc facing the car, their faces lifted and rapt. Williams knelt in the burned grass. He felt like a fool but he had felt more of a fool standing. Out of common courtesy he tried to look rapt but probably failed. He did, however, assume the proper angle of his head and saw — Don Q. What now? he said to himself. What now indeed.

There passed a weary time with many signs of the cross, murmurings, sighs, groans, and meditations. Williams meditated: he found that his head hurt, that the ground was hard, that he was hungry, and that his legs would soon become useless, to say nothing of painful. Before he could starve, however, or fall impiously on his face, the leader of the fishermen — it had come to Williams that these men were fishermen because they had with them a bright blue plastic milk case overflowing with fish — the one who had given Williams the high five, crossed himself one last time, stood up, and looked with disgust on those still kneeling, those trying, in a word, to be more Catholic than the pope. He climbed up on the car and kissed the Don's hand. The others scaled the car from all sides, kissed hands and feet, and placed their hands on the Don's iron bosom, where the mystic heart must be supposed to beat. The pious son was glad of the iron, knowing full well whose bosom was really involved, hard and dry as it was.

The formalities now concluded, the leader stared without ceremony at the Don, inspected him with the hard glance of a shopper, thumped his chest, swung up his visor as if it were the lid of a trash bin, and looked in. He was neither surprised nor impressed by the Cortez mask, which was the first thing he saw. He lifted it out and looked further. He grunted as if he had known all along and began to unlash the Don. Other men helped him, and among them they lifted the Don from the car and laid him on the ground.

Now they poked and prodded the Don, moved his arms and legs, rattled his visor, and thumped him soundly. They talked among themselves and eyed Williams askance as if wondering whether this was the sort of man from whom they would buy a suit of used armor. It was that speculative look that prepared Williams for what followed.

The leader pointed to Williams. He pointed to the Don. And he pointed to himself. Then he held out a handful of coins that any self-respecting beggar would have been ashamed to take home. They were smooth and shiny and seemed to represent denominations long forgotten. They might have been washers.

Williams said "No," shook his head, and shaped large refusals with his hands.

The men now dismantled the Don and made a clanging heap of his elements. The leader rejected the ironware with a disdainful gesture. He pointed to Williams, to his mother, to himself, and once more held out the coins.

Murmuring an apology to the Don, Williams gave the pile of scrap iron a great bonging kick and hurt his foot but made his point.

The men conferred among themselves and began to carry off the mummy. Williams screamed denunciations and anathemas. He reached into the car and blew the horn. The men stopped short. They might not have known that the horn blared the challenge of Our Lady, but they certainly knew a fight song when they heard it. They set the mummy down at the edge of the beach. Perhaps they felt they had established a bargaining position. Williams, at least, felt they had. He felt they had left him no position whatever.

He paused for a moment to regroup. He would have to negotiate from nowhere. They had possession on their side to begin with and made up another nine — or a dozen — points of the law by outnumbering him fifteen to one. He called for a parley and again suggested a smoke. They agreed, which was a good sign because they didn't have to agree to anything. He had perhaps reduced the legal odds against him, but there were still fifteen of them hunkered in a ring around his mother. Then, as if at a signal, they all took something out of their pockets. Switchblades. The bright blades went off like flashes of cannon fire. They began to pare their nails. Williams's computer went down, and he no longer thought of odds.

He went to the car for cigarettes, still without a next step in mind, still without having in any way regrouped. He brought back the cigarettes and passed them out. He lighted the leader's cigarette, and the leader passed the light to the man next to him. It was the Olympic fire passing from hand to hand. Williams lighted his own cigarette while he watched.

When all the cigarettes had been lighted, each man stuck his cigarette upright in the sand in front of him, where it burned like a joss stick. And they began to sing. Williams began to sing with them. He dropped to his knees; he was not about to hunker and ruin his circulation, fall on his head when he tried to stand up. There was no mistaking the music this time — church music. "Tantum Ergo." He had learned it by rote when he was a child sitting in a corner of the choir loft while his mother practiced. "Tantum ergo sacramentum," he sang. Now she was getting some long-delayed return on her investment of his time.

When the singing was over and the last cigarette had gone out, Williams began with a simple statement. It was the only one he could make. He rocked a baby in his arms, pointed to himself, pointed to his mother.

The leader smiled and drew a circle in the air over his own head and pointed to Williams's mother.

Williams didn't know how to disabuse him of the notion that his mother was a saint. But since the fishermen hadn't — so far — simply cut his throat, he felt somewhat encouraged. He could see how they might like to adopt a patron saint. He wouldn't mind one himself. But he couldn't see what had ever led them into this ridiculous mistake.

Then, having nothing further to say for himself, he rocked the baby, pointed to his mother, pointed to himself. He thumped his chest. It hurt.

The leader now ventured into more complicated explanations. He appeared well practiced in dialogues with recalcitrant keepers of the mysteries. He began to haul in his net hand over hand. He held up the net. He shook it to show it was empty. He looked sad. Then he smiled. Pointed to Williams's mother and once again hauled his net. He hauled it slowly and with great effort. He lifted it like a great burden. He took out fish in great numbers. Williams could see them. Red snappers. Tuna. Herring. Not a skate among them. Not a rockfish. Not a puffer.

Williams was elated as much by the splendor of the catch as by the understanding of the issue. He still didn't see a way out, but he felt there had to be one now that he knew they simply thought his mother had worked the miracle of the fishes for them. Perhaps he could convince them that the magic was really in the hubcaps of his car. He rejected that idea.

The leader of the fishermen, in the spirit of compromise, offered to cut off his own right arm—no, he meant he would be satisfied with Williams's mother's right arm.

Williams was appalled but alert. He could see his mother's arm, like Grendel's, hung up as a trophy. Stranger things had happened. He himself had seen shrines to scraps of questionable skin, flakes of dubious bone. He was really entering into a negotiation. What, however, could he offer?

Hair. Hair was readily detachable and not really integral. But he couldn't remember hair as a relic in any shrine or sanctuary. Pubic hair, perhaps as a force for fertility in the sea. That might appeal to them. But it didn't appeal to him.

Then he saw her stockings, her poor, dear, imperishable nylons, trailing off her feet like the contrails of her mystic taking off for glory. He hauled the net. He made a mesh with his fingers. He touched the stocking. He made a mesh. Sympathetic magic.

The leader smiled. He touched the stocking. He stood and gave Williams a high five.

Williams peeled back the stocking as carefully as he could. The toes still had a tendency to come off, but Williams persisted. There were two toes left in the stocking. He hesitated, then passed it over. Let the toes be the fish in the net. No negotiation is perfect.

The leader's eyes gleamed. Perhaps he had had the same thought. He said nothing, however, and received the stocking with all piety. Perhaps he hadn't noticed the toes. Perhaps he thought Williams hadn't noticed them. But in the spirit of fair exchange he gave Williams a fish shaped like a small tuna. Although Williams would have preferred a red snapper, he didn't press the point.

After a final ceremonial cigarette, the fishermen stood up to return to their boat. The leader laid his hand on Williams's arm and with his other hand apologized for delaying him for the smallest moment longer, his thumb and forefinger almost touching. He pointed south along the coast. He grasped a steering wheel with both hands and drove a car. He touched Williams on the chest. He nodded his head as if he knew all about it. He pointed north, shook his head, and waved vast negations with both hands.

Williams nodded and touched himself on the chest. He pointed south. He grasped the steering wheel. Why not? He offered the leader a high five and, while their right hands were in the air, used his left to touch the stocking one last time for luck. There might, after all, be something to it.

The fishermen carried off their relic and their basket of fish, and left to himself, Williams cleaned his fish, impaled it on a green stick, and crouched to broil it where the slow fire still crept through the grass.

He drove south. There was only south and north and into the sea. It was perhaps all a trap but perhaps not. A tossup either way. Now that he was away from the beach and the fishermen and their bright knives, he began to edit the scene, to try to create a new script in which he would say . . . wonders, in which he would do . . . miracles. But nothing came to him. There they all were with their cigarette smoke ascending to heaven, a pleasant odor in the nostrils of his mother, as if she were basting a roast in her own kitchen with her cigarette dangling, her ashes showering a blessing on this food. And there he was, still frozen as in a nightmare. He was only making it worse, so he gave up editing.

But one of the fishermen remained before him, a man he had not particularly noticed at the time, a man who hung back and kept his head down. Williams felt he had seen him somewhere before, sitting, it seemed, against a wall with his hat over his eyes. He dismissed the notion—a stereotype, a tourist painting. The exercise yard of the prison. The same man or not, but the idea of the prison comforted him. If he ever went back there, he would be safe, and until then the prison alumni association was looking after him, for what reason he still couldn't imagine.

He went on south, not in utter despair, and just after noon began to pass through the usual sea of trash that indicated the approaches to a town. This was not just the ordinary sea of trash, however. It was larger and thicker and more malodorous, as if the local people had been discarding tin cans and plastic since long before the Conquest. The trash even encroached on the road and left him only a narrow, devious path, itself mined with jagged glass, dead dogs, and plastic sacks oozing into black puddles better not thought about. He avoided them all and was rewarded at last by descending into what is usually described as an undiscovered or unspoiled fishing village. Who would want to discover it? he said to himself as he drove tentatively through the brook that came down the hill and seeped across the road. It was green and seemed to be the liquid form of all that was unspeakable in the town's protective ring. How could it be spoiled?

The village street was unpaved, not even cobblestones. In fact, the place was so unspoiled there wasn't even a speed bump. A solitary blond, blue-eyed drinker sat in the shade of an awning in front of a café. He had the complexion of something under a stone and stared out at the street with petrified delight. There was something that might pass as a hotel. There were fishing boats with powerful outboard motors drawn up on the beach — nets drying, of course. Farther along, a woman — not Mexican, although some sort of well-tanned leather — strode toward the boats and the real Mexico. She carried a sketch pad and glanced bitterly toward Williams as if he were the beginning of the end, as if he were the original discoverer and spoiler.

Almost at once he came to a second brook even more revolting than the first and inscrutably deep. This marked the limit of the town. He cringed and began to turn around. And it was here that his car, his faithful Rosinante, failed him.

It was necessary then to make a more detailed survey of the town. There were three cafés, not one. What might have been a hotel was, in fact, a hotel, El Refugio. It even had a sort of beer garden on the water side and two palmetto shelters with tables on the beach itself. There was a city hall. A bank. Four shops of general merchandise. And a Taller Automotriz, which was, of course, closed, although a formidable-sounding dog was alert inside. There was nothing to be done. It was obviously time for a beer.

He avoided the solitary drinker and settled at a café on the other side of the street. The sun was so high that neither side could properly be called shaded. In fact, the light poured in through the open end of the street, for both street and beach seemed to be running east and west at that point, further disgusting Williams, who knew perfectly well that the Pacific Ocean was supposed to be in the west. But wherever he himself was supposed to be, he had already furnished the drinker with an exciting day. In the past half hour a car had gone by and then two men on foot and now there was someone drinking at the café across the street. It was practically a parade.

Williams drank a beer and nothing happened. He drank another beer very slowly and nothing happened. He was not accustomed to sitting still so long and having nothing to do but think — at least not since he began his travels. And what he thought was that he would let his mother's lawyer know where they were and that they were on their way and that they were still alive — at least some of them. So he went to the hotel and rented a room in order to get a sheet of paper and an envelope.

The clerk spoke English and received him with aplomb as if he were accustomed to hordes of guests, although the register clearly showed that the last guest had signed in for one day two months before. "Welcome," he said. "Welcome. Goddamn."

The hotel was unexpectedly luxurious, although it had the air of having decayed without ever having blossomed. It had once been the Convent of Saint Agatha and had been carefully restored by someone who expected to be discovered and devoutly hoped to be spoiled. In all the renovations, however, the saint's attributes had been piously left in place, so that over the door to his room a pair of highly glazed and delicately tinted breasts protruded into the passageway as if the saint herself were about to escape from her long immurement. There was also a scrap of faded wall painting and a dim slogan that announced: This Place Is Sacred. He entered humbly and wrote his letter, feeling more secure and protected than he had felt since he left prison.

When he had finished his letter, he came out and asked to be directed to the post office. "Post office?" the clerk said. "Turn left. It's on the other side of the street near the city hall." But apparently fearing he had made no intelligible sounds, he led Williams into the street and pointed. "There," he said. "By the sleeping dog. Goddamn." There was indeed a dog sleeping in the street, so Williams had no trouble finding the city hall. The post office, however, was nowhere to be seen.

He looked into the city hall, one room with three desks and no people, and he crossed to the bank, where there was at least a corpse laid out on the counter. He stood at the counter and waited. Sooner or later someone would have to do something about the corpse, if only to take it up on the hill, where it wouldn't be noticed.

The corpse opened its eyes. "Hola," it said.

"Hola," Williams said. "The post office?"

The corpse closed its eyes. "By the city hall," it said and died again.

This time Williams inspected the city hall more closely. He could see at a glance exactly what he had seen on his last glance, three desks and no doorway except the one he stood in. He went down the street to the right and passed a closed shop, a café, and came again to the Taller Automotriz. It was still closed. Even the dog must have been asleep.

When he passed the city hall this time, he found a stairway going up to what he supposed was the house of the people who owned the next shop (closed), and then he came to the café of the drinker. Williams felt foolish about passing the drinker for what would have been the sixth time, so he stopped and turned back. Now he went into the city hall and quickly found a man asleep on the floor behind a desk.

"Post office?" Williams said as if he were part of the man's dream.

"Next door," the man said without opening his eyes.

"I've looked next door," Williams said. "I've looked to the left and I've looked to the right, and I have found no post office."

The man groaned and pried himself from the floor. He took Williams by the arm as if to lead him, but since his eyes didn't seem to be open he might himself have wanted to be led. In any case, they moved together to the door and went out into the street, where they made a complete about-face and were at the foot of the stairs Williams had noticed. The man pointed up the stairs like an admonishing saint on the front of a church. Williams went up. There was nothing else to do. But at the top he stopped. There was somebody's house door, exactly as he had suspected, and nothing else. He turned and looked down at his guide, who now raised his arm again, straight up. To be sure, there was another stairway, but it clearly led out onto the open roof. It seemed to be a matter of leaving no stair unclimbed, so he climbed.

He climbed into the pure, undisputed sunlight, and he faced a bank of post office boxes, which stood under the shelter of a striped awning. There was also a counter. Both the boxes and the counter had the look of having been abandoned in the middle of a move, but Williams felt by now that he knew the ropes, so he stepped around the counter and woke the clerk, who reared up off the floor long enough to sell him thirteen enormous one-peso stamps for his airmail letter.

"Smaller?" Williams said. "Larger?" Size, he meant. He meant denomination.

"Only," the clerk said in his sleep. Williams contrived to frame the address and cover the back of the envelope with stamps. He was glad he had prudently left off a return address to avoid being traced.

He was now confident enough to go back to the garage and pound on the gate. The dog barked like a true dog. A man said, "Hola."

"Hola," Williams said. "I want to talk to the maestro."

"I am the maestro," the man said. A bolt scritched. The gate jolted on its little iron wheel along a rut worn deep in the stone of the courtyard. Ah, the courtyard. There were mounds of old tires and heaps of corroded batteries. Tubs of oil or dirty water. Parts of engines lay about on newspapers. It was beyond a doubt the ninth circle of automotriz hell. Three cars and an old Ford truck lay about in various stages of despair.

Now that the gate was fully open, the maestro himself appeared from behind it. He wore overalls that might originally have been blue, and he had the tribal markings of grease on his face. Clearly he had just risen from the newspapers after some arcane confabulation with the well-oiled parts.

"Is all this yours?" Williams asked politely.

The maestro nodded. "And what is your problem?" he said.

Politeness was working so well that Williams continued it. "My motherfucking car has fucking crapped out, fuck it," he said.

"Ah," the maestro said. He was obviously impressed by the language of the great world. "And where is your motherfucking car?" he said.

"Near the brook," Williams said.

"Shall we go?" the maestro said and started out the gate. Williams followed. He looked about for the tow truck, but there was no tow truck. They were going to walk, no doubt about it. Sanctioned now by the maestro, Williams nodded to the drinker, who waved, glad to recognize an old friend.

"This is a beautiful car," the maestro said.

"Thank you," Williams said.

"This is beautiful armor," the maestro said.

"Thank you," Williams said.

"This is a very sick car," the maestro said. "There will be no parts nearer than Guadalajara. That will take a week. Mexico City is ten days. And if we have to send to Dallas, you can marry my sister and raise a family."

"Thank you," Williams said. "Thank your sister. But let us begin to telephone at once."

"Ah, telephone," the maestro said. "You Yankees are impetuous, no matter how well you speak Spanish."

So Williams settled in at El Refugio. As the days passed, he began to look at the wall over his door in hope that he might catch the good saint in the act of trying to back out of the plaster, but the wall was too thick, and she was too well stuck. He read ancient *Newsweek*s and worried about the war in Vietnam. He avoided the street and the drinker and drank carefully rationed beers in the garden by the sea. But mostly he walked like the good Yankee he was, early and late and in the heat of the day.

The clerk at the hotel produced binoculars and a bird book

abandoned by some earlier guest. He did not say what had happened to the guest, but he knew that all Yankees spied on birds. Goddamn. So Williams became a bird watcher. In the morning he stalked them among the coconut palms. With Dr. Peterson's help he found three kinds of orioles and a cacique. He found the gray-headed kite and the blue-throated hummingbird and the rufous-backed robin. He found the groove-billed ani and the boat-tailed grackle. He found the purple finch where it wasn't supposed to be and a small black bird that didn't exist anywhere. In the afternoon he watched the sea and sorted out the terns and the gulls and a blue-footed booby and frigate birds soaring over everything. He also watched whales and tankers on their migratory routes and wondered what would have happened if the clerk had produced an easel and a set of oils.

From his seat in the garden, and from the window of his room, he could see the rocky headland that closed in one end of the bay. He thought it would be pleasant to be up there looking down on the village and on the sea and on the backs of birds soaring below him. On his walks he explored approaches to the high ground but could find no path, although he traced the beach out to the point where the rock dropped sheer into the water, and in the other direction he followed faint trails far inland but found none that bent the way he wanted to go. Sometimes, however, as he studied the headland from the hotel, he could see small figures moving about, and he knew there had to be a way. Each morning he tried once more to find it, but each morning he failed and had to return to the hotel for the comforts of his breakfast and the *New York Times*.

It was a venerable copy of the *Times* that he read, yellow now and nibbled by mice. Nothing was resolved from day to day, but the tapes were never explained, and the President never approached closer to disgrace, and the Chicago Cubs never sank farther toward the bottom of the league. Reassured, he turned to the crossword puzzle, which he did very lightly in pencil and immediately erased to be ready for tomorrow. The crumbs on his table were orts. The bird in the bush was an ani. He was ired by the delays in repairing his car. And the clerk at the hotel, goddamn, was a oner. His life was inane, he knew, and what he needed was some élan or elation. He needed to leave this agora and seek the purer air of that tor or arête, to find some oread or nymph at least, preferably wearing a Pacific A-bomb atoll, beginning with *b* and ending *i* blank *i*. As he sipped his chocolate, he thought about the maestro's sister and wondered if he should make discreet inquiries.

And then one evening when he was exploring a cove he had often explored before, he heard a woman singing in the woods on the side of the mountain just above his head. The place, he had always thought, should lead by a gentle slope up to the spine of the ridge, but the gentle slope always ended in the precipitous bed of a dry stream. As he listened, the woman's song passed him and faded. He went on into the glen a step farther than he had ever gone and found there was a path, a steep and rocky path that crossed the brook back and forth recklessly. In five minutes he was standing on a well-worn trail that led in one direction God knows where back inland but in the other direction to the high point he wanted to reach. The trail had obviously once been used by wagons or trucks, but it was now washed out in many places, and the dumps along the edges had been long abandoned, ancient tin cans collapsing into the ground, rusted the color of dead leaves and rotting wood.

The path led out of the woods onto an open neck where he could see the bay on one side and the sea on the other. The drop was sheer to a pebble beach on the sea side, and he looked down, as he had hoped, on the evening glitter and the towering spray as the sea battered the outlying rocks. Then he pressed on to reach the farthest possible vantage point.

The trail plunged back into a bit of woods, traced the edge of a rock pinnacle, and again came into the open at an even narrower neck than before. As he stepped out of the woods, he saw a woman painting. She was seated on a little camp stool with her back to the rock. It was the same leathery woman he had seen when he first drove into town. He hesitated but his feet went on walking. He would have to pass close before her, and he knew she despised him. He would have to drag his shape across her scene. He made himself as small as possible and prepared to go on. He half-raised his binoculars, pretending to contemplate a distant bird. He would pass her as he would have passed Dr. Livingstone in Darkest Africa—unless, of course, it was his specific duty to speak.

"Hello," she said. "You must be the new boy in town."

"I guess so," he said.

"Where do you keep yourself?" she said. "How come I never see you?"

He looked at her now. She was indeed brown and lean and seemed very fit, but the hair that showed beneath her big straw hat was white and made her look like an old man, one of the Impressionists but he couldn't think which one. "You saw me once," he said. "The day I drove into town. You didn't like me."

"I never saw you," she said. She was seeing the water and the sun and made a quick pass at her canvas. "I can go for days without seeing anything."

"Oh," he said. She was very different from what he had thought but no less formidable.

"That must be your car at the garage," she said. "I've sketched it. What's with the armor?"

"Oh . . ." he said. He had been meaning from day to day to do something about the armor. But although he was quite used to his mother on his roof, he couldn't quite reconcile himself to the idea of her standing in the corner of his room watching him sleep. He saw now the danger of exposure he had risked. This woman before him was clearly the kind who might well want to see the inside of the armor before she sketched the outside.

"What do you do with yourself?" she said, en garde before her painting.

"I walk," he said.

"Then I should have seen you," she said. "This is the only place to walk."

"I walk all over trying to find a way up here," he said. "I've only just found it."

"And what else?" she said. She hesitated. Almost touched the canvas. Drew back.

"I read the *Times*," he said.

"You get the *Times*?" she said. Her voice was excited but her eyes were judicious.

"Only one," he said. "It's very old. All about Watergate."

With great care and perfect assurance she touched her painting once and began to lather her palette. "You read the same one every day?" she said. "Next thing you know you'll be going eccentric."

"The *Newsweek*s are even older," he said.

"You'd better come sketching with me," she said.

"I look at birds," Williams said. He thought birds might be more acceptable.

"You can sketch birds," she said. "What do you think of it?" She gestured toward her painting with her elbow.

Williams cautiously circled and looked over her shoulder. There was no sea and there was no sun. The painting was green at the top and black at the bottom with a clear dividing line two-thirds of the way down. He wondered where she had made that one last assured touch. He looked back at the sea. He looked at the painting. He looked up and saw the prairie and the midwestern sky. "It speaks to me," he said.

"Yes. Well," she said, putting down her palette and rising. "It's time to admire the sunset." She led off toward the end of the headland, a little knob of rocks he had selected through his binoculars as the very place. She simply assumed his consent and spoke to him without looking over her shoulder.

As they finally got into the open, clear of the rock where she had been painting, they saw the man. He was lounging against the rock. He did not exactly belong to the place, although he was clearly Mexican. He looked like a waiter in his off hours, white shirt and black pants. He was young. He was unshaven. He did not greet them or even look at them but stared into the middle distance as if preparing a commentary on the seascape. In one hand he carelessly held a small clear plastic bag smeared with yellow. Perhaps he had captured some marvelous butterfly and then absently reduced it to pure color as he waited for the sunset.

"That place," she said, "is the only place. It's as close to flying as you can get." She ignored the man as easily as he had ignored her.

"It must be you I've seen there — with binoculars, I mean," Williams said.

She shrugged. "I never suspected binoculars," she said.

"They're not very good," he said. He caught up with her as they came to the last rocks. They arranged themselves to face the sea, to look along the blood lane to the sun. He was also sitting where he had to include her in his view.

Except for the white hair she did not appear old, nor did she give the impression of premature aging. Rather, age was irrelevant to her. He thought that perhaps she was as old as his mother. He tried to concentrate on the sunset, but her image, touched softly with pink, was the largest part of it.

"I could paint that boy," she said without losing the play of a single ripple.

"Could you paint me?" he said. He had always wanted to say that to someone and hoped that this was the time.

She shrugged without bothering to look — she had looked, he knew.

"I'm probably not an interesting subject," he said. "Not like that boy."

"A man who drives around with a suit of armor on his roof is bound to be interesting," she said. "A man who reads the same copy of the *Times* every day."

"That's not very interesting to me," he said.

"Oh" — she turned toward him, apparently trusting the rest of the sunset to take care of itself — "would you like some brandy?" she said. She plunged her hand at once into her purse and caught a fine silver flask. The flask had a cap that held about a jigger. She poured it full and held it toward him. He took it.

"Why, yes," he said. "Thank you. I'd like that."

She saluted him with the flask and appeared to knock back a long drink. He was not impressed, however, for he remembered the feats of his undergraduate days, with his head back and his tongue in the neck of the bottle. He tossed off his jigger. And strangely he found himself wondering how it would be to make love to her, a woman so old.

"We'll have something to eat at my place," she said. "There won't be much."

"Come to the hotel," he said. "They'll have something."

The sun had settled on the rim of the horizon and was ready to roll all the way around to the east and start over again. "Now," she said, "this is it." She filled his cup again without really taking her eyes off the sun.

They held their drinks up to the sun to incorporate its last direct rays, and at that moment Williams saw a terrible head rise above the rock behind her. It was the head of the man they had seen near where she painted. But now, up close, he was clearly mad or drunk or spaced out on drugs. His eyes, which were turned directly on them, were unfocused, and his mouth was lax, glistening.

"Hello," Williams said. That was the best he could do, but it alerted her.

She turned. "Hello," she said. The glaring eyes didn't move. "What is your name?"

"Do you live around here?" Williams said.

The head began to slide to the left, and the whole man began to rise out of the earth until he stood towering over them.

Williams scrambled to his feet. The brandy slopped over his hand. "Have a drink?" he said, holding out the brandy and the sun.

A hand reached toward him, apparently of its own volition. Fingers touched and the cup passed. But the hand, its ideas exhausted, stayed exactly where it had received the cup.

"Here's how," she said and raised the flask toward the cup. Nothing happened. "How," she said. Williams guessed it was a real drink this time.

"Would you like to sit down?" Williams said, gesturing toward the rock where he had himself been sitting. He seemed to be pulling up the rock and holding it politely.

But the man turned his back and stepped to the edge of the cliff. His toes were at the limit of the rock or just beyond. His arm, holding the cup precisely as he had received it, projected into the void and saluted the darkness that began to rise out of the sea. It was clear to Williams that when the darkness was complete, he would drink the elixir, go beserk, and fling them both over the cliff. And then, terribly, the man began to shout.

Nothing about him moved, but he spoke in tongues. The language was rhythmical and repetitious and passionate. "Perhaps he is only a poet," she said. But she hadn't convinced herself. She had aged. Her hair was whiter than ever and seemed thin. Her tan had faded to the color of ashes.

"Let's get out of here." Williams moved his lips and gestured. He helped her to her feet and then down the rocks to the level ground. "Your cup," he said. She shook her head violently.

They walked as fast as they dared, anxious not to throw the maddening scent of terror into the air. "Your things," he said as they passed the place where she had been painting. Again she shook her head. She clutched his arm and hurried on. As they entered the woods, he glanced back. The man had not moved. His voice came to them faintly, mingled with the heavy sound of the surf rising up the face of the cliff.

In the woods they hurried, fearing ambush. They slid and scrambled down the dry stream bed and reached the level ground, the familiar palms, the beach where fishermen were preparing to go out for their night's work. The hotel was not far. He barely noticed that his car was at the door.

"You'll feel better when you've had something to eat," he said.

She shuddered and shook her head. "Your room," she said.

"Oh," he said. "Of course." He needed that too. Flesh on flesh. And arms. The breasts of Saint Agatha gleamed faintly as he helped her through the dark hall and into his room.

Once inside, she wilted. She stopped just past the door. "Lock the door," she said. He locked it. "Undress me," she said. With care and proper ceremony and eyes averted, he removed her chambray shirt, her sandals, her Penney's jeans, her impeccable white underpants. He left the heavy necklace of what he took to be pre-Columbian beads. "Put me to bed," she said. He led her gently to the bed. "Cover me," she said. He drew up the sheet. "Kiss my forehead," she said. He kissed her forehead.

"You will watch?" she said. "I can sleep if you watch." He retreated to the corner and watched. It was the corner where he would have placed Don Q.

He watched for hours. Her hair hung in damp strands about her face. Her mouth fell open. Her cheeks fell in. She was in an agony of singing or in the midst of a scream. From hour to hour her color became more ashen. At times he glanced from her to the blank plaster over his door. The faint words out in the hall had eaten their way through and now burned in all their original color: This Place Is Sacred. And it was.

Toward morning he must have slept. He would have sworn he was just lowering his eyes from the plaster to the bed, but the bed was suddenly empty. She was gone.

Before full light he had settled his bill and was gone himself. He drove through the stinking brook and climbed the long hill out of town. At the top, mindful of ancient precedents, he did not look back. If he were to become a pillar of salt, he would prefer to choose some other place for it. If his Eurydice were to disappear from behind him — but of course he had no Eurydice. His mother — He paused. Considered. But in the end he did not look back. Ahead of him the path was clear through the ring of garbage. The rising sun caught everywhere in slashes of gold and dazzle among the trash. Mesquite and cactus were vertical gold. Stones were pure gold and faded as he passed. He knocked the mirror askew and turned his outside mirror against the side of the car. Its silver rim still sparkled.

He began to follow the road back along the coast. As he passed the turnoff for the beach where he had seen the fishermen, he wondered if their plan in sending him to that village had been fulfilled. He wondered what he would have seen if he had looked back from the top of the hill. He imagined palm trees and a deserted beach, a harbor undiscovered and unspoiled. He drove as nearly north as possible, following the winding road now east, now west, sometimes even briefly south as it circled some bay or mountain, some torrent or forbidden ravine. Sooner or later there would have to be a way back up to the central plateau.

VIII

He knew it was Sunday because the fields were full of boys playing soccer. Wherever there was a flat place there was a soccer game. Sometimes there wouldn't be a house in sight, let alone a village. Sometimes he would look down into a deep valley and see the game streaming across the land, the white flash of the ball, the black authority of the referee. All else would be still, only the pale tracks winding down the hillsides and concentrating on the game like lines of force. He would stop then and watch like a god, at once hopeful and indifferent, exhilarated and depressed by every move. When being a god wore him out, he moved on and replenished himself in solitude, so he was always ready for the next struggle, to be yearned over and seen only at a great distance and in miniature.

He knew he had come to a town because the pavement stopped and cobblestones began. He slowed down until he came to the first of the speed bumps. He was used to them by now, far more used to them than he was to the sign warning of them. *Topes*, it said, and the symbol looked like a lewd boy's drawing of a brassiere or of a woman, front or back. He might have ignored the warning if he hadn't seen the bump itself looming in the distance, a monster. Even the Mexican drivers came to a complete stop before easing over it. The local cab driver coming the other way crossed himself before attempting it.

At this rate of speed, it was easy to take in the sights of the town, which were: three Dallas Cowboys T-shirts, all number 12; one Plattsburgh (N.Y.) State Teachers College; six Fernando Valenzuela; one The World's Biggest, on a woman, but they weren't. It was the kind of town where the saints on the façade of the church all looked disgruntled. They hadn't expected this. Only the Christ remained serene. Under the outstretched hand of John the Baptist, a natural roost, he stood in a perpetual drizzle of pigeon shit. He had known from the beginning how it would be.

It was a town to pass through, so he passed. There was nothing he could recognize as a hotel, nothing he would trust as a restaurant. Fruit and meat were sold at every corner, flies and dirt blowing over everything: instant ptomaine, just add spit. He drove on until he saw the white walls of a cemetery set back in a field. He drove off the highway and parked beside the wall.

His guide book — which he rarely followed but always read with pleasure and only incidental profit — happened once to mention that a cemetery was a very quiet, satisfactory place to camp. He felt it was worth a try in any case, not that he had ever dreamed of trying most of the other things suggested in the book. He was not about to build a thatched hut, for instance, or dig a well. He had dug wells in his time, and septic tanks too. He had even driven well points into the ground, including the one that hit a rock and came up behind him. Digging a well was something you did once in your life; you used it forever and passed it on to posterity. Your grandchildren blessed you even after they sold the place and moved to California.

Still, the *People's Guide* was amusing and well written and full of useful things he hoped he'd never have to know. He read it each night before he went to sleep, although as a general rule anything, or any person, labeled of/by/for the people he regarded with suspicion and hostility. *People*, like *gay*, was a word that needed to be rescued from its pre-emptors and rehabilitated for general use.

He read by the fading daylight with his back against the cemetery wall. He had punched two holes in a can of Campbell's soup, *sopa de res*, and he drank it neat. He also had Saltines and a Hershey bar *con nueces*. He chose tonight not to read the anecdote about automobile repairs because he couldn't bear to consider what might happen if his car should again become disabled, giving whatever was following him a chance to overtake him. He read instead the anecdote about the elephant's head being loaded into a truck in the middle of nowhere. Just about where he always was, he imagined, and he was always on the lookout for wonders. He never saw any, although that winter many motorists reported to the author that they had seen a car with a suit of armor strapped to the top, here, there, and just about anywhere. They asked that they be given credit for the sighting in any future editions of the guide.

When it became too dark to read, he built a little fire for company. One reason for selecting this site was its isolation, but another was a sense that it would provide some suitable companions for his mother, whom he had come to feel he had rather neglected in his concern for his own safety. Then he wrapped himself in his poncho and lay down with his back against the sun-warmed wall and wished he could think of some way to disguise his car as a burro.

When he opened his eyes, he knew he couldn't have slept long, for the fire was still burning brightly. But across the fire sat a man, who surely hadn't been there a moment before. Williams tried to convince himself that this was some campesino, some shepherd, perhaps, attracted by the fire and the hope of a friendly word or two, but it was hard to make the hypothesis hold up when he found he couldn't ignore the automatic weapon ready in the man's lap. Most shepherds, he knew, controlled their sheep simply by throwing stones at them. It was quite possible that they had caught up with him.

"Hola," he said to start things off.

"Hola," the man said and stopped them.

Williams shuffled the various possibilities in his mind. None of them particularly delighted him. He felt rather inclined, however, among what was available to him, to prefer police and prison to unknown enemies and an unforeseeable end.

"Federales?" Williams said.

The man spat into the fire, which Williams chose to consider noncommittal. Entrapment was not an impossibility.

"If this is a bust," Williams said, "I'm clean."

"If you're clean," the man said, "you need a smoke." He tossed a cigarette case across the fire. It landed on the edge of Williams's serape. Williams picked it up guardedly. It looked and felt like heavy gold. He sensed more than ever the danger of entrapment, but the danger of refusing the smoke was even greater. He might be hassled for smoking if the man was the law, but if he was not the law, Williams could find himself shot dead for discourtesy. The choice finally was not difficult.

The smoke was very good. "Nice," Williams said.

"The best," the man said.

"Very elegant," Williams said as he handed back the case.

"Naturally," the man said.

Picking his words carefully, calculating the risk, Williams said, "Perhaps you are not what you seem."

"Nor are you," the man said.

They nodded solemnly together. They were getting nowhere. The real problem for Williams would come when the officer—if he was a policeman of some sort—tried to sell him anywhere from a kilo to a ton of marijuana. He decided that the best thing would be to pretend to have no money.

"A very nice car you have there," the man said.

"Thank you," Williams said.

"Not everyone travels with a suit of armor on his car."

"No," Williams said. "not just everyone."

"I like that armor," the man said. "It has class."

"I call it Don Q," Williams said.

"Very good," the man said. "Don Q. I like that." They laughed together very politely.

"I like that armor," the man said again. He seemed to be coming to some point.

"It is something of the family," Williams said. Inspired by his surprising invention, he added, "Very old. From the Second Crusade."

The man smiled. "Anyone can see it was made last year in Guanajuato," he said. "I know the shop."

Williams saw that he was trapped. "Take the car," he said. He saw himself crossing Mexico with Don Q on his back, but he knew that he could always call it a pilgrimage, a holy vow.

"It's a very fine car," the man said.

"Take it, please," Williams said.

"But I have no use for a car in these hills," the man said. "The armor I can carry on a burro. The car, no."

"Take my money," Williams said.

"Oh, of course," the man said. He laughed and patted the barrel of his weapon. "I hope there's lots of it."

"Then you'll leave the armor?"

"Of course not. I've always wanted a suit of armor, something very old, something of the family, grandfather, Don Q."

"Well—" Williams said.

"Look at it this way. We leave you your car. We leave you your shoes. We even leave you your life. In this world you can't have everything."

Williams gave up. Perhaps life would be simpler without the Don and without his mother.

The man whistled a burro out of the darkness and strapped the Don to its back. The burro, which seemed to have seen everything, received this burden like any other. Williams groaned for his mother with each jolt and clank as the Don was wrestled into place and lugged off like so much firewood. "Please be careful," he said.

"Of course," the man called and urged the burro to greater efforts until it couldn't be told from a rattletrap car, climbing straight up the mountain and out of hearing.

Again Williams slept — it had been a good smoke — and when he next woke up, he saw his old bandit strapping the Don back on the roof of the car.

"Hola," Williams said.

"Hola," the bandit said and went on strapping until he was done.

"What's up?" Williams said. He was not wholly pleased to see the Don back once he had been rid of him.

"You did not tell us," the bandit said, "the true nature of your suit of armor." He seemed offended.

"I'm sorry," Williams said. He knew he'd better be, even if he didn't know what for.

"If you had told us it was a religious object, a reliquary, we would have honored your wishes. Just because we are communists, you don't have to think we have no feelings."

"I didn't know you were communists," Williams said. "I thought you were bandits."

"Freedom fighters," the man said. "We have freed your money, but we leave you your faith. We are not pigs, in spite of Karl Marx."

"I thank you for your courtesy," Williams said. The form of their dialogue was clear enough, although the content continued to elude him.

"When we opened the armor and saw —"

"Ah," Williams said, "you saw —"

"Yes," the man said. "One man's god is another man's garbage, but we respect it."

"You are very kind," Williams said. He knew real nobility

when he saw it, but he felt the Don settle onto his back once more like a curse.

"We apologize for any inconvenience," the man said.

"It's nothing," Williams said. He knew what good manners required.

"Even so," the man said, "we want to offer you something. Chucho," he called.

A man stepped out of the dark background of a Rivera painting, better dressed, better armed, but still clearly the classic guerrilla. He advanced and held out his closed hand to Williams, who thought he was about to say "guess."

"Take it," the first man said. "It's peyote. The ancients said it put them in touch with their gods. At least it will help you sleep. Take it."

Williams was not surprised, in the moment Chucho crouched and extended his hand, to recognize in him probably— perhaps— the same man as the fisherman he remembered from the beach. He was surprised, however, when he felt something fall from Chucho's left hand onto the dark side of his leg. "Thank you," he said in general, for the peyote, for the return of the Don, for whatever Chucho had dropped, for being left alive. "Thank you." He groped for Chucho's gift and at a touch recognized his own sheaf of traveler's checks. At least he wouldn't have to drive until he ran out of gas and then walk, crawl, squirm north into stillness.

At some time, the man vanished. The car vanished. Don Q vanished. Across the fire, which was burning as if just refreshed, his mother sat, glowering at him.

She was dressed in an Indian costume with a woven ribbon headdress of many colors and a richly embroidered huipil, but she was easy to recognize by the white, diamond-shaped patch that always appeared on the bridge of her nose when she was angry. It was always the first thing he checked. Other than that she was unrecognizable because she had chosen to appear in the form of her own mother as a young woman, a soft, billowing Edwardian shape, a lush compensation, Williams conjectured, for the lean times upon which she had fallen. He knew this shape only from old brown photographs, for his grandmother had always been to him a small, thin woman, victim of changed fashions in medicine and in women. He recognized his grandmother by the old photographs, and he recognized his mother by the white on her nose.

"Well," she said, "you've made a mess of things as usual."

He groaned in spirit. This was about where they left off before she made her last trip to Mexico. "I'm doing my best," he said bravely. He felt obscurely aggrieved that his best was once again going uncredited.

"I was perfectly well off," she said, "until you came along."

"But those people staring — "

"I loved it," she said.

"You said no one was to stare," he said. "It was in your will."

"I was wrong," she said. "Are you trying to tell me I wasn't wrong?" She had never once hit him in her life, but she seemed very close to it now.

"No, no," he said. "You must have been wrong."

"Your mother is never wrong," she said more out of old habit than any present conviction.

"Of course," he said out of eternal and unshakable conviction. "Even when she's wrong."

"Of course," she said, responding to his tone of conciliation rather than to any sense or nonsense in what he said.

"It was a party," she said. "You took me away from a party. A masquerade. For once in my life I could do as I pleased and no one knew who it was. I could laugh and show my teeth. I could roll my eyes. I could shake my ass — "

"Your what?" Williams said, aghast on multiple levels.

"Didn't know I had one, did you?" she said. Without getting up from the ground or appearing to make any effort at all, she quivered violently from top to bottom.

"Oh, it must be jelly — " she sang.

" — 'cause jam don't shake like that," he added under his breath. But nothing was escaping her, even in the midst of her cataclysm.

"What did you say?" she said sharply.

"Nothing," he muttered.

"That's better," she said. "You say nothing because you know nothing. Not about jelly and not about jam and not about delicious honey dripping from the comb. Mmm." She licked her lips.

He didn't answer but privately reviewed jelly and jam and honey to his own satisfaction.

"Wrong," she said. "You know nothing and what you do know is all wrong."

"All?" he said, feeling she was being unfair.

"All," she said. "You've got us into this mess and now I suppose it's my job to get us out — and, by the way, if you were going to do this at all, why were you so long about it?"

"I was detained," he said.

"A good son is never detained from his duty," she said. She seemed to have forgotten that he had no duty of any kind to break up her party at the museum. He hesitated. "Well," she said, "I'm waiting."

"It was business," he said.

"Not good enough," she said. "Nowhere near good enough."

"I was in jail," he said.

"More interesting," she said. "But another lie." She had always prided herself on bringing up her boy not to lie, but she prided herself more on her ability to catch him at it.

"It was all a mistake," he said.

"It would have to be," she said with all the assurance of total contempt. "You never had the character to do anything wrong." *Character* had always been one of her bludgeons, but now it all seemed somehow to be coming out backward.

"I was just driving your car home, and I got searched at the border—" He stopped because he knew it was beginning to sound like an accusation.

"Holy Christ," his mother said, "and they caught you with the dope."

He hung his head in shame.

"Without me there to tell them what to do, they couldn't even get the dope out of the car before they let you have it. Holy Christ."

Williams began to have a sense that she was not only reading his mind but was reading out of it things he himself didn't know were there. "You knew about the dope?" he said.

"I put it there," she said.

"You?" he said.

"Wise up," she said. "How did you think I paid for your fancy school and your summers in Europe? How dumb can you be?"

"You?" He remembered one night in college when they were all high on cocaine they had bought from the governor's son, and they laughed about the legendary little old lady, head of a big ring, who ran it in. "May she never be caught," they shouted and snorted another line. "You?" he said.

"None other," she said.

"I've done seven years for you," he said.

"It seems to have been good for your character—you never complained before."

"Seven years," he said.

She waved seven years away. "It's little enough," she said, "after what I've done for you."

"Such as?" he said.

But she froze him with a glance, the old trick. Perhaps his character had not been improved as much as either of them thought. "And now I've got to get you out of this, I suppose."

"It would be very helpful," he said.

"What seems to be the problem?" she said.

"They're waiting for me on all the highways to the border."

"How do you know this?"

"Some other 'they' keeps telling me."

"Perhaps a lie to keep you here."

"Perhaps not."

He had been over this so many times in his own mind that it had a comforting familiarity.

"Perhaps both of them think you know something."

"Such as what?"

"Such as where I hid it, of course. One side wants to leave you free, so they can follow you while you lead them to it. The other side wants to grab you and squeeze it out of you. Elementary."

"Where did you hide it?" he said.

She looked at him as she knew how to do. "When have I ever trusted you with business details?" she said. "I thought you might be able to manage the funeral — everything written out word for word — but no, you even contrived to make a hash of that."

"You liked it at the museum," he said under his breath.

"Through no fault of yours," she said.

A cock crowed. She faded slightly but quickly righted herself. "Stupid Mexican roosters," she said.

"They crow all night," he said.

"And the dogs bark," she said.

"And the church bells ring," he said.

"And the people shoot off fireworks," she said and glared at him, daring him to claim a sleep more disturbed than hers.

"Sometimes they have parties," he said in spite of everything.

"They have rock bands with amplifiers as big as outhouses," she said definitely, and that was that except for a gratuitous coda: "And they go on until daylight."

He listened peacefully to crickets and nighthawks and a distant burro roaring like a mythological beast.

"Now what is it really that you want me to do for you?" she said.

Williams didn't dare even think that he wished she'd just get back into the Don and lie down.

"Besides that," she said sharply. "Let's not fool around."

"All I'm trying to do is get you home," he said. "That's all."

"So I have to do that too," she said. "Rob my own grave."

"I didn't ask—" he said.

"Enough," she said.

"I—"

She rode right over him. "I must think," she said. But her thinking seemed to be as audible to him as his did to her. "The roads are watched," she thought. "We've been there before. We ford the rivers where there are no roads. We fly. We go by sea."

"We can't fly the car," he thought. "The Don would rust in the river."

"I've grown attached to the Don," she thought.

"Then by sea," he thought before she could get it out.

"Wiseass," she thought and thinned and towered and spiraled upward like smoke from the smoldering fire. Last of all, her one wretched stocking dangled briefly before him.

"But where?" he shouted, too late repentant.

The last bit of wood fell from the stones, showered sparks and ash, and died. The cock crowed again. This time there was genuine light in the sky. A large black goat was inspecting him solemnly. A number of sheep and goats were cropping their way along the cemetery wall. At a little distance the shepherd, his pants down, was squatting against the wall.

So it was to be by sea.

IX

IT WAS no more than he expected that when he came down to the sea there was a rusted landing craft drawn up on the beach. He drove across the sand and stopped before the gaping jaws, the waiting ramp. In the throat of the ship, a man motioned him to drive aboard.

Williams hesitated. The man was dressed like a working sailor: white skivvy shirt, faded dungarees, small white hat. He even had a package of cigarettes rolled up in his sleeve at his shoulder. But he had long white hair tied in a ponytail and a long white beard. He wore heavy Mexican sandals with tire soles. If he was indeed a sailor, he was a very ancient one.

Now he waved Williams aboard with sweeping hand signals suitable for directing an airliner to its gate. Williams responded by nearly missing the ramp altogether on the left and then veering almost off on the right in spite of the fact that the way was clear and broad.

"Tricky passage," the man said as Williams stepped from the car.

"I guess we made it, though," Williams said.

"We sure did," the man said. "My name's Sewell Hutton, but you better just call me Kid like everyone else — at least the last person who called me anything called me Kid."

"Williams," Williams said, surprised out of half a dozen carefully prepared aliases. "Marc Williams." They shook hands, the quick-shifting Mexican handshake, from the conventional straightforward five, sliding into the grip favored by blacks, athletes, and others who knew what was what.

"What do they call you, Marc Williams?" the Kid said.

"Marc," Williams said. "Hey, you. Shithead. Take your pick."

"I'm going to call you Bills," the Kid said. "I knew a man once, had the only name worse than mine I ever heard of — Williams Leveret. We called him Bills. He had balls too. He was killed along with me at Guadalcanal."

"What do you mean," Williams said, "along with you?" He didn't think he was up to dealing with another ghost. He was also distracted by something that kept popping at the back of his head. He was afraid it was blood vessels breaking and he was having a stroke.

"Oh, I'm dead," the Kid said. "This ship is dead. That's why I call it *The River Styx*."

Williams started to get into his car in preparation for backing out. "No, no," the Kid said. "Officially dead. Not really dead. Off the records. Cases closed. It's very convenient. We can always manage to slip through."

Williams gave up any idea of backing out, especially when he saw that the ramp was up and the jaws were closed. "You were expecting me?" he said. He felt relieved, although the popping noise at the back of his head went on. Surely, he thought, he would be dead by now if that were blood vessels.

"Someone always shows up," the Kid said. "It's a way of life."

"To go by way of the River Styx," Williams said.

"Oh, I like that," the Kid said. "I like that, Bills."

"Use it in good health, Kid," Williams said. He felt foolish, the way he would feel if he called his grandfather Kid.

The Kid laughed and showed his teeth, all delicately chased in gold. "I want you to meet Alice Jo," he said and gestured over Williams's head so that Williams didn't know whether to expect a bird or an angel. But he turned and saw a girl staring at him from the catwalk above his head. While their eyes held, she consummated and burst an enormous pink bubble.

"Hola, Alice," Williams said. He waved vaguely in her direction. She responded only by gathering in the wreckage of her bubble with her slow pink tongue.

"She doesn't have much to say," the Kid said. "She's always high on bubble gum or something."

"Gimme a cigarette," she said. She was stretched out on her stomach, looking over the edge. She wore a modest blue bathing suit and appeared to have no cleavage and no hips and no other recognizable appurtenances, primary or secondary. Her pale hair was cropped short, and her uncolored nails were bitten to the quick.

The Kid unrolled his cigarettes, shook one directly into his mouth, lighted it, and passed it up to her. She simply held it while her eyes, still fixed on Williams, grew wide and large and very very dark. His own eyes wheeled about in crazy circles, flickering past her and gathering a sort of stop-action view of her slow unfolding. Not only did her eyes widen but her nostrils as well. Her earrings, vast gold hoops, turned slowly as her ears stirred. Here Williams placed a strict limit on his imaginings of openings and closings. With the cigarette, half burned and wholly unsmoked, still in her hand, she blew another bubble in his direction, deftly gathered it in, and lay down out of sight.

"She goes with us on this trip," the Kid said. "She's baggage."

"Whose?" Williams said.

"Yours," the Kid said.

"Jesus," Williams said.

"When you land," the Kid said, "you take her with you in the direction of Nevada."

"I didn't know I was going to Nevada," Williams said.

"Why not?" the Kid said.

"Why not indeed?" Williams said. "Cómo no?" They quickly exchanged the lodge grip once more and got down to cases. The price was almost exactly the value of the traveler's checks Williams had left, but cheap if they really did get past the border, especially as it included new engine numbers for the car, a new paint job, and two coats of silver paint for the Don, an infallible disguise. The date of departure was at once plus the time needed for painting and altering. And the date of arrival, one week from the above, to include all time spent laying up and taking evasive action. The Kid insisted on including an article binding himself to deliver Alice Jo into Williams's hands in good condition at the moment of arrival. "She's spacey," he said, "but she's all there is."

On the first day of the voyage, Williams noted strange variations in Alice Jo's appearance. Sometimes she looked fourteen. Sometimes she looked forty. If she stood against a freshly painted bulkhead, her slim, light figure—to say nothing of her incessant bubbles—spoke clearly of youth. On the other hand, if she lay on a patch of scaly and rusted deck, the dark smudges under her eyes came into prominence, and the light would catch a hint of crepe at the corners of her jaws. She seemed to him a sort of chameleon, and he wondered what she looked like when she lay in the Kid's arms. He resolved he'd never let her get close enough to him to take on any visible signs by which he might see himself reflected. There was a good deal he didn't want to know.

"How old are you, Alice Jo?" he said that first day.

"I been married," she said. "I been divorced." She unwrapped another piece of bubble gum and chewed heavily. "I had me a baby."

"Oh?" Williams said cautiously. Tense might be everything.

"She's eight," Alice Jo said, promoting the child to the ranks of the living.

"Do you have a picture?" he said. He didn't know much, but he did know one or two civilized gestures.

"No."

"Where is she now?" That was the other gesture.

"With my mother," Alice Jo said. She blew another bubble and stared cross-eyed into it as into the future.

This conversation reassured Williams, although not much. Up to then he had heard Alice Jo say only, "Gimme a cigarette," and he knew very well that a parrot could easily be taught to say that.

On the second day of the voyage, Alice Jo said, "I'm going to see my mother. She's finally got a place I can go."

Williams noted that nothing was said about seeing her child, who, at least as of yesterday, was alive and supposedly with its grandmother.

That night the Kid said to Williams over their canned beans and Spam ("Good navy food"), "She sure talks a lot to you. You must know how to bring her out."

Williams told a joke about Calvin Coolidge firing a guide for talking too much. The man had asked twice in eight hours of fishing, "Any luck, Mr. President?" Even as he told the joke, he wasn't sure how it applied. But the Kid laughed. After all, Calvin Coolidge went back to his childhood and was always good for some affectionate fun.

"That's a good one," the Kid said. "It ought to make me think of a joke, but it doesn't." The best he could do was tell again the story of going down with his ship, both of them dead in the surf at Guadalcanal. It wasn't very funny, except that there they were, both of them, not quite so good as new but very far from dead.

On the third day of the voyage, the first thing Williams saw when he came on deck was Alice Jo up on top of his car, sitting on the Don's chest. She had lifted the visor and was looking into his head. "Neat," she said. "How about you give him to me?"

"Why?" Williams said. That was all he could think of to say, but it sounded reasonable. It seemed to him that if he was going to be giving her a ride in the direction of Nevada, she was the one who ought to be doing him favors. The thought of her favors made him waver perceptibly. Perhaps once he was in the United States he would have no further use for the Don. God knows what Alice Jo would do with him, but that was her problem. Still, he was cautious. After all, it hadn't been that long since the witch. He expected that remembering the witch would always make him cautious.

"Not him," Alice Jo said, rapping the Don on the skull with her knuckles until he echoed in all his caverns.

Williams winced for his mother and her migraines.

"Him," Alice Jo said. She pointed into the open visor with imminent danger to his mother's eyes, such as they were.

"That's a her," Williams said. He felt he owed it to his mother to quibble even of such tenuous grounds as she left him.

"No way," Alice Jo said. "I know a him when I see one. How about you give him to me?"

"I couldn't do that," Williams said. "Something of the family. Very old. First Crusade." He knew he was getting his cases muddled, but he hoped Alice Jo would laugh at his pretensions just as the bandit did and forget the whole thing.

"When we've been on shore a few days, you'll give me anything," she said. Her assurance was a huge pink bubble, which she exhaled and inhaled without breaking and which left her looking exceedingly well fed.

That was an interesting proposition. She might know fantastic arts to drive men mad. Williams shivered with delight. But at the same time she might simply have serene confidence in her ability to bore him until he would do anything to be rid of her.

"What about it?" she said.

Williams could think of nothing to say, so he climbed up beside Alice Jo and looked into the Don's head. He did not see his mother, and he did not see the Cortez mask, which had a way of sliding off into the more remote reaches of the Don. What he saw was a distinguished gentleman with a silver mustache and a silver beard. "I beg your pardon," he said and averted his eyes.

A moment's reflection, however, convinced him that it had to be his mother really. When the Kid was spray-painting the Don, he must have forgotten to seal off the vents in the visor.

"Well, what about him?" Alice Jo said, giving the Don another intolerable rap and starting up migraine echoes in Williams's head.

"We'll see," Williams said.

"We will for shit sure see," Alice Jo said. "That's as close to God the Father as I'm ever going to get. And I'm going to have him, case and all."

Williams decided that Alice Jo didn't know any mysterious arts, just the same old ones, and he knew he was in trouble. After all, he thought for his mother's benefit, it was only another disguise and a good one—the best. Now she could shake her balls. But he could already hear her thinking, "I always have."

"Mine," Alice Jo said. And she closed the visor with a snap.

Williams made placating but unconvincing gestures with his hands and jumped down to the deck. Alice Jo was the kind of girl who could be left at truck stops or abandoned at motel swimming pools. There was a lot you could do with Alice Jo.

"Mark my words," the Kid said, and stopped in order to take advantage of the pun he had fallen into. "Mark my words, Marc, that's one that won't bear too much bringing out." His long life and the habit of being alone had brought him to a point where conversations went on in his head with days—and often years—between statement and response. There was no such thing as a remote reference in his discourse, only an eternal present.

"It would be just another bubble," Williams said. They were standing on the bridge while they looked down on Alice Jo, to the great peril of a flotilla of small fishing boats they were passing through.

"Maybe yes," the Kid said, "maybe no. Just remember, Bills, that one of those bubbles laid over a man's nose and mouth at the wrong time would be the end of him. I always sleep in a gas mask."

Williams couldn't be sure how serious the Kid was being about the gas mask, but he stored up the information anyway. It was always well to pay close attention to the experiences of others. Besides, this would go a long way toward explaining why the chameleon Alice Jo often looked long in the nose in the morning.

The fourth day of the voyage Alice Jo said, "I had me a shop in Taos. (pop) Sold all kinds of Indian things. Made most of them myself. (pop [and a long, meditative pause climaxing in] pop) Hell, I was better than any Indian." She closed her eyes and turned her face to the sun. She was visibly drying out. He could practically see the sun drawing moisture from her in a nimbus, although where the moisture came from he couldn't imagine. He never saw her put into her mouth anything but bubble gum.

"Take her," the Kid said as he dropped anchor for the night. "Never mind until we land."

"A deal's a deal," Williams said quickly. "Not until we land."

"I'm landed, stranded, and dead on the beach," the Kid said. "I thought at first it was enough for her just to be there. But she isn't even there. She slips through your fingers and goes pop."

"No way," Williams said. He blanched at the thought of Alice Jo in midocean, where there was no place to hide.

On the fifth morning, Williams found Alice Jo sleeping in his car. "Watching my property," she said.

"Locked myself in," the Kid said. "I think she was monkeying with my gas mask."

"Sweet mother of Jesus," Williams said. And he took the precaution of locking the car the moment he saw Alice Jo stretch out on the deck in her favorite patch of sun.

That night when he was stealthily checking the car and the Don and his mother, he was startled to hear a hiss in his ear: "Watch yourself." He was peering into the Don's head trying to make out by moonlight the beloved features behind the silver beard and mustache.

"I do my best," he said humbly. He did feel she was being unreasonable. To be sure, she had had to suggest that he go by sea. But since then he had, he thought, managed very well. He had even, accidentally, provided her with a new and splendid identity. She had no reason to be angry now, except, of course, for her ancient wrongs, which could always be brought out if all else failed.

"That's mine." This time the voice clearly did not come out of the visor but out of the air above him. He winced, sat back on his heels, and faced a large pink bubble at the edge of the catwalk just over his head. He stood on the roof of the car and confronted the bubble, which was attached to a long, lean naked body prone on the deck, sexless as angels.

"My karma is out of whack," the bubble said. "I've got to do something about my karma. Too much sun and not enough moon. I've got to soak up some moon rays."

"Good luck," Williams said and climbed down from the car.

"Pop," the bubble said. And only the short, pale hair shone in the moonlight.

On the sixth day, Alice Jo kept out of sight, doubtless redressing her karma by avoiding the sun altogether. "Be good to her," the Kid said as they watched the California coast slip by. "She doesn't deserve much, but there's no reason why it has to be bad."

"Why me?" Williams said.

"Like the feller says," the Kid said, "you're there. After tomorrow you're all she's got."

"She's got her mother," Williams said. In the frenzy of his self-protection he forgot the general nature of mothers.

"I don't put much stock in that mother," the Kid said.

"You mean she doesn't have a mother?" Williams said. That would certainly explain her anxiety to take over any mother she could get her hands on, even under the impression it was a father.

"Everyone has a mother," the Kid said, shocked as only a person who has faith in nothing can be shocked. "Except that some mothers you can't put stock in."

"And this mother is one of those?" Williams said.

"She never had a place for her kid from the day she was born, and she isn't going to have much of a place now."

Williams thought of Alice Jo's own child, for whom there could never have been a place, and he marveled again how the most agonizing patterns are passed on generation after generation by their victims. "Is Alice Jo's kid a boy or a girl?" he said.

"Girl," the Kid said.

"Figures," Williams said.

A submarine was stalking them. The eye of the periscope peered from behind every wave. Williams took it personally and believed he was caught at last, on the very brink of success. "They do it all the time," the Kid said. "They like to practice sneaking up on people."

"You're sure?" Williams said.

"I saw him before he saw me," the Kid said. "By all the rules, he's dead and he knows it. Don't worry."

Williams didn't see how this was at all comforting, but they went on their way, and soon the submarine abandoned them for the profile of a tanker low on the horizon. "Now that's a target," the Kid said. "That pays all his bills. He can go to the bottom now."

This struck Williams as an extremely interesting idea. He wondered at what point all his bills would be paid. He couldn't imagine it, but he hoped it would be the moment he laid his mother to rest in the family plot in Alpha, Illinois. It was improbable but still it was something to aim for.

Alice Jo, like the full moon, rose as the sun set. She came out on deck like a dancer, her toes pointing, her ass, such as it was, held tight. She paced as if onto a ritual altar. For a moment she was magnificient, but when she had commanded her stage and had dominated her audience, she could only lie down, sink from their sight, and offer herself, they assumed, to the moon. "If only she fucked like that," the Kid said.

"You'd be dead," Williams said.

"Gladly," the Kid said.

Before light on the morning of the seventh day, Williams woke when the ship touched the beach. He came out on deck and saw that the jaws were open and the ramp was down. A jogger staggered past the ship. Then another. Then two plus a dog. "Not very private," he said.

"Don't worry," the Kid said. "They don't know we're here. If they remember it later, they'll think it was a dream."

"How about the cops?" Williams said. "Somebody will report the marks on the beach, and they'll be after you."

"Not me," the Kid said. "You. They'll think the whale came in to spit up Jonah. Everybody loves whales but nobody wants Jonah. So you better get started. Get a long lead. Nevada is east."

"Thanks for everything," Williams said, but the Kid had spoken his last. And Alice Jo was already sitting in the car in spite of the fact that he had carefully locked it before he went to bed. She was sitting in the middle of the front seat, snuggled up against the space he would occupy.

"Here we are," he said and drove down the ramp onto the beach, narrowly missing a jogger. He could imagine the jogger saying at work, "Came right out of the sea at me. Brand new Buick with a silver hood ornament as big as itself. Damnedest thing."

To Williams, the damnedest thing was that he was there at all.

X

HE TURNED his back on the coast and plunged inland. Alice Jo slept. She drew away from him into the corner of the front seat after he refused to lash her to the roof, where she could soak up some rays and protect her property. He was disconcerted at first to discover that the road inland was taking him north, although he needn't have been if he had remembered his childhood wisdom: What is the largest city west of the Mississippi and east of Reno? And the triumphant answer: Los Angeles. So the Kid was wrong. Nevada was not east. It was west — and north.

But none of that much mattered. He still traveled in the blank spaces, and when these failed, he improvised by seeking out the creases in his map where the names of cities were rubbed off, where all roads failed, and where there was no mileage to anywhere. In this manner, he managed to approach his orientation point, Elko, Nevada, from the east as if he had badly overshot Illinois.

Beyond Elko, the road turned south to the town of Jiggs,

which he nearly drove through without noticing. Fortunately, Alice Jo happened to have her eyes open at the time. She saw the sign and she saw the town, mainly a café where they were to ask for directions.

"Hippolyta?" the woman at the counter—and the grill and the cash register—said when Williams asked. "Straight on from here, and where the road turns left, you keep going straight. But," she added after a struggle with her conscience, "you're not going to like it."

"Oh, I'm not going to stay," Williams said. "I'm just delivering a girl to her mother."

"Poor kid," the woman said.

Williams ordered a beer, hoping it would be the price of further information, but nothing was forthcoming. He noticed a yellowing VW ad taped to the wall: The Entire Population of Jiggs, Nevada, Can Fit into a VW Microbus. He didn't doubt it. The only other resident in evidence was a girl of about six. She was wearing a green eye shade and dealing blackjack to a table of ghosts.

"She's getting ready," the woman said. "They all get out." She selected a toothpick from a shot glass on the counter and clamped down on it. "But not to Hippolyta."

"So I won't like it?" Williams said.

"No," the woman said.

"And the girl won't like it?"

"Depends on the girl," the woman said.

They drove straight on. The country was as blank as anyone could wish. It looked like Mexico. Alice Jo thought he had got lost and gone back across the border in a fit of absent-mindedness. Particularly the line of mountains off to the left looked suspiciously like the one that had followed him wherever he turned from the moment he left Guanajuato. The barrenness was the same. The scattered cattle were the same. The spotty vegetation was like a man whose beard wouldn't grow properly. And here and there someone had managed to grow a crop of alfalfa, except that now it was lying in green bales in the fields rather than riding to market in elegantly contoured truckloads.

When the blacktop turned left, he went straight on, reluctantly. Things were getting a bit blank even for him. The blacktop seemed to be heading straight for the mountains. He would have liked that, although his experience with Mexican mountains had made him wary. There he had driven for days heading for mountains that somehow never materialized. On the other hand, he remembered, there had been times when he got into mountains no matter how he tried to avoid them.

The road was barely a road at all and became less so. Finally, when he seemed about to strike out into terra completely incognita, he rattled over a cattle guard — what cattle? guarded against what? — and stopped at a gate: hippolyta, keep out (no capitals). The vague misgivings he had picked up at Jiggs came into unpleasant focus.

Beside the gate was a telephone: ring and wait. Alice Jo jumped out and rang, although she had been largely inert since the first time Williams saw her. Often the only sign of life was the regular rise and fall of her bubble like some device the movies would use to dramatize a patient's vital signs.

"Hey, Mom," she said into the phone. "I'm here." Williams would have thought she couldn't be excited by anything.

"Well," she said, more like herself, "tell her I'm here."

"Alice Jo, that's who." She slammed the telephone back into place. The gate buzzed and she kicked it open.

Williams drove through. "Better close the gate," he said.

"Stupid woman," she said, but she closed the gate.

The way was now straight and clear but there was no house in sight. In the middle distance, shovels flashed in the sun where a gang of workers labored in some incomprehensible ditch. And farther off than that, a brown, half-naked figure urged a yoke of oxen to no amended pace.

"Cows, Jesus," Alice Jo said. "They use cows to pull their wagons. I thought we were in the U.S."

"Oxen," Williams said.

"Cows, oxen," Alice Jo said. "What's the difference?"

"Sex," Williams said, wondering, not for the first time, if she knew anything at all about that subject.

"So bulls," she said, suggesting that she knew very little.

"Not exactly," Williams said.

"They're exactly bulls or they're exactly cows," she said. "What are you giving me?"

"They're neuters," he said.

"Like a cat?" she said. "That's dirty. It's filthy. It's disgusting." She sought comfort in a bubble, the first since she had tried to speak to her mother.

"They're quiet and strong," Williams said. "They're very useful."

"I'll bet," Alice Jo said. "No, thank you."

The house had suddenly appeared before them, although it looked as if it should have been visible from far away. It was very large, a Victorian monster, towered and turreted, trimmed everywhere with gingerbread. It was obviously a gentleman's house, and, to judge by the location, an eccentric gentleman's. The house and outbuildings were freshly painted and impeccably restored. Care and competence spoke from every brick and shingle, from every fence and watering trough — and money too. Money spoke loudest of all.

"Some spread," Alice Jo said.

Williams was about to drawl some appropriate movie talk — "Right on, podner," or something — but he stopped. He had driven around to the back of the house, knowing that much at least about country manners, and there he found a sort of welcoming committee drawn up one step from the kitchen door. There were two women — good — but they were dressed in what he supposed to be saris — identical — and wearing on their heads the kind of kerchiefs he had last seen in a movie about Africa.

He stopped driving. But Alice Jo jumped out of the car and ran at the two women indiscriminately. "Mom," she shouted.

"Her," the larger of the two women said and waved her thumb at the other woman.

Alice Jo checked and said, "Mom?"

"Sister," the large woman said as if pronouncing a blessing. "We are all sisters here." But she broke off when Williams got out of the car. It was close to suppertime and he was hungry. He had earned a meal and a bed, if not eternal gratitude, which somehow did not appear to be in the cards.

"Who's she?" the woman said. "And what's that?"

Williams and Alice Jo looked around for the mysterious *she* but found it easier at the moment to deal with the obvious *that*. "Oh, that's a suit of armor," Alice Jo said. "It's mine." Williams could see that the showdown over his mother was very near at hand.

"I can see that," the large woman said. She was really very large, Williams could see as he drew near her, and he stopped before she got too large. He preferred to limit her to the dimensions of a modest linebacker.

"I can tell a suit of armor," the woman said, "and I can tell that armor is male. We can't have it here. Take it away."

"If it goes, I go," Alice Jo said. She didn't have to think at all before making a choice between the mother in the sari and the mother in the armor.

"We must remember," Alice Jo's mother said in the humble manner of a novice refreshing the recollection of the mother superior, "we must remember that Saint Joan of Arc wore armor."

"And much good did it do her," the other woman said.

"And hippolyta herself — "

"Whatever she wore, it was not medieval armor," the woman said, but she seemed mollified. "But do I hear you saying that armor might properly be considered androgynous?"

"Yes," Alice Jo's mother said like a woman who had lost rather then won the argument.

"Let it stay," the woman said. She seemed to be pronouncing a blessing. Alice Jo and her mother fell into each other's arms. "But who is she?" This time the large woman pointed directly at Williams, who felt his stubble but still looked over his shoulder.

"Oh, that's Bills," Alice Jo said.

"Welcome, Bills," the woman said. "Welcome to hippolyta. Welcome, sister." She embraced him as if she were sacking a quarterback. "And welcome, Alice Jo." She repeated the entire formula, although Alice Jo slipped the tackle and seemed ready to run for at least a first down.

"Well," Alice Jo's mother said, "you've been welcomed and that means you can stay at least one night even if you're as much of a shit as I remember you. It's a rule."

"Thanks, Mom," Alice Jo said.

"My name is Marc Williams," Williams said. "I appreciate your hospitality, but I'm not really a sister."

"All women are sisters," the woman said beatifically. She seemed to be pronouncing the salvation of All Womankind.

"I mean I'm not really a woman," Williams said. "Feel my beard."

She frowned. "All women are women," she said. She still spoke from the heights, although sternly.

In the instant before rage, there was genuine confusion. "You mean you're a man?" the large woman said. She seemed to shrink into herself the better to expand. "You mean that's not padding in your pants?"

"I should hope not," Alice Jo said.

"What?" She went off like Mexican fireworks. "What? What? What?" All flashes and bangs. Big and pink as an Alice Jo bubble.

"Alice Jo," her mother said, "you have deceived us."

"Out. Out. Out." She was sputtering now.

"You can't put him out," Alice Jo's mother said. "You have pronounced the blessing on him."

"By mistake," the large woman said. "He deceived us."

"He didn't fool me for a minute," Alice Jo said. She blew an insolent bubble.

"You deceived us," the woman said to Alice Jo.

Alice Jo drew in her bubble. "You deceived yourself," she said.

"He must stay," Alice Jo's mother said. "It's your own law."

"Then I can break it," the furious woman said.

"Not and remain sensai," Alice Jo's mother said. "We all have to meditate on it, center right down to the heart of our vaginas."

"He'll have to stay in the barn," the large woman said. She was now huge and still growing.

"What a good idea," Alice Jo's mother said in the manner of a woman who had long since learned when to stop winning.

"Put him where we put the last one, that spy." And she turned on her heel and went into the house.

"While there's life, there's hope," Alice Jo's mother said, not very happily. "Drive into the barn." She opened the massive barn doors with a strength surprising in a woman who had been worn down to the point of knowing that the next step beyond winning a little is to lose everything. Williams drove in and parked behind a very dusty car with long-expired New York registration.

"In here," Alice Jo's mother said. She opened a wide, tall door of extremely heavy wood. Over the door was the word *Prince*. Williams went in.

"The royal suite," Alice Jo said. "Hey," she said as the door slammed shut behind him. Chains rattled and locks clicked. Williams found himself in a box stall apparently intended to contain a vicious beast.

"It's the best we can do," Alice Jo's mother said.

"I'll bring you something to eat," Alice Jo said.

"That will have to be voted on," her mother said.

At that moment a TV screen in a high corner of the stall lighted up. "It will keep you company," Alice Jo's mother said through the door. But Williams didn't believe her, because all he could see on the screen was the interior of the stall and himself in it.

He turned his attention directly to his surroundings. There wasn't much to see. The walls were wood, stout and closely joined. There was a small barred window high up. Close-set bars above the door. A square hole in one corner of the ceiling, and on the floor below it a small pile of old hay. A manger with hay still in it. And a water bucket. Nothing else. No water.

"You could at least wear underpants with that nightgown," Alice Jo said somewhere out in the barn.

"We don't believe in undergarments here," her mother said. Her voice was strained and curiously muffled.

Williams tried to visualize the scene but got nothing except the old picture of Marilyn Monroe walking over a wind machine and her skirt blowing up over her head.

"Oh, for God's sake," Alice Jo said, "let me climb up there for you."

"You wouldn't know what to do if you got up here," her mother said. Her voice was clearer as she finally hit the old maternal snarl. Then Williams heard her walking over his head. A dust of hay filtered down from the hole in the corner.

"Over here, you, man." Alice Jo's mother's voice filtered down along with the dust. Williams cautiously approached the corner. "I can't see you," she shouted. Williams took another step, looked up, and caught a rush of alfalfa hay in his face.

There was a great chorus of female laughter from the TV, and a woman's voice said, "Let's have that on instant replay." The TV flickered, and Williams saw himself looking hopefully heavenward and suddenly turning green. He shed the hay like water and stood, still hopeful, dripping hay and faintly frosted with hay dust.

"That's one for the permanent file," a voice said.

"That's a dirty trick," Alice Jo said. She had climbed up the outside of the stall and was spread-eagled on the bars like a monkey in the zoo—except, Williams thought, he was the one who was shut up.

Then Alice Jo dropped lightly from the bars, and he could hear her mother walking overhead. The female voices came loudly over the TV.

"We can keep him for laughs," someone said.

"If we decide to keep him at all."

"We can keep him at stud."

"We can't keep a man on the place."

"We can neuter him, turn him into an ox."

"What's the good of that?"

"He can work for us."

"But stud is an idea too. We can't let the community of sisters die out."

"The way the Shakers did."

"There you are."

"Sisters, this is Alice Jo."

"Alice Jo is Shulamith's daughter."

"Shulamith?" That was Alice Jo and she was angry.

"We call ourselves by our true names, which we discover by meditation." This was clearly the voice of a guru.

"Jesus," Alice Jo said.

"Here we swear by Mary, the mother of gods."

"Holy shit," Alice Jo said.

"And by the sacred functions of our bodies," the same voice said, and even Alice Jo was silenced.

"Alice Jo and Shulamith," the Voice of Authority said, "we are about to begin our meditation on the male subject. What to do with him."

"How about feeding him?" Alice Jo said.

"Our options are keeping him at stud or giving him the beautiful gift of true androgyny."

"What about his options?" Alice Jo said.

"After thousands of years of male oppression, he should have options?"

"He's a good guy," Alice Jo said.

Williams was gratified and also a little ashamed. He hadn't been as kind to Alice Jo as he might have been. He didn't see, however, that he could go so far as to give her his mother — if, that is, he should ever be in a position to give or withhold anything.

"In actual fact," a cold, reasonable voice said, "with modern techniques we could do both — freeze his . . . stuff and then neuter him."

"Good thinking," the Voice of Authority said, "and that would see us through very nicely until the great day — "

" — the day we solve the problem of parthenogenesis — " This sounded to Williams like Alice Jo's mother trying on a pious voice.

And Authority continued unruffled, " — the secret hidden so long by paternalistic power."

"The day," a ragged chorus echoed.

"Now let us meditate," Authority said.

"I should like to point out," a new voice said in the odd, coldly ranged English of her majesty's late empire, "that my people have been meditating for six thousand years to no appreciable end."

"Now that we have had the usual comment from the Inscrutable East," Authority said, "let us meditate. Let us begin to put down roots. Let us close our eyes and feel our roots extending. From the soles of our feet. From our anuses."

"Ani," the Indian woman said.

"From our vaginas. Close your eyes, Alice Jo."

Williams closed his eyes, but he couldn't feel anything. Not from his feet. Not from his anus. He couldn't begin to imagine his vagina. And he didn't dare to contemplate the only real root he had, no doubt growing moldy and shriveled in the flickering gloom of the stall. He tried to think of his mother, snug in the bosom of the Don, growing arabesques of vines from all her hardened orifices.

"I brought you some supper," Alice Jo said. He opened his eyes and looked at the screen, but all he saw was himself, profoundly rootless, forlorn, and covered with hay.

"Over here, you dope," she said. She was waving through the bars above the door. She began throwing plastic bags of unspeakable substances down on his head.

"What's all this?" he said.

"Tofu," she sang, "and alfalfa sprouts and veggies. All they eat is veggies." The contempt in her voice was as great as that he felt himself. But he also felt hunger, so he opened the least revolting of the bags and began to eat the half-cooked vegetables.

"Did they decide to let me live?" he said with his mouth full.

"They didn't decide anything," Alice Jo said. "I stole this shit."

"They'll see you," he said.

"They can't see me up here," she said. "Besides, their eyes are closed. They'll keep them closed for hours."

"Someone will peek," he said. He poked the tofu with his finger and tried the sprouts.

"No one would dare admit it, no matter what they saw. They're thinking about their cunts."

"Always thinking of something to eat," he said. Even a handful of fodder and a mouthful of sprouts made him feel frisky in spite of the uncertain future.

"Me too," Alice Jo said. She held onto the bars and stuck her legs through at him. Apparently she had already been converted to the community's rejection of undergarments.

"Too bad I can't get up there," he said, feeling perfectly safe.

"I brought a rope," she said. She tied it to the bars and threw him the loose end. Just imagining the gymnastic feat was enough to unman him.

"Christ," he said, "I can't climb a rope."

"Tie it around you," she said, "and I'll pull you up. I'm a lot stronger than I look."

And a hell of a lot hornier, he thought. "I'll tie knots in it," he said.

"Good thinking," she said. "Just hurry up and serve it hot."

He was as clumsy with the knots as he dared to be, hoping all the while that the women's meditation would come to an end somewhere well short of six thousand years. But Alice Jo's patience held up for less than six minutes. She drew the rope up, tied the knots herself, and dropped the rope to him again.

"Climb," she said.

"I can't climb a rope," he said. But he climbed anyway.

The act was not remarkably more arduous than any other stand-up quickie, but at the height of her passion Alice Jo exhaled a bubble in lieu of a shriek, drew him to her, and jammed his face into the bubble. All three exploded at once —*pop pop pop.*

Gently they drew apart. Tender strands of bubble gum prolonged the sweet parting, becoming more and more tenuous, more and more subtle, and finally separating only to lie against their cheeks in one last caress, to entwine in their hair like shredded clouds of glory, to dangle from their chins like gently falling dew of passion, stopped, caught, and eternalized in the permanent file of memory.

"That was more like," Alice Jo said.

Williams groped for an appropriate reply. "Thanks for the veggies," he said, although he was not truly grateful now that the edge was off his hunger. He thought of the tofu, still in its plastic bag in the hay. He was revolted. His gorge rose and he slid back down the rope. Still, he knew that by morning he would feel differently about the tofu, especially if he should be voted no breakfast and the women should open their eyes.

XI

TIME PASSED but nothing seemed to be decided except that he was to be fed. In the morning he was led out to the trough and allowed to fill his water bucket. He was also required to dig a slit trench behind some bushes in the corner of the paddock for his beastly necessities, which somehow, in spite of close analogies and even identity, were not to be considered sacred. While he was in the paddock, he was allowed to take whatever exercise he chose. His main exercise at first, however, was still climbing up the bars to Alice Jo during the nightly hour of meditation. He had very quickly learned to clamp his mouth to hers at the first sign of a bubble, and he decided that feeling his cheeks swell and his ears block was decidedly sexy after all. The additional interpenetration added a new dimension to their frantic coupling.

"I have a right to be heard," Alice Jo said one night out of the TV.

"Everyone has rights," her mother said.

"I want to talk about his rights," Alice Jo said.

"He has no rights," the Voice of Authority said.

"Certain inalienable rights blah blah blah," Alice Jo said. She emphasized this with a particularly loud pop.

"I wish you wouldn't do that," her mother said. "I brought you up better than that."

"You didn't bring me up at all," Alice Jo said.

"Order, sisters, order," the Voice of Authority said from great and benign heights.

"I mean he's a human being."

"We have abandoned that category," said the cold, precise Voice of Science. "Now there are women and animals."

"Even animals have rights," Alice Jo said. "Each beast has his or her rights."

"We have also eschewed that cumbersome locution," Science said. "We no longer say *he or she*. We say *na*."

"Jesus Christ," Alice Jo said.

"Mother of gods," her mother corrected.

"I'm sure even you wouldn't use the barbarism *he* to stand for both animals and women," Authority said.

"I never had much schooling," Alice Jo said.

Williams fell asleep at that point. The conversation was much the same every night. He wondered what they would talk about if he had never appeared. He was awakened when Alice Jo threw the rope down on him. "Alice Jo," he said, "don't I ever get a night off?"

"Not if you want to eat," she said. "They haven't decided anything, but I've decided to keep you at stud."

"You learn very fast," he said. He sighed and swarmed up the rope as if he had been doing it all his life—as he was indeed coming to believe he had.

Later, when he lay in the hay with the rope dangling loosely over him, Alice Jo said, "I'm splitting. I've had enough of working in that stupid ditch with a bunch of stupid bare-chested dikes. Every time they toss a shovelful of dirt, they throw their tits over their shoulders. It's disgusting."

"How will I eat?" Williams said. His sense of priorities had been honed by imprisonment, although his sense of reality was being eroded. He was well aware that he was beginning to talk filthy Spanish to the stable rats.

"You have a problem," Alice Jo said. "I'd take you with me, but you'd just make a fuss about my property."

Williams had by now reached a point where he had no trouble choosing between his mother and his balls. "O.K.," he said. "It's yours."

"It's about time," she said. "You're a stingy bastard."

"When do we go?"

"Tomorrow night," Alice Jo said.

"Great," Williams said. "It can't be too soon." He got up and rattled the door with a few good kicks.

"Quiet, Prince," Alice Jo said. "They're having an extra-long meditation tomorrow night — six thousand seconds, a second for every year of Indian meditation. They're going to show that fancy-talking cunt that a second in America is better than a year in India. Then they're going to decide about you."

"But then we'll be gone," Williams said. There was something to be said for escaping from prison and from his mother at the same time.

To help pass the time during the next long, laborious day, Williams reviewed the circumstances of his imprisonment. After the first week, they had set him to cutting wood down in the dry bed of the river. Limbs and whole trees brought down by past floods lay silver in the torrent of sunlight. "Everyone contributes to the welfare of the community," they said. "The cows contribute. The goats contribute. Even the oxen contribute." They gave him a two-man saw — they slipped up on that one — and a dog. The dog's contribution was to keep an eye on him. "She's very fierce," they said. "She hates men, and if you try to run away, she'll eat you up."

The dog was a large Irish setter. Her name was Sappho. She

turned out to be very amiable. She licked his face and went about her business, which was to lope in great circles over the countryside and check back with him from time to time. When she ranged too far, he could always whistle her back. The first time she seemed about to disappear forever, he opened his mouth to call her back but stopped. He looked about him. He tried again but found he could not bring himself to pronounce that name even to the rattlesnakes and the vultures. So he whistled. "Good dog," he said as they admired each other. "Good, good dog."

Each night in his cell he decided to run away the next day, but each day, halfway to freedom, he couldn't bring himself to abandon his mother in such a place. He knew the dog would gladly go with him—he would call her Red—but he couldn't quite reconcile himself to a trade of a mother for a dog.

"Let us meditate," the voice of the TV said. Williams glanced up and saw himself on the screen crumbling into the lotus position. He sprang erect and prepared to leave. That is to say, he used the TV as a mirror and combed what hay he could out of his hair. He gave himself a brush and a shake and was ready. And Alice Jo was there. "I'm ready," he said.

"There's a small problem," Alice Jo said.

"Never mind the details," Williams said.

"I hate to tell you this, Bills," she said. "But I can't get you out of there. No key. Tough luck."

"You bitch," he screamed.

"No hard feelings," she said. "I'll just take my property and get the hell out of this nut house."

He kicked the door. He kicked the walls. He punched the walls with his fists. He ran around kicking and screaming—and tripped and crashed headlong into the wall. As he gathered himself for fresh efforts, he felt among the hay for the thing that had tripped him. He found it, grasped it, ready to annihilate it, but it was firmly attached to the floor. It was an iron ring. It raised a small trap door. He knew the trap had been used in cleaning the stall. He knew what was down there in the dark, but he also knew that his mother, his balls, his sacred honor, to say nothing of his very life, were at stake, so he dropped through the trap.

It was a short fall and a soft fall onto a mound of ancient hay and dry manure. He had visualized the stinking wells of barns he had known in wetter climates, so he was agreeably surprised. But he wasted no time in self-congratulation. He ran out from under the barn and around to the door and discovered Alice Jo still fumbling with the dismembered Don.

His mother was leaning against the car, glowering with disapproval. What he thought at first was the white angry patch on her nose was really the silver paint the Kid had used in disguising the Don, but he could tell she was angry just the same.

"It's about time," Alice Jo said. She pulled out of the Don's leg a stocking containing an errant foot. "Let's go." She picked up his mother protectively.

"No, you don't," Williams said. He made a lunge to retrieve his mother. Alice Jo dodged. And he was left with half a leg in his hand. Cursing, he threw it to the ground. Alice Jo ran around the car to safety but managed to knock off the rest of the leg on the back bumper as she went. The other leg went on sympathy strike and fell off.

"See what you've done," Alice Jo said. He grabbed her arm, which did not come off. "You're hurting me," she said in that tone which makes a man automatically loosen his grip. She spun away. But he recovered in time to catch her by the hair.

"Goddamn it, that hurts," she said. But this time it was the wrong tone.

"It's supposed to," he said. They struggled. Pieces of mummy flew about until Alice Jo was left holding only the head. She tucked it under her arm and faded toward the barn door. Then she turned and hurled it at him. Amazed, he caught it and stopped. Alice Jo was gone.

Piously, he began to gather up the fragments. Now they would fit easily into an old grain sack he found. There was no further need for the Don, but when he thought of just leaving the Don dismembered on the barn floor, he found he was fully as attached to the Don as he was to his mother. Having collected his mother as best he could, he now began to reassemble the Don. Reverently, he placed his now compact mother in the Don's bosom and lashed the Don to the top of the car.

The women had left him his pocketful of change in spite of objecting to the fact that it hung down his leg like a spare scrotum. Among the change was an extra key to his car. He crashed the big doors of the barn. The dog began to bark. "Quiet, Red," he shouted. The dog was quiet. Lights began to flash on in the house. Women screamed insults and imprecations. Perhaps his struggle and escape had taken six thousand seconds. Perhaps not.

He drove very fast down to the gate. He was going to crash that too but thought better of it. The gate might not have been horse high or pig tight but it was certainly bull strong. As he got nearer he saw that it might even have been tank strong. He heard no sounds from the direction of the house and concluded he had plenty of time. And a good thing too. When he got out to open the gate, he found that all the crashing and jolting had knocked the Don loose from his moorings. He was hanging on by his eyelashes. His belly door was flapping in the wind.

Williams composed the Don in his rightful place, listening carefully all the while and hearing nothing but the distant barking of the dog, let out, no doubt, to run him down and eat him up. He knew, though, that she was more likely to eat up a rabbit, particularly if it wasn't too fierce. Even so, he seemed to be moving at a nightmare pace. He trudged the gate open and started back to the car as if he were walking in knee-deep molasses.

When the car moved toward him, he thought, Good car. It was like the milkman's well-trained horse. But when it gathered speed and came on in a blare of light and horn, he dove for the roadside. Even his flight through the air was in slow motion, and he had time to map out his fall and to see Alice Jo at the wheel. "Goddamn you, Alice Jo," he shouted and landed in a decidedly hostile bush.

He did not, however, scratch out both his eyes or even one, and he got up and began to follow Alice Jo's receding tail lights. After a certain time, they didn't seem to get any farther away, and he hoped she had stopped to wait for him. But he followed on until morning and and never caught up with her.

He passed through Jiggs just as the crescent moon was rising over the mountains, the biggest moon he had ever seen, deep orange and dragging the day up with it. Jiggs was much more noticeable at a foot pace, and he was glad to pass it before anyone was awake. He wasn't sure what he could manage to say to the woman who told him he wouldn't like hippolyta. He was very sure he didn't want to sit in on a game of blackjack with the little girl who practiced on ghosts.

For a long time traffic was against him, that is, two cars of fishermen going up into the mountains and a power company work crew off to some improbable site. In the growing light, cows lifted their heads and eyed him judiciously. He looked at them and grew thirsty. The smell of fresh hay was everywhere, and he couldn't choose between lying down in it and eating it.

The first truck that came along gave him a ride. The driver was an Indian. He looked suspiciously like a Mexican, but Williams felt safe. In a confused way, he believed he had been reborn. He was free of his mother. He was free of the Don. He was free of his car. He had done his best and he had failed. No one could possibly want anything of him. He had nothing anyone would want. He was going nowhere anyone would follow him. He was out of it all. As soon as he stopped walking, he fell asleep.

XII

WHEN HE woke up the next day—perhaps it was the next day and perhaps it wasn't—he seemed to be in a motel. The room was light, so it was some day at least. Shouts and shrieks and mammoth splashes let him feel safe in deducing a swimming pool. The bed was firm, the linen better than necessary, and the air conditioner barely audible. The picture over the bed was familiar. He had seen it before and not just in the Chicago Art Institute. He knew he should be able to remember what motel chain had bought *Grande Jatte*s by the gross, but the effort was too great and he fell asleep again.

The next time he woke up, someone was pounding on the door and shouting, "Housekeeping."

"Go away," he said.

"Do you want the room made up?" A key rattled, and the door opened as far as the chain would let it.

"I want to sleep," he said.

"Are you going to stay another day?" The face at the door was an eye, a nose, and part of a mouth. Another Mexican, it appeared.

"No moleste," he shouted. He woke himself up.

"No dirty talk to the maids," a man's voice said. The door slammed.

Jesus, he'd give them dirty talk. But when he soberly reviewed the transaction, he got hung up on "another day." He wasn't sure he'd be able to pay for a single day, let alone another or some others. He was going to have to tell his lawyer to send money pronto, and he lay awake trying to imagine how he could send the message without its being traced back to him by his enemies or, worse, his friends.

He checked the phone book on the desk and found that he was in Elko. A matchbook told him that this was El Rancho Grande Motel, corroborated by a white plastic pen in the form of a quill. Put that in your code and send it, he said to himself, but of course he didn't have a code, and if he did, the lawyer wouldn't know it. Then he remembered that the lawyer was addicted to crossword puzzles. A large deer, he said to himself, E-L-K. He left the O dangling and went on to *Nevada*. A Russian river, he said, four letters. A-R-A-L. L-E-N-A. Even he couldn't remember N-E-V-A. It looked hopeless. Paternal parent, two letters. "D-A," he shouted, pleased with himself, but the echo came back P-A. Good God, the money was going to go to Pennsylvania.

He sank back on his bed and contemplated the mirror. Behind his back the good Parisians were taking their Sunday stroll. None of them would ever wake up lost and broke and far from home. From the tops of their silk hats to the farthest reaches of their bustles, they proclaimed fiscal and geographical responsibility. Only then did he remember he was free. If his friends and his enemies were looking for anyone, they were now looking for Alice Jo. Good old Alice Jo. Served her right.

He got dressed and went out to call his lawyer. Innate caution still made him bypass the motel switchboard. "Where in hell are you?" the lawyer said, pinning Williams against the door of the phone booth and freezing his hand to his ear. He would brook no fudging on cross-examination.

"I'm in Elko, Nevada," Williams said meekly. "Send a thousand dollars to Western Union."

"O.K.," the lawyer said. "And get your ass back here. There's enough funny business without your staying lost, you hear?"

"I hear," Williams said. "One thousand dollars. Elko, Nevada." But the connection was a bad one, and the money went to Elkhart, Indiana. Williams took himself out to breakfast, satisfied that all was right with the world, and if it wasn't, help was on the way.

"Huevos rancheros," he said to the waitress, "con jamon. Pan tostada. Jugo de naranja."

The waitress coiled. "I want you to know," she said, "that I'm a Mormon, and I don't stand for any dirty talk."

Williams reviewed in his own mind what he had said and changed his order to "Number Two." He was afraid as he said it that she might take further offense, but she simply looked him in the eye and shouted, without turning her head, "Chuckwagon Special." It was very loud, and if it had been a pink bubble, he could have climbed into it and floated away.

The Chuckwagon Special turned out to be eggs on a tortilla with a piquant sauce, ham, toast, and orange juice. He had forgotten to mention coffee but it came anyway. And kept coming, although none of it tasted as good in English.

"Anything else?" the waitress said as she circulated past his table.

"My check, please," he said, placing his hand over his cup to prevent her from filling it for the seventh time.

"One moment, please," she said and scalded the back of his hand with precisely a cupful of coffee.

The check was $4.35 and when he explored his pockets, he found a five-dollar bill and a few pennies. He left it all and went out into the street prepared to be a new man.

He went directly to the Western Union office to inquire for

his money. "Not yet," the woman said. She was doing a cross-word puzzle in a book of puzzles.

Williams was glad he hadn't tried to get a coded message past her, but he gave her the password. "A table scrap," he said. "Three letters."

"Ort," she said. "A baseball player. Three letters."

"Ott," he said.

He felt he had made a good impression and could see the money zipping along the wires.

"Sometimes it takes hours," she said. "Aloha."

"Oahu," he said.

He decided to walk around town and try to imagine what he would do with the rest of his life besides getting on a bus and riding to Alpha, Illinois. He walked for an hour, although there was really no place to go. As he lifted up his eyes, he could see the hills at the end of the streets, but no help came to him. The trees were green. The snow was white. The great letters—painted or carved—on the dark stone stood out white: EHS 79. But none of this gave him any useful ideas.

Every hour on the hour he returned to Western Union, but when the office closed at seven o'clock, the money still had not arrived. He visualized it hung up on the wires, a very large and very dead green bird. "In the morning for sure," the woman said. "Good sera."

"Good soir," he said.

But when he stood outside the office door in the morning and looked in, she saw him and shook her head. He turned away. He had been abandoned. The lawyer had doubtless invoked some obscure clause in the will to cut him off, and Williams couldn't blame him. The whole odyssey had ended in fiasco. He didn't deserve any thousand dollars. He deserved . . . to be abandoned. Now he had to begin a new life, but not any life he had ever imagined, without money, without goals, without reputation, and without hope. It occurred to him, however, that when people need money they sometimes get jobs, so he went directly to the restaurant where he had had breakfast the day before. It also occurred to him that he was very hungry.

The waitress who had served him stood at the cash register. She didn't even offer to show him to a table. Obviously she could tell he had no money. "Need any help?" he said. "I'd like to wash your dishes in exchange for breakfast."

"We've already got a drunk Indian," she said. She ruffled her feathers and swelled to occupy all the space between him and the kitchen.

Considered as an average, zero for one was not a very good percentage, but considered as an indication of serious intent, it was very encouraging. He told himself he was taking hold, and he was encouraged.

He tried a service station and a grocery store and a K Mart, all places that, he had observed, preferred to hire people with no experience and only limited intelligence. His recent imprisonment had made him feel particularly stupid. He hadn't been able to learn much of anything from the stable rats, nor had they seemed at all anxious to teach.

He comforted himself with the ancient folk wisdom that assures you you will always get a job at the last place you apply, but he also reminded himself that he had better check out of his motel because he couldn't pay for another night. And in this way he came to the last place.

As he stood before the motel, he regretted having to leave it. He hadn't realized how very secure it was. Three sides of a square were solid blocks of rooms, two stories high with a balcony facing inward. The fourth side was plugged in large part by the office. Only a narrow drive remained open. In the very center of the court an Astroturf deck surrounded a swimming pool. That, in turn, was surrounded by a vast parking lot with a ring of cars all pointing outward. It was the wagons drawn up in a circle. It was a fort. It was a prehistoric earthworks crowning a hill far on the lone and rolling downs.

There was a sign in the window of the motel office: Help Wanted, Maintenance Man. He had to admit to himself that he had never maintained much of anything, but he applied just the same. And it was well that he did. The job description spelled *handyman*, not that he was particularly handy either. But he felt he could sweep the parking lot or hose it down as required, that he could skim and vacuum the pool, although the idea of walking around on the bottom of the pool with an electrical appliance didn't much appeal to him. Perhaps they had a rubber suit that would insulate him. If not, he wouldn't have to worry about what he was going to do with the rest of his life. But the interview itself posed no great problem. The manager did all the talking, answered all his own questions to his complete satisfaction, and hired himself to do whatever needed doing.

"You aren't a wino, are you?" he said.

"No, of course not," he said. "Clear eyes. Steady hand to start the day."

"How long will you be keeping the job?" he said. "Winos don't last. They never last. A week at most. I'm always training a new man."

"Out here for a divorce, I suppose?" he said.

"That will hold you for three months," he said.

"Oh, very good," he said. "Let me show you around."

There wasn't much to show. There were all those rooms on the two decks. There was the swimming pool surrounded by soggy Astroturf. There was the parking lot. And there was a strange device for vacuuming the pool. Williams was relieved to see that it was powered by water rather than by electricity and that he wouldn't have to get into the pool at all. There was also the supply room.

They entered the supply room through a door at the back of the office wing. Stairs led down into the smell of dry cement and airless rooms. They passed through aisles of crude wooden racks holding cartons of toilet paper, enormous but light. Rubber shower curtains, small but heavy. Stacks of sheets and towels, both old and new. Boxes of cleaners and disinfectants and ammonia. Light bulbs to outlast a siege. Broken boxes spilling out shoals of the plastic quill pens he had noticed in his room. Boxes of matches too. There was also a squat, throbbing machine with laboratory equipment on a shelf over it.

"The pool filter," the manager said, "and the pool chemicals. I take care of that."

"You don't have to worry about it," he said. He led the way to the back of the supply room to a corner where a miserly bulb shed a gloomy light on enigmatic piles of salvage. Williams could pick out torn and soiled shower curtains, ripped sheets and ragged towels, bits of pipe and lumber, but there was still much that defied recognition, the sorry annals of the motel's construction and decay.

"And this," he said, "is your work bench." It was ramshackle and seemed to have reared itself up from the material at hand. The legs were crazy. The top gaped and heaved. It was a wino's nightmare of work. Williams would have hesitated to trust it with his lunch if he had one.

"And these are your tools." The tools were clearly all stolen from the toy box of a reckless child. The saw had a double bend in it. The handle of the hammer was cracked. The wooden grip of the screwdriver was missing, and the two parts of the pliers were close to having a falling out.

"And this is your big straw hat to wear when you work outside."

It was precisely the hat Williams had been offered at his marriage in the wilderness of Mexico. What goes around has to come down, he thought, and he committed himself to his inescapable fate.

"Very good," the manager said, "very good. "You'll want to know if a room goes with the job?"

"Well, it doesn't. Not usually. But there's a little apartment at the back of the second deck I can let you have. It usually goes with the assistant manager's job, but since my wife is the assistant manager right now, I can let you have it."

"And if you want to know if we can work out a deal for the apartment?"

"We can. When can you start?"

"Tomorrow?"

"That's fine."

Williams cleared his throat.

"Aha," the manager said. "I've been expecting that. I never hired a man yet who didn't want an advance on his first week's pay, and the answer is no, but I'll tell you what I will do. You paid for two more nights when you came in—without baggage and all—and I'll just refund those nights to get you started."

"Fair enough," he said.

Williams skimmed the top and vacuumed the bottom of the pool every morning and even learned to notice when the tiles at the water line needed to be cleaned of their bathtub ring. Lift that sponge, tote that pail, he sang to himself as he shuffled on his knees around all the edges of the pool.

His main job aside from the pool and the parking lot was changing light bulbs. When he was settled into the routine and was accepted by the maids, he was also able to take little naps in the afternoon under the sink in one of the rooms. A maid would thoughtfully disconnect the drain plug mechanism and then call the office to report a malfunction. He would pick up the work order, go to the room, crawl under the sink, fix the drain in thirty seconds, and go to sleep just where he was. The heavy carpet was soft. The room was quiet. The maids usually remembered to wake him before they went off duty, although there was one embarrassing day when the police came to investigate a guest's report of a body under the sink.

"Working overtime, eh?" the manager said.

"Good man," he said and raised Williams's pay a nickel an

hour. Williams began to dream that in due time and with good behavior he might someday rise to the dignity of the minimum wage.

Since Williams never spoke to the manager and only rarely to the guests, his social possibilities were limited to the maids, who were either Mormon high school girls or married Indians. The Indians were easy to get along with, although they offered no more than hello, how are you, a light bulb. They had a tendency to fall asleep with their heads on a bed if their duties happened to cause them to kneel beside the bed, and if they had no such duties, they could always drop down for a quick prayer. When he discovered them asleep, he would wake them as an act of mercy rather than leave them to be discovered by the manager's wife, who was incapable of mercy and would dock their pay for each moment of supposed oblivion. He sympathized, although he was usually able to find his own oblivion with his eyes open and his hands and feet doing all the things he preferred not to know anything about.

The Mormon girls, however, were another matter. They marked him down as something to use like a target ship, anchored off shore and dumped on by bomber crews on practice runs. Their wiles were not many or sophisticated. In fact, almost their only move was to try to steal his hat and wear it as if he were a member of the high school basketball team.

"Give me my hat," he would say.

"Yah, yah, yah," they would say, and they always returned it at the end of the day so they would be able to steal it again in the morning. But they were always coming on even if they didn't know what they were doing, and at one point he considered inquiring into the age limit for statutory rape in Nevada. He gave that up when he realized he didn't want to be rated inferior to some steam engine of a high school boy. He thought very briefly about one of the older Indian maids but abandoned the idea as racist because he couldn't convince himself that he would think the same lewd thoughts about a white woman. He didn't even get as far as worrying about how he'd compare to her wild Indian lovers. He did worry a little about these thoughts, but only a little.

Basically it was a very quiet and restful sort of life. Work went on evenly with only minor variations like cleaning up a pool of vomit here or a pile of dog shit there. Little things. In the evening he went to softball games. He particularly enjoyed the Indian teams, both women and men, for they seemed to lack something of the true competitive venom. Instead of becoming angry when a teammate made an error, they would laugh and throw water on him. If legging out an extra-base hit was too difficult, they would lie in the base path and wait to be tagged. Even so, they hit strongly and fielded well and played a really crafty game. But above all they enjoyed themselves. He enjoyed them, too, but steered clear of any moral.

The player that he yearned for, however, was on a different team. She was a first baseman, well over six feet tall, and she had the best hands he had ever seen in this world. She could play so close to the bat that it would have been suicide for anyone else. Williams had once tried to understand cricket, and he knew that the spot where she stood is called silly mid-off. At night he would lie awake creating dialogues for the two of them, dialogues far more intelligent, sensitive, and attracting than anything the motel manager ever cobbled up for Williams and himself.

In his efforts to make certain he was treating her just as one ball player to another—he had played in high school, not well—he invented the name Joe DiMaggio for her and ran the dialogue first as Joe and then as Joan, the name he had seen on her nameplate when she cashed his check at the bank.

"Well, Joe," he would say, "what kind of figures do you expect this year?"

"Oh, somewhere around .350, 120, 40."

Since that sounded O.K., he ran it again.

"Well, Joan, what kind of figures do you expect this year?"

"Oh, somewhere around 38-30-38."

It didn't always work.

In his embarrassment he would withdraw to his room and watch the game from his balcony. He used the binoculars he got when he opened a savings account, and when she came to bat and was of necessity looking directly at him, he reversed the binoculars and removed himself to a discreet distance. He wasn't at all sure he liked what was happening to him. He was becoming altogether too ambivalent about skinned knees and grimy thighs, sweat-stained crotches and the endless debate between the bras and the no-bras— Hey, Joe, that's sure some raspberry you got on your ass (the result of a slide into third on a single to right, because she could do it all).

He continued to watch but without much conviction after his first baseman was transferred to the Reno bank to bolster the flagship team. When she was replaced by a very ordinary weightlifter, he put the binoculars away and went in for a thin aesthetic of distance. It was a life but he didn't seem to be getting anywhere. A job was not the magic solution to his problems that jobs were rumored to be. To be sure, he ate, he slept, but he had no control of his lot. He often dreamed he was back in prison, but then there had been a date clearly marked in his mind when he would be released into a whole new life.

Then one night after he had watched a game between the Seagulls and the Kachinas, his favorite team, he had a visitor. The man wore a Kachinas jacket with the letters MGR over his heart. Williams wished he had thought of managing a girls' softball team, but it was now much too late for that.

"I see you're a great fan," the man said. He nodded in the direction of the balcony even before Williams could ask him in.

"Oh, yes," Williams said, to be agreeable. In spite of his tricks with the binoculars it had never occurred to him that someone down on the field could actually see him or could be bothered to look.

"Nice place you've got here," the man said. He kept looking at the balcony without even pretending to run his eye over the nice place.

"It's O.K.," Williams said without quite endangering his immortal soul.

"O.K.?" the man said. "It's terrific."

Williams looked around him. It was not terrific. Nevertheless he said quickly, "It's not for rent."

"Terrific," the man said. He was by now out on the balcony.

Williams knew that when you have someone on your balcony, the only thing to do is offer him a drink, no matter how things are going. "Have a beer?" he said. He sidled onto the balcony, and they both looked down into the ball park. Even with the lights off, the design was clear. The relentless white foul lines funneled into home plate like an exercise in perspective. The rounding sweep of the red infield held off the outfield grass — classic.

"You got Coors?" the man said.

"Sorry," Williams said. "All I've got is Bud." If there had been a beer brewed closer to home than St. Louis, he would have had that.

"Terrific," the man said. He made a face. "What can you see with those binoculars?"

"Not much," Williams said. "They're not too good."

"I'll bring you a spotting scope."

Williams didn't think he wanted a spotting scope. In fact, since distance lent abstraction to the view, he much preferred that the ritual be performed by nymphs and goddesses. "Well," he said, "thanks." Of course, he didn't have to use it.

"Let me tell you the setup," the man said. "You got a beer?"

"Bud," Williams said.

"Terrific," the man said. He winced.

Williams brought out two very cold bottles he had forgotten to drink during the game.

"My name is Mason," the man said and held out his hand. "George Mason. Maybe you've seen my sign around town. Real Estate and Insurance."

Williams hadn't. "Oh, yes," he said. He extricated his hand from Mason's fumbling grip, which was either a lodge greeting or a proposition. He wanted no part of either.

"You're quite a fan, aren't you?" Mason said.

"Oh, yes," Williams said. Déjà vu wasn't quite the word for it. It was more like a rut.

"And you like the Kachinas, my team," Mason said as if the name wasn't writ large all across his back.

"Why do you call them Kachinas?" Williams said, although he probably didn't want to know.

"Because they're magic dolls, that's why," Mason said. "I thought you'd never ask. Besides, it's the name of my firm, Kachina Realty. Pretty neat?"

"Terrific," Williams said.

"I'll bring you the spotting scope," Mason said. Williams nodded. "And I'll bring you a two-way radio." Williams's mouth fell open. "And I'll give you twenty-five dollars a night." That was the only sensible thing he had said so far.

Since there was money going around, Williams said, "Make it fifty."

"Thirty-five," Mason said.

"O.K.," Williams said.

"Terrific," Mason said.

They still didn't seem to be getting anywhere, but now there was money in it.

"This is what it is," Mason said. "You just sit here and watch the game as usual — "

"Thirty-five dollars?" Williams said.

"Thirty-five real ones," Mason said. "You have the scope and you have the radio. You read the catcher's signs, and you radio them down to me."

"That's worth fifty," Williams said.

"A deal is a deal," Mason said sternly, almost shocked.

Williams left it alone. The pay was good and the work was light and every week he'd be seventy dollars closer to getting out of there.

"I'll show you how to read the signs and how to work the radio," Mason said.

"I know how to work the radio," Williams said. "I know the signs — one if by land and two if by sea."

"It'll be O.K., Bills," Mason said.

"Bills?" Williams said. He took a good look at Mason. This was surely no one he had ever seen before: 40–50, 6'1" or 2". Bald with black tonsure. Large nose on the diagonal. No scars, moles, or tattoos. High, tight paunch but thin arms, legs, and face. Fancy boots, turquoise ring and slide — big ones. Never saw him before. Didn't know him. "Bills?" he said.

"Where I come from," Mason said, "Brockton, Mass., home of Marvelous Marvin Hagler, home of Rocky Marciano, used-to-be shoe capital of the world, everybody named Williams is called Bills, everybody named Campbell is called Soup, everybody named Heinz is called Beans. All the Fords are Liz. All the Rogerses are Buck. All the Hazards are Hap. Like that. Get it?"

Williams got it. He knew he hadn't mentioned his own name, but he couldn't imagine anyone inventing all that on the spur of the moment. Of course, Mason would have had to do his homework before he came around with any such project. He would have had to know that the name was Williams and that when he did go to the games, Williams only threw a couple of nickels into the bucket. He might also have known that anybody working as a handyman at El Rancho Grande Motel had to be interested in a fast buck and a bottle of cheap wine.

Two nights a week when the Kachinas played, Williams became a reluctant voyeur. Disguised as his own laundry hung out to dry, he studied the crotches of the opposing catchers, fringed with fingers and dark with sweat. Three, two, one, he counted the fingers. Two, one, three. "Curve," he said to the radio. "Fast ball," he said.

The Kachinas prospered. But Williams himself was not doing well. One, three, two, he read. Two, three, one. He wearied of his bargain. He wearied of the game. He even wearied of the pale thighs and tautly outlined mound of the peppery little catcher for the Seagulls, who sometimes threw in an extra finger for her pitcher when they had had a lovers' quarrel or turned the finger against herself when they had not. But most of all he wearied of himself. He wanted to quit but he went on. He continued to get his thirty-five dollars after every game, and money was piling up for a getaway if he could ever imagine anywhere he wanted to go. "Fast ball, in," he said. "Curve, away," he said. "Change-up."

One night after a game the Kachinas had barely managed to win, he was waiting for his thirty-five dollars. Things had gone badly for him. He had been missing signals all night. Things must have been going badly for the Seagulls' catcher as well, for she was giving more fingers than usual, more even than the night she finally walked out to the mound and decked her own pitcher with a single punch.

When the knock came at his door, he was expecting his thirty-five dollars, but he was also expecting a lot of flack. "They kept changing the signals," he was prepared to say. "Every time I had it right, they changed on me."

"Bad night," Mason said. "It happens."

"You don't have to pay me," Williams said. He hoped this was the way out, but he didn't feel any better.

"No, no, here it is." He counted out the money on the coffee table.

Williams remembered to thank him. He knew his mother would be proud, but even that didn't help.

"You're doing a great job," Mason said.

"Not tonight," Williams said. "Tonight somebody could have got brained."

"No sweat," Mason said. "After the third inning, I told them the system was down and to hit away. It was O.K."

"I guess," Williams said.

"Don't worry," Mason said. "Just don't worry. I tell you what. How'd you like to meet some of the girls?"

"I —" Williams began. He had, of course, seen much more of the Kachinas than any of the other teams, and the days were long since past when he was taken by those brave vibrations in the skimpy uniforms, when he gave himself extra points for detecting a nipple in a sweat-soaked T-shirt. If he had been able to fathom what went on between the Seagulls' pitcher and catcher, he had much more opportunity to sort out the Kachinas. He understood now which high fives and pats on the ass were pro forma and which meant something. He knew why the third baseman threw well to the second baseman and kept drawing the shortstop off the bag. He knew why the first baseman could dig out of the dirt any throw except one coming from third.

"I think it had better remain anonymous," he said.

"Suit yourself," Mason said. "They're great girls."

"I'm sure they are," Williams said. "They're great players." How anonymous, he wondered, can anyone get? Can he really go all the way? Shuck it all off? Disappear?

That night a legend visited him in a dream. He turned from the spotting scope and saw a man standing beside him, a baseball player dressed in an old-fashioned uniform. Williams recognized him at once, even before he saw that the man was wearing black stockings and no shoes, even before he read CHICAGO on the man's shirt.

"I didn't know your hair was red," Williams said.

"It is now," the man said. No hair had ever been that color. It was the color of a comic wig, but it inspired horror.

"I suppose it is," Williams said, knowing and not knowing at the same time.

There seemed to be nothing further to say. Williams could

not grant absolution, although he was empowered to do so. There was something beyond absolution in tampering with the faith of millions. But there was still one ritual line he must speak: "Say it ain't so, Joe."

The man gravely nodded his head. "But it is," he said.

In the bathroom mirror, Williams's own appalled face stared back at him. His hair was flaming red.

In the morning he got up and went to work as if nothing had happened, as if, in fact, his conscience was as good as anybody's. He vacuumed the pool and skimmed off the leaves and trash that had blown in overnight. He swept the lot. He changed light bulbs and fixed drains. He carried heavy boxes of soap to the laundry room for the Basque laundress, who could easily have lifted the soap and him along with it. "We need it any soap," she shouted from the laundry room door and wiped her forehead with her forearm. He washed windows and polished shower rods.

"Have to polish them," the manager said.

"Because it's inspection time, that's why," he said.

"We're on probation right now because our rods were water-spotted," he said.

"Every spare minute," he said.

Williams reassembled a broken bed and found a new lampshade.

But that was only one Williams. The other Williams treated his moral nature like a bad tooth. He picked at it. He prodded it. He bit down on it. He had always wondered how he would turn out. Now he knew but he was not surprised. He had always hoped for better things but only wistfully and against the grain. He was glad his mother wasn't on hand to deliver a few words.

During his lunch hour, supplies had been delivered and left stacked beside the door to the supply room, so when he came back to work, he began to carry boxes down the stairs. He thought his legs would be good for half a dozen trips now and another box every time he went down for the rest of the day. But it wasn't that simple. The stock on the shelves had to be rearranged, almost all of it shifted to accommodate what he was bringing down. Years ago when he worked summers for Ho-Jo, he had grasped a principle: rotate the stock. He wasn't sure that the principle applied to bottles of bleach as well as to bottles of milk, but he pulled down the old stacks and put the new cases on the bottom. After all, there are few principles to hold to.

Another principle — well, not exactly a principle, although he held to it religiously — was to brighten his afternoon by keeping his eye out for the blond beauty who showed up every day, driving cars from California mostly, but also from New York, Florida, for example, North Dakota, Idaho, Maine, mostly white Cadillacs or at least white. Marilyn Monroe league, strictly. She looked great in a bathing suit and lay around the pool with her eyes half shut, checking, constantly checking, to make sure he, the only man in view, was admiring her. He admired her. She looked like the actress who would play the part in the movie.

But late in the afternoon it was a woman of a different color who accosted him. He had just carried yet another box into the basement when a woman said behind him, "What you doing, honky?" He turned quickly. She must have followed him down the stairs just when he was listening to the blood pound at his ears rather than staying alert for footsteps behind him.

He recognized her at once: the delicious black woman who had checked into the motel in the company of a large white Mercedes, a small Mediterranean sort of man, and an enormous cigar. Her hair was cropped short and showed to perfection every bone in her head. Pale gold hoops shone against the café au lait of her neck.

Well, Williams said to himself without sending any particular message to his tongue. He hadn't got as far as lewd thoughts about her, let alone trying to place his thoughts on a scale of racial equality.

"I'm talking to you," she said.

"I'm, ah, putting away the supplies," he said. "The new stuff has to go on the bottom and the old stuff on top."

"I see that," she said. She wasn't supposed to see, and he was left without the recourse of explaining the principle. He was left, in fact, with nothing to say. But fortunately, she sat down on a case of Kleenex.

"Would you mind sitting on the bleach?" he said. "It's stronger."

"You saying I got a fat ass, honky, chauvinist pig?"

"Ah, no," he said. This was more familiar territory, doubtless something he could handle. Not only was she in a position to call him a pig and a honky, but she was a guest as well.

"Don't y'all know me?" she said. She was looking at him through narrowed eyes, like a gunner glaring from the slits in the watchtower at the Museo Leon Trotsky.

"No, ma'am," he said.

She beckoned him closer and suddenly blew a large pink bubble in his face. He sprang back. "Alice Jo," he whispered—a whisper was the best he could do.

"Right, Bills, the same," she said.

"You didn't use to be black," he said. He was floundering, but she knew exactly why she had followed him into the basement.

"Where is He?" she said.

"Who?" Williams said.

"Him," she said. "The one I want." Williams was afraid she might mean her small Mediterranean, who could be coming at him any minute now with a switchblade like a machete hidden in the palm of his hand. He looked around vaguely and in fear. He wasn't communicating.

"Him," she said. "The one you promised me."

"Oh," he said. "Him. Yes, where is He? I want Him back."

He was so in the habit of calling his mother He when Alice Jo was concerned that he forgot even a mental apology.

"I'm here to make a trade," Alice Jo said. "The car and that stupid armor for Him."

"Where is the Don?" Williams said, deflected for a moment.

"You turn Him over," she said, "and I'll turn over your traveling junk yard."

"I don't have Him," Williams said. "He's in the Don."

"No way," Alice Jo said. "I've taken it all apart, and He's not there."

"He's got to be," Williams said.

"But He isn't," Alice Jo said. They looked at each other, weighing the probabilities. Williams knew he didn't have his mother or the Don or the car. As far as he knew, Alice Jo had all three. He couldn't see what she was up to.

"Come on, Alice Jo," he said. "Don't play games."

"For your information," she said, "the name is Alijwan." She highlighted it in pink. "Who's playing games, honky?"

"Look," he said, "I don't have Him. You say you don't have Him. What are you trying to pull anyway?"

"I don't have Him," she said. "Period."

For a moment a sense of his mission swept back over Williams. "If I had Him," he said, "would I be rotting here in Elko, dabbling in vomit, spooning dog shit?"

Alice Jo's — Alijwan's — eyes spun like a slot machine about to come up with a bunch of lemons. "Maybe," she said, "not."

"Reaming Kotex out of shit-filled plumbing? Fishing condoms out of light shades?"

"O.K., O.K.," Alijwan said. "But you don't get your car or your Dawn until I get Him."

"I don't need a car for what I do," Williams said. "I don't need a hat." He trampled it to shreds. "I don't need gloves." He flung them against the wall.

"You don't need pants either," Alijwan said. She laid a hand on his belt buckle.

"I don't need pants," he said and began to unbuckle.

"Not here," Alijwan said. "You got a room?"

Later, as they lay together on his bed, he said, "I should think he would notice your white ass."

"I make him put out the light before that," she said. "So that's O.K. You know how they say, 'At night all cats are black.' "

"Oh," Williams said, "yeah." He had never had a black woman before and was beginning to feel racist for enjoying it so much.

"How come you got to be black?" he said.

"All that work on the bare-tits gang browned me up good," she said, "so he thought I was some kind of funky nigger girl with bleached-out hair."

"I never thought of that," Williams said.

"Now he's trying to teach me culture. He won't let me chew bubble gum. I have to sneak a quick one under the stairs or in the ladies' room. He makes me dye my hair black — natural, he says — and have it kinked."

"Is he O.K. to you?" Williams said. He was surprised to discover that he felt a sort of proprietary interest in Ali — in her.

"Hell, yes," she said. "I've never had it so good. His skin is so white that he gives me whatever I want, except bubble gum. He says he's trying to bring me up to my inner essence. How about that? But if he tries anything, I'll shoot his balls off with one of his own guns."

"He has guns?" Williams said. He wasn't at all surprised to feel his lunch rise to the top of his throat.

"Guns?" she said. "Has he got guns? He's got guns you never even thought of. He's got guns for shooting through steel walls, and he's got guns for shooting around corners. He's even got a special gun for shooting people at the bottom of swimming pools. And he's got silencers for all of them. You want a gun?"

"No, no," Williams said. He felt as if his pants had been stolen and there was nowhere to hide.

"All he does at night is take his guns apart and oil them and put them together. I don't know what he wants me for."

"You better be careful," Williams said.

"If he tries anything funny," she said, "I know what to do." *Pop.*

"I don't know," Williams said, edging away from her as far as he could with her legs locked around him. "I don't know if I like the idea of messing around with any woman who belongs to a man with all those guns."

"I hear you say *belongs*, honky?" Alijwan said.

"Sorry," Williams said. It hadn't occurred to him that Alice Jo might have picked up an idea or two out at hippolyta, and if it had occurred to him, he probably wouldn't, in the stress of the moment, have remembered to clean up his nasty old habits of speech.

"You didn't mind guns back at the ranch," she said, "and they had a machine gun and a bazooka."

"A machine gun?" Williams said. "A bazooka?"

"They bought them from some crazy minister out east. I think they were afraid of Indians."

Williams settled down to merely normal panic and was able to say, "Machine guns and bazookas are pretty phallic, aren't they?"

"They meditated about that a lot," she said. "And they were practicing with bows and arrows, but none of them were any good at it."

"Arrows are pretty phallic, too," Williams said.

"Arrows are all right, but I can't remember why," she said. "Something to do with the Amazon River."

"That figures," Williams said. "What's he do when he isn't oiling his guns?" Perversely, he was probing for something that would hurt him.

"He's crazy," she said. "He just rides around looking for

some guy driving a black Buick with a black suit of armor on top of it. How about that? Good thing your car is red and your armor is white.''

"Silver," he said.

It was ironic that Alice Jo's gunman was so close and didn't know it. It was ironic that they were catching up with him just when he was the wrong one to catch. It was more ironic that the right one was even closer at hand than he was himself. It was all very ironic, but Williams was unable to enjoy the irony.

XIII

ALICE JO and her gunman went away and came back like the tide. They went to Reno, and they went to Las Vegas. Williams wondered what kind of person they thought he was. They went to Wendover, and they went to Sparks. They tried Winnemucca, and they tried Hawthorne. But there was no black car and no black armor to be found.

Each time they went away he was relieved, and each time they came back he was appalled. He should have cut and run for it while they weren't looking. Without the car and without the Don to attract attention, he would have been untraceable even if he had gone only as far as Jiggs.

He was at his most regretful one afternoon when he had a visitor in the supply room. He was standing at his work bench, fiddling with a lamp that kept shorting out. He looked up after one more failure and saw that Alice Jo's gunman had materialized not three feet away. Williams still didn't know the precise nature of this gunman, but he was apparently about to find out. He took no pleasure in the prospect. They were all killers, but the short-run killers would kill him outright as a means of wringing information out of him, whereas the others, the ones he sometimes thought of as protectors, the long-run killers, would kill him only after he had led them to whatever it was they were looking for. And it might be that the long-run killers had finally run out of patience.

The gunman said nothing but let his presence sink in. It was a sinister presence. For one thing, he was standing on a spot that was miraculously clean. This in itself was an effortless display of a talent Williams couldn't help admiring even at that moment. He himself was up to his knees in bits and pieces, broken this and worn-out that, dubious relics saved by a long succession of handymen against the day when they would be just the thing.

The gunman was, moreover, wearing a discouraging seersucker suit. It was as fresh and unwrinkled as when it still hung in the cleaner's plastic bag. He looked and smelled as if he had just stepped from the barber's, but if he had, the scent was not known to any barber this side of the Donner Pass. His shoes were shined. His nails were polished. His cravat — it was certainly not a necktie — was rich and modest and modestly underscored by a plain gold pin that matched his cufflinks. His cigar was so expensive it didn't even smell like a cigar. In short, he was a man difficult to imagine out of the context of an enormous white Mercedes and an astonishing black woman. Williams couldn't guess where on this trim figure the big gun with the long silencer could be hiding.

When the man felt he had been properly appreciated, he said, "You are the custodian, I presume?" His voice had been manufactured along with the rest of him. It was simple and expensive.

"Yes," Williams said. "Handyman, janitor, whatever." He wondered if, at the last moment, he could take comfort in being killed by a gentleman.

"Lars Pederson," the man said and held out his hand. Williams clutched it, for a moment at least immobilizing one hand full of murder. The grip was gentle. The hand was damp and cold and as unyielding as one of the Don's iron gloves.

"Marc Williams," Williams said, unable to think of anything else. He was sure, however, that there was nothing in their records about a Marc Williams, although John Doe and Richard Roe must have been rampant.

"Nice place you have here, Williams," Pederson said. "Private." He was the kind of man who would have said the same thing to Dante on the Grand Tour, and it would have had the same ominous ring.

Williams nodded. He could be as polite as anybody provided he didn't have to say anything.

"I'm with the FBI," Pederson said. "My credentials." He flashed something that looked like what Williams had seen flashed on TV, but actually saying "my credentials" gave the show away. No one had said that since *Gangbusters*.

Williams nodded.

"Don't be alarmed," Pederson said. "We only want some information."

Williams was not reassured. In fact, he was speechless.

"We're trying to run down a man known as John Doe or Richard Roe. We have reason to believe that neither is his right name."

Williams shook his head.

"It occurs to us that in your official capacity, you might have noticed something."

Williams shook his head. If he had had six hands, he would have placed them over his eyes, ears, and mouth.

"This Doe — or Roe — is a very average sort of man, no scars, birthmarks, or tattoos. But there is one thing. He was last seen driving a black Buick Electra with a black suit of armor on top. Have you seen or heard of anything like that?"

Williams shook his head, but his mouth terrified him by saying, "A few weeks ago, I heard some hunters say . . ." He listened avidly to hear what it was the hunters had said. "They said they had followed something like that south of Jiggs — you know where Jiggs is?"

"I can find it," Pederson said.

"But when they turned up into the mountains — Harrison Pass, that is — the other car went on straight. I don't think there's much down that road."

Williams and Pederson both listened for more, but there was no more.

"Thank you," Pederson said after a decent interval. "Here's a little something for the lead." He laid a bill on the work bench. It was a fifty. That would buy a lot of bus ticket, and Williams could be long gone before Pederson got back from Jiggs, where he would have been directed to hippolyta, where . . . Perhaps it wasn't such a great idea to send him off in that direction.

"The road gets pretty rough out there," Williams said. "I wouldn't want to take that beautiful car out there."

"Good thinking," Pederson said. "I'll rent a car."

"Maybe a four-wheel drive," Williams said, "something with a fierce name."

"Oh, very good thinking," Pederson said. "Thank you for everything."

They shook hands again. Williams wondered how he could manage to immobilize both of Pederson's hands when he came back — but no, he wouldn't be here. He'd be somewhere else with a tattoo and a birthmark and dyed hair. His scars wouldn't show, but he'd fool them all. But, again, no. He couldn't lose track of Alice Jo, not as long as there was a chance of making a deal for Him. Williams found it convenient to think of his mother as Him when it came to buying and selling her or losing her or even reducing her to rubble. He hoped she would never appear to ask for a strict accounting.

"Geezus," Alice Jo said. "You sent him out there? He'll be bullshit." She had come to find Williams as soon as Pederson left in his rented Bushwhacker. She found him still in the supply room, fiddling with the lamp, giving himself small shocks in the way of penance.

"I didn't mean to," he said. "It just came out. All I could do was stand there and listen to my mouth."

"It may be O.K.," Alice Jo said. She shrugged Alijwan's delicious shoulders. "You want to take a ride in the Mercedes?"

"I'm working," he said. The last thing in the world he needed was to be seen tooling about in Pederson's car with Pederson's woman — correction, with Alijwan. "Where is He?" he said. "At least tell me He's safe."

"If you don't know, no one does," Alice Jo said. She had been looking forward to taking the car and having fun, ruffling Pederson's feathers — in complete safety, of course. Pederson was as thorough a gentleman as he looked. He believed firmly (but not ardently) in women and blacks and wouldn't encroach in any way unless it became necessary to shoot them, and even then he would wear gloves.

Williams pretended to give up on the lamp. "To work, to work," he said.

"You know, Bills," Alice Jo said, "you aren't much fun since you got a job."

"How about I quit the job," Williams said, "and you come across with what you've got, and we'll go have fun?"

Williams went out to sweep the lot, but he was already so far behind schedule that it wasn't surprising that he was barely half through the job when he was overtaken by incoming guests, in particular a Greyhound bus and a large truck that parked right across the windrow of sand he was driving across the lot. Both bus and truck flaunted banners announcing the Happy Aardvark Convention, Elko, 1986.

He threw his broom down. He threw his hat down. He kicked the shovel he used to pick up sand. The bus door opened and a man hurtled out. He ran a few steps as if the bus had been moving at high speed, fell on his face, and began

to vomit. Williams had the presence of mind—but barely—
to stir the man's head with the toe of his boot and prevent
choking. That was as far as his altruism went.

The ramp of the truck slammed down like a drawbridge.
Horns blared. The portcullis rose. And an army issued forth.
Well, eight or nine tiny cars driven by old men wearing caps
with long visors warped into the shape of aardvark snouts.
They raced in line around the parking lot in a figure eight
with Williams inside one loop and the prostrate man inside
the other. Their timing was flawless. They crossed in their
pattern with the precision of bullets fired through a propeller,
although they were red-faced and glassy-eyed, and more than
one brandished a bottle.

Last out of the truck was a large old-fashioned bathtub. It
was powered by a small motor bolted to a platform where the
pipes should have been. Williams wondered if the motor should
be dusted and was relieved to observe the absence of a shower
rod. The driver was a fat old man wearing a blond wig like a
new mop, a black bra stuffed to enormous proportions, a little
boy's Halloween makeup, and two diaphragms for earrings.

The other drivers broke off their figure eights and formed
a rolling circle around the tub as it chugged toward the office.
The sound of the cars was the high whine of cicadas, but the
sound of the tub was a lobster boat leaving the harbor before
light on a foggy morning. Williams wanted to roll over and
go back to sleep. Trying to figure out the old men's dance was
just too hard, especially in the absence of masks and canes
and a helpful legend of Cortez.

Men now began to come slowly out of the bus like survi-
vors, blinking in the sunlight and resigned to disaster. "Fall
in," someone shouted. They sidled, backed, and spun into a
line against the side of the bus, propped against it like toy
soldiers with sore bases.

Even when he saw the manager skirmishing across the lot
from somewhere in back, Williams was unable to mount a

suitable action. The manager had apparently wanted his wife to handle the registration and had lurked, perhaps, under the stairs, Williams's own secret observation post. Williams felt betrayed.

"I can never imagine . . ." the manager said. "Hose."

He was speechless.

He went on toward the office, cautiously feeling for the safe path, the surprise route.

"Have you got a mop and pail?" the bus driver said, placing the blame squarely on Williams.

Williams turned and started for the supply room. He flapped his hand without conveying anything to himself, whatever the driver might have made of it.

He came up the stairs from the supply room and stepped out into the lot with a pail in one hand and a mop in the other. He had a bottle of disinfectant in the pail just as if he were going to do the job himself. So much, he thought, for the theory that men are animals and that among animals altruism exists only where domination is complete. He hoped that this unnatural generosity would be taken into account and that he'd get a break when he needed it.

He needed it at once, for the moment he stepped into the lot, he saw Pederson bearing down on him. "I've been looking for you," Pederson said.

There wasn't even room to swing the mop. Williams shortened his grip and prepared for a thrust. He advanced the pail to raise as a shield. It might count for something that the lot was maggoty with people even if most of them were drunk.

"I just want to thank you," Pederson said. He held out his hand.

Williams retracted the pail, set it down. Pederson's hand was as hot and dry and firm as the mop handle.

"There's something out there," Pederson said. "I felt it the minute I got to the gate of hippolyta — that's where they sent me from Jiggs. Ever hear of it?"

"I've heard of it," Williams said. The ice wasn't thin. He was skating on water.

"If they've got what I think," Pederson said, "you'll hear from me again." He put his hand to his heart or perhaps to his wallet — perhaps to some pretty little gun — and he went off up the stairs as fresh and unwrinkled, as expensive smelling as in the morning.

"Glad to be of help," Williams said to Pederson's ex-space. He hadn't a clue, but he was reasonably sure he was still alive.

He took in a lot of money that day and into the night simply by standing around looking picturesque with a big straw hat and a bucket and mop. Ever since Alice Jo's karma got out of whack on the Kid's ship, he had mistrusted the moon and gave day and night equal time with the hat. He made five dollars for knowing the way to the nearest drug store. He made another five out of knowing how to find ice in the ice machine.

Just after sundown, Alice Jo ducked in under the stairs. "He's up in the room," she said, "getting ready. He's got black makeup all over his face and hands. He's got a black watch cap over his hair. Everything is black. Even the knife strapped to his shin is black. He's just waiting for it to be dark so he can go out there again."

"What does he think is out there?" Williams said in spite of himself. He knew that sooner or later Pederson would start blaming him.

"What happened," Alice Jo said, "was that he got to hippolyta in the middle of Boadicea Day."

"Boadicea?" Williams said. "As in British tribe, five letters, I-C-E-N-I?"

"All I know is she stomped the Romans," Alice Jo said.

"I think they got her in the end," Williams said diffidently.

"The usual lies of male-oriented history," Alice Jo said in a voice he had heard before. He knew better than to object.

She said, "I heard them planning it while we were all digging the ditch. What he ran into was a bunch of naked women painted blue and shooting arrows at him. Their aim was terrible, as bad as when they opened up with the machine gun. But the bazooka took out his vehicle and he had to catch a ride back to town on a cattle truck." She blew one last bubble and said, "I better get back. I was just on my way to the ice machine."

"That will be five dollars," Williams said.

There was money to be made, so he made it. For an introduction to a taxi driver, any taxi driver, who knew where the action was—wink, nudge—he made a series of fives that stretched from the arrival of the bus to the moment he couldn't keep his eyes open any longer. There were other opportunities he declined, having heard, as the invaders apparently had not, of AIDS. His getaway fund was in great shape.

He was still drifting toward sleep when there was a light rap on his door and an urgent whisper, "Bills, Bills. Open up."

There was only one woman who called him Bills.

"Hurry, Bills."

Tired as he was, he was glad of a visit from Alice Jo. He was glad he had resisted the blandishments of drag queens and leather boys, sadists, masochists, moon walkers, and tarts. He was glad virtue was once again to prove its own reward.

"For God's sake hurry, Bills." There was a gratifyingly frantic ring to it.

He opened the door and grabbed her. She fought him off like the noblest virgin of them all.

"There's no time for that," she said. But at the same time she landed a self-defeating kiss high on his cheek.

"What is there time for?" he said. She eluded his riposte.

"Time to get dressed and get the hell out of here," she said. "Oh, hurry, hurry. They're almost here."

"They?" Williams said. Half asleep, half blonked with lust, he still didn't like the sound of them.

"Killer," she said. She shook him. "Move. Hurry."

He stared.

"Oh, hurry," she said. "Killer—my gunman—Pederson—
got a message: *Disregard color.*" She was emptying his dresser
drawers, throwing his toothbrush and razor on the bed. "Suitcase," she said. "For God's sake, suitcase." He dragged it from
the top of the closet. "The dumb shit thought it was in code.
He spent a week with his code book. I was able to hold him
off that long. Then he got suspicious of me. I woke up and
found him trying to wash off my tan with paint remover. He
won't try that again."

"I should say not," Williams said. He put his straw hat in
the suitcase. Alice Jo threw it on the floor.

"Get dressed," she said. "We've got to move."

"We?" he said.

"I'm with you now," she said.

"Hey," someone shouted. "Open up." Alice Jo laid her finger across her lips. Blows on the door. Kicks. "Where's the
nearest drug store?" A five-dollar bill slid partway under the
door. More blows. More kicks. The bill was withdrawn. "Fuck
you." Footsteps diminished.

"That wasn't Killer," Williams said. But it was bad enough.

"We don't know who it was," Alice Jo said. "He's sent for
reinforcements. They're coming tonight. They may be here
now. When he got back today, he called for help. They'll blow
hippolyta up if they have to, and that's only the beginning.
So give me my Him and let's get going."

"Your Him—" he said. He was trying to get the right grip
on it.

"You gave Him to me on the ship," she said.

"I said I'd see," he said. "I've seen."

"Oh, for God's sake," she said. "Mine, yours, we've got to
get out of here. We've got to hurry. We need disguises. Wait."
She opened the door cautiously, stepped out, and retrieved a
very large parcel she had left beside the door. She came in
and threw it on the bed. It clanked and rattled and moaned
most piteously.

"The Don," Williams said. "You've got the Don."

"I've got the car too. It was in a garage not a hundred yards from here. Now it's just around the corner. I took the armor apart and hid it in the trunk. They weren't looking for that."

"I wish I'd thought of that," Williams said. "Come on," he said. "Where is He?"

"I don't have Him," Alice Jo said.

"I could wear the armor," he said.

"I could wear the armor," she said. "They'd open the visor and see you and blam blam blam—there're three of them now."

In the pit of his stomach, and in other places, he felt the force of her argument. "That's O.K. for you," he said, "but what about me?"

"When I'm a knight," she said, "you can be my horse or my hound or my lady fair."

"How about your dwarf?" he said, trying to look small. "How about that? How about your squire?"

"You're too big for a dwarf," she said, "and you're too obvious for a squire. You aren't spotted enough for a hound, and you don't have the right tail for a horse."

"Hawk," he said. "How about hawk?"

"Turn your head," she said. "Your beak isn't quite right." She was already laying out her makeup kit. "Off with those clothes," she said.

"Oh, shit," he said. He undressed.

Alice Jo stripped off her head scarf and her long African gown. "Put it on," she said.

"Don't—" he said.

"Sit on the edge of the bed," she said. "We'll only do what will show—eyes, fingernails, toenails." She knelt in front of him and set to work.

When she was finished, he stood up and took a few practice steps. He fell in love with his little scarlet toes that peeped from under his dress. "It's all I can do to keep from copping a feel," he said.

"Now for the yashmak," she said. She took off her underpants and cut out the crotch with her nail scissors. She held
up her creation and admired it. "Yashmak," she said. "Veil."
He shied when she tried to slip it over his head, but she
persisted and adjusted it just beneath his eyes. "Now don't
look in the mirror," she said, "or it will be rape."

He looked. The beautiful eyes of a pagan princess flirted
with him over the lacy trim of the veil. "Jesus," he said.

"Help me with this armor," she said.

Together they buckled on the greaves and the cuisses, the
breastplate and the back plate, the brassards and the gauntlets.
They fitted the gorget and the sollerets. They put on the helmet and anchored it fast.

"What we have to do," she said in the voice of the ghost
in *Hamlet*, "is watch how we talk. If anyone speaks to me,
you answer in your man's voice — "

"It's the only one I've got," he said.

"And if anyone speaks to you, I'll answer for you. Got it?"

Williams truly believed he had it and they set out.

Alice Jo clomped and squeaked along the walkway. "I'm so
excited about the masquerade," she said for the benefit of all
sleepers and murderers. "You're so handsome in your armor."

"If it were not for my armor," he said through his veil, "the
virtue of my dark-eyed Mahometan captive would not be safe
for a moment."

"I have a dagger in my bosom," he/she/Don Q said.

Williams groped hastily under his dress and found no dagger
and scarcely any bosom to speak of.

At the head of the stairs, Alice Jo said, "Give me your arm.
I feel unsteady on stairs." Indeed, she was teetering and
scritching and seemed likely to fall all aclatter down the length
of the stairs.

"Your servant, madam," he said and daintily took Alice
Jo's — the Don's — arm in his steeliest grip.

She went very slowly — clank, squeak, and scritch. "You

drive," she said aloud and added in his ear, "they won't be expecting the armor to be driving the car."

"I—O.K.," he said. He was having trouble remembering that *I* was *you* and *you* was *I* and holding his clanking companion upright and still keeping his skirt elegantly out from under his feet.

They had reached the bottom of the stairs and were about to congratulate each other on reaching level ground and on superb costume management, saying, You (meaning I) were marvelous, when the motorized bathtub dashed out of ambush and blocked their way.

"How about a little spin, cutie?" the driver said. He was dressed as before, his bra more stuffed if possible and his diaphragm earrings punched full of holes.

"No, thank you," Alice Jo said. Williams slapped the driver's hand away from his ass.

"Leave that woman alone," Williams said. Alice Jo made a threatening gesture with her mailed fist.

"You stay out of this," the driver said, "or I'll take a can opener to you."

"I'll pull your plug," Williams said. Alice Jo clanged one step forward. Williams slapped the driver's hand away from the hem of his garment.

"Spirit," the driver said. "That's what I like to see. You come with me, little lady, and we'll be just fine."

He put his machine in gear and threw an illegal block on Williams with the rim of the tub and toppled him in. "We're off," he said. And they were.

Williams's legs were waving in the air. His toenails ravished him. They must have ravished the driver as well, for he drove with one hand in circles around Alice Jo and with the other hand ran quickly up Williams's leg. Williams fought off the hand and fought down his dress. Deprived now of Alice Jo's voice, he fell back on a gibberish of fingers.

"One of the quiet ones, eh?" the driver said. "So much the

better. There's nothing to worry about," he said. "I'm not really a woman." He took a grapefruit out of his bikini and hurled it at Alice Jo—at least his intention was obvious, although she could scarcely have felt threatened by the object itself. Alice Jo revolved slowly and clanked out of the parking lot. Now Williams was truly abandoned.

The driver's idea of a little spin was to dart among the cars in the lot and try to cop a feel at the tightest corners. Williams was jackknifed into the tub with his feet in the air and wasn't able to get any leverage to right himself even if he hadn't been fully occupied in defending his honor.

"Whoopee," the driver said as he achieved a bit of thigh with his hand and a bit of paint with the edge of the tub.

Whoopee? Williams thought, and he thought this guy must have been in on the rape of the Sabine women. He hoped for some reprieve when he saw a car enter the parking lot, but instead of running for cover, the bathtub charged it head on and darted between two parked cars only at the last moment. Williams saw that it was his own car. The Don was driving, advancing implacably on the tub, following it, finally cornering it.

Just when Williams expected deliverance, the tub darted up the laundry room ramp and scuttled along the first floor walkway. The Don nudged the railing and blinked his lights in a rage.

The tub stopped. The driver jumped out and unlocked a door. He was wearing the obligatory grass skirt. Williams, with more room now, was getting himself organized. When he got one hand on the edge of the tub, the driver clamped his wrist in a device like half a pair of handcuffs and twisted it tight and then a little tighter. "Come along quietly now," he said. Williams would have cried if he hadn't been afraid for his mascara. Being a woman was turning out to be very hard work.

With his back to the locked door and his belly blocking

access to the bathroom, the villain slipped the key into his bra, mixing his metaphors but making his point. "Now isn't this cozy?" he said.

Williams warily kept the bed between them — cowered, that is — and struggled with rage and frustration — i.e., terror. His fingers blinked a message, all red lights.

"Well, in that case," the man said, "we'd better have a drink. I forgot all about that little old dagger." He lurched toward the desk and poured two heavy slugs of Jack Daniel's. He slid one along the shelf at the head of the bed and stepped back respectfully. "And then," he said, "we'll lie down and have a little talk, and you'll tell me everything you know about John Doe and Richard Roe and what they've got and where they're taking it."

Williams forgot his womanly fears for a moment and trembled in his own right.

"Here's how," the man said and waited for Williams to reach for the glass and secrete it under his veil. Williams poured the whiskey down his chin with a convincing gesture. He felt it run cold over his chest and belly, across his loins, and down his thigh. He moved by stages along the side of the bed to spread it around.

"That's how I like to see a woman drink," the man said.

I'll bet, Williams thought, whatever his fingers said.

"Another?" the man said.

Williams made the O.K. sign.

"My name's Lowry," the man said. "Fred Lowry from Carson City. Who are you?"

Williams typed *Alice Jo West* in the air.

"Pleased to meet you, Dulso," Lowry said. "That's a nice name. Dulso. I never had a Dulso before in all my life. God, it's hot in here." He whipped off his bra, and a grapefruit and the key hurtled about the room. He had something like an acre of white hair on his chest, and out of it rose two old man's breasts like drumlins in a field of grass on a hoarfrost morning. Alice Jo had more reason to pad her bra than he did. He poured two more drinks.

"Aren't you hot, Dulso?" he said. "Don't you want to take off your clothes?"

Dulso shook her head modestly. Fortunately, the soggy carpet around her feet was keeping her cool.

"Hope you don't mind if I do," Lowry said and stepped out of his grass skirt. The sight was not edifying but neither was it horrible. His little nubbin didn't rise as far out of its ground cover as his breasts did out of theirs. His scrotum hung slack and empty. His balls, at a guess, were the size of marbles.

Dulso watched herself in the mirror register shame—her nails fencing her eyes—and lust—her eyes evading her nails. She was pretty hot stuff.

"So let's lie down," Lowry said. "We can do a lot for each other." He reached across the bed. Dulso put her glass in his hand. "What a woman," he said.

They drank again.

"You'll be the fourth tonight," Lowry said. "A Tiffany and two Debbis." No wonder he had so little to show for it.

He lay down and started to snore.

Dulso picked up the key and, as an afterthought, the grapefruit. She didn't know how she and the Don were fixed for provisions.

The Don had the car at the door. He was blinking his lights and revving his engine.

"Jesus Christ," Alice Jo said. "You could at least have broken down the door and got me out of there."

"It's not so easy in this iron clothing," Williams said. "Besides, my shoes are full of whiskey."

"Go east," Alice Jo said.

"Right," Williams said.

The Don ran through the gear box and got the hell out of there.

They stopped at a motel in Winnemucca—the Don was

confused and drove west—and changed clothes all around. Alice Jo put on a minidress and boots. Williams put on the suit he had worn to his mother's funeral and started a fad for seventies clothing all up and down Route 40. And the Don, freshly painted white, lay down on the top of the car to rest.

Alice Jo went out to have her hair bleached and came back with it flame red and standing up four inches all around her crown. She demanded that Williams go forth and do likewise. But he compromised by staying in and shaving his head.

In the morning she was gone. "Take care of my property," her note said. "I'll pick it up later." He was glad he wasn't wearing makeup anymore. Makeup might make stoics of us all, but the price was just too high.

XIV

ONCE THE DON had started them off in the wrong direction, Williams found it hard to get turned around, especially since his own tendency was to go north. He had long since forgotten why he was going north. He only knew that he felt comfortable when he had Rosinante pointed in the general direction of Banff and the Great Slave Lake, Yukon and Klondike, and the Alcan Highway of his heart. Even-numbered roads made him nervous. He automatically turned onto the odd numbers. Interstates, U.S. routes, state routes, farm roads 101 and 103 eased his distress. So it wasn't strange that when he left Winnemucca, they went north on U.S. 95. In fact, 95 felt so good that he followed it all the way to Coeur d'Alene, which, unfortunately, turned out to be the wrong heartland, and despairing, he turned onto Interstate 90 until he couldn't stand the strain and veered off onto 287, south. This brought him to Yellowstone, and he rested. He marveled at how long it had taken him to go so short a way east.

As soon as he stopped moving, he felt that he was floating

free in a car spinning on glare ice and that sooner or later there would have to be a crash. He no longer had a mission. He no longer even had a job to disguise the fact that he had nowhere to go. He had enough money for now, to be sure. There was Pederson's fifty and all the fives from the Aardvarks. When his first baseman left the bank, he closed his account and kept the money on him in a money belt. What was the use of a savings account when there was no one to smile and say thank you, to touch the deposit he had just touched, to send him her touch on the savings book?

His life was out of control and headed for ruin. But he took heart—a very small heart—from the memory of a time when he had spun twice at 60 mph and continued on in the same direction. The guard rail beside him flicked twice before his eyes. The astonished face of the driver behind him peered twice through the murky arc of his wiper blade. The great white wall of the semi was before him and behind him and beside him on both sides, and then everything was as if nothing had happened. The picture recomposed itself into its proper pattern: *Cars in a Storm, Rain, Night, and Speed*.

In the morning he looked down from the top of the tallest of the hot-spring terraces. He looked on his car—on the Don—and regretted he hadn't been able to bring the Don up to see this marvel of nature. In Mexico he would have done it, but in the United States, unfortunately, carrying a suit of armor uphill on your back is not one of the recognized forms of self-flagellation.

He admired the clear water flowing over the yellow stone and was pleased by the thought that even the clearest water still deposits its sediment. He was more pleased, however, by the realization that, not being a poet, he didn't have to do anything with the idea.

More sobering was the warning given to one and all that the spring was dangerous. A dog had recently jumped in. Its owner had jumped in after it. Both had died. He wondered if he himself would have jumped in to save the Don. His mother? Alice Jo? He stopped. He wasn't required to think such thoughts. He wasn't required to think at all. From his earliest memory had had been required only to do what was right. Perhaps it was fortunate that he now had nothing to do, for he no longer had any idea what was right.

He sat the rest of the day contemplating Old Faithful, shifting only as the wind shifted and blew hot spray over him. He felt there was something to be learned from that loyal pulse, but in the end he decided that whatever it was he had already learned it, that the geyser, in fact, could learn from him.

Just before nightfall he followed a well-worn path along a river. He thought of plunging in but changed his mind when he tested the temperature. Bathing in a mountain stream was not a form of self-flagellation that he himself recognized. The path crossed small meadows close-grazed, he deduced from droppings, by deer, and scrambled over rugged outcrops. It became muddy where a rock face forced it almost into the river and finally, after one last scramble, slid him down to the edge of a hidden pool connected to the river only by a narrow channel in a low ridge of rock. Streamers of mist hung over the pool, although the rest of the river was clear. Investigation turned up a brook of very hot water flowing down from a spring nearby. His bath was ready and steaming. Cautious testing found exactly the comfortable spot, so he undressed and eased himself into the water. By now it was full dark.

He settled into a niche in the bank and prepared to become all white and wrinkled, a particularly ascetic saint, Saint Marc Fluvites, with a particularly well-contemplated navel. He also contemplated the brilliant stars in the moonless, and smogless, sky. As the night wore on he addressed more than one apostrophe to Alice Jo, whom he located somewhat to the left of the Pole Star.

Well after midnight he began to be aware that being a saint

was decidedly tedious. He had had some intimations of the
trials and endless labors in Mexico, but then he had been
enduring it all with a goal in view. Here in the warm bath in
the middle of nowhere, endurance was an end in itself. He
prepared to abandon his life in the river. But while he lingered
for yet another peek at his belly button, he heard shouts and
laughter on the path. He began hastily to assemble himself
around the omphalos, snatching an arm here, a leg there, an
entire head, which he might or might not have put on backward. He searched for his genitals, which were so easily mis-
laid, and was still searching when the advance guard of the
raiders broke over the crest and slid down to the pool. Williams rubbed night-fighter mud on his face, sank in the water
up to his chin, and faded into the shadow of the bank.

Golden lads and girls, they flung off their clothes. Their
bodies glimmered in the starlight. They entered the water and
splashed across the pool to some imprinted assembly point.
More and more followed. Some carried Styrofoam coolers on
their heads like bearers in an antique frieze. They anchored
cases of beer out in the cold current of the river. From their
shibboleths and imprecations, Williams made out that they
were waiters and waitresses from the hotel and were, therefore, probably college students come to the spring to purge
themselves of all indignities.

Williams lurked in the shadows, immobilized and sorely
tried. He remembered vividly the Mexican priest's account of
his struggle for sainthood in the face of the temptations of
the flesh. "Saint Anthony, preserve us," he said. A Styrofoam
cooler of beer floated past on a gentle circulation. He took a
can. Shouts and laughter drowned the hiss of the can as it
opened. A long, smooth body glided over his outstretched legs.
It was even more erotic than minnows nibbling his toes.

The surface of the pool was littered with heads in pairs
floating nose to nose. Swimmers surfaced and dove, surfaced
and dove. More bodies slipped across his legs, surfacing and

diving, the amours of seals and swans. The beer passed him again. He began to hoard against the worse to come, night and silence. He was glad he wasn't a salmon susceptible to impregnation of a million eggs in the milt-filled spawning pool.

A Styrofoam chalice approached, reeking the mystic veil of prophecy—or, rather, a smoldering joint. He held the ashtray while he toked and let it pass only after he had toked again. He closed his eyes and all his orifices and sank beneath the surface.

When he came up again, still another cooler was coming on, but it was coming from a very great distance, sharply etched in the starlight. As it came closer he could make out a tiny figure seated on the cooler—actually the flat lid of a cooler. It was a long time approaching, growing ever larger. He began to have misgivings. Something deep inside him rumbled, about where his soul should have been. At last, enormous, it stopped in front of him, blotting out the pool, the sky, and all his foolish fears. This was a real fear. This was his mother in the lotus position with all her attributes about her, huipil, headdress, cigarettes, playing cards, knitting needles. The diamond patch on her nose was like leprosy.

He tried to slip beneath the water and dissolve. "Sit up straight," she said before he was even over his chin. Her mind was obviously on something else. "I don't have much time." He sat up and folded his hands. She didn't move, so she couldn't be said to have composed herself, but when she spoke again, her voice was fully engaged—in overdrive even. "Meet me in three nights at the gates of hippolyta," she said.

"No way," he said.

"Beware the gates," she said as if she had been taking lessons in spirit communication from a real pro, Madama Sosostris, perhaps, or Julius Caesar, maybe Princess Spotted Tail.

"Never fear," he said. "I won't go near them." In three days he could be in Alaska.

"The gate is now electrified," she said.

"Well, then—" he said.

"Take the jumper cable from the trunk," she said, "and clip it to two places on the wire beside the gate. Cut the wire between the clips, and cross the fence." She had obviously been getting some good advice. This time it sounded like Mr. Goodwrench or Thomas Edison. Still in her most prophetic voice, as if from deep in the bosom of the Don, she said, "I hope this works."

"Are you sure I want to do this?" he said.

"Once through the fence," she said, "turn and approach the gate from the rear. Then—" The crowing of a cock blew her out of the water. This was no giddy Mexican cock but a forthright American who knew what was what. The sky had just begun to lighten, the stars to pale.

He was alone at the side of the pool. There wasn't a beer can in sight, no crushed and abandoned coolers. The air was pine freshened. He wondered what those kids mixed with their pot and how they had managed to get home.

After a breakfast served by a dazed waitress in the coffee shop, he checked his compass and headed north. It was his plan to go to Alaska and cross on the ice to the peace and security of Siberia. All day he failed to notice that the sun rose perversely in the west and set defiantly in the east. It wasn't until he saw the Mormon Tabernacle that he realized his mistake. He bought a new compass and started again. When he found himself entering Nevada rather than Wyoming, he stopped and wept. "We never had a chance," he said to the Don.

Resigned now, he made a big loop in order to avoid the impertinences of Elko and Jiggs and to approach hippolyta from the south. All day he kept crossing and recrossing the route of the Donner Party—"ill-fated" was their epithet on the roadside markers. He wondered if he, too, might become a dotted line on a map. It would only be fitting. He lurked at

McGill and skulked at Ruth. He surveyed the approaches from Little Antelope Summit and from Pancake. And just after midnight on the third day, he stopped his car well back from the gates and went on cautiously on foot.

There was no sign of his mother, but two burned-out four-wheel vehicles had been pushed into the ditch just before the gate. He touched the rusted bodies and smelled the odor of disaster and old burning. He stepped back up to the road and saw a figure silhouetted against the gate. "I've come," he said as in Childe Roland's finest hour. He didn't think he was doing badly. There was no response, neither word nor gesture.

"I've got the jumper cable," he said. He held it up. "Wire cutters," he said, "with rubber handles." He had bought the cutters at Wendover, where he had tried to foretell the future by winning thirteen dollars from the first slot machine in Nevada.

He was close enough now to see that he had been talking to a two-dimensional man, black turtleneck and black pants with black watch cap, and all of it nailed to the gate like a pelt. Through the chest of the jersey a commando knife had been driven into the wood. There was still no sign of his mother.

Now he was set to follow every instruction down to the end. He attached the cable, cut the wire, crossed the fence, and strode forward to the very brink of the dash. "Now what?" he said.

He heard the dog bark up at the house. Women shouted. There were repeated pistol shots and someone shouting "gee" and "haw," so perhaps it was a bullwhip and not a pistol. A short burst of machine-gun fire, the real thing. They must have mounted the machine gun on the ox cart and gone mobile. It was time to get the hell out of there.

But when he tried to move, he was held by a firm hand on his shirt. "O.K.," he said. "I give up." He knew a second stretch at hippolyta would be much worse than the first with no Alice Jo to see him through. Clearly his mother had abandoned him in the face of this latest failure.

But when no alarm was given, Williams turned to see what sort of person it was who had collared him. It was no person at all but a scrap of wire that had been twisted to close the mouth of a burlap bag full of stones. The bag had apparently been added to the counterweight to make the gate easier to open and close.

He felt sufficiently ridiculous. No wonder his mother had abandoned him. The pistol shots and the "gees" and the "haws" were closer now. He reminded himself that even oxen eventually arrive. He wrenched at the wire, but instead of his getting loose from the bag, the bag came loose from the gate. He clutched the bag to him and ran as well as he could to the car.

He threw the bag on the seat beside him. A wiser person would have turned the car around to begin with. He was glad no one from his Mexican prison was there to observe his lapse. He backed and filled and finally turned. The machine gun opened up. They must have been practicing. He heard the Don moaning and taking punishment. "Excuse me, excuse me, excuse me," he said as he drove out of range.

Again he avoided Jiggs and avoided Elko. He cut over through Harrison Pass and went up by Ruby Valley and Wells. By good luck he crossed Interstate 80 just before daybreak when there were no witnesses. He was avoiding Wendover and Salt Lake City and anybody who was trying to catch up with him along that route. It was well into the morning when he stopped at Jackpot, just before the Idaho line. He and the bag had not yet been separated.

He found the wire cutters in his hip pocket and liberated himself. He felt, quite reasonably, that a great weight had passed from him. He dropped the bag by the roadside but looked up in time to see a police car bearing down on him. He picked up the bag and put it back in the car.

He kept going north with the bag on the seat beside him.

He got nearly to Missoula before he stopped again in a deserted area and tossed the bag into a ditch. Some large round stones rolled out together with some thin gray fragments like a hornet's nest or wet cardboard. He stooped to examine them, carefully removed the remaining stones, and contemplated what was left of his mother. Life among the stones had not been kind to her. Riding up and down on the counterweight had mashed her and ground her to the essential woman — a rag, a bone, and a hank of hair — but she was unmistakable. A weight heavier than any sack of stones settled on him and bowed his neck. He drove on into Missoula and headed east on Interstate 90. At least he had somewhere to go.

Once he was on 90, he began to notice the motorcycles in their twos and threes. Their tens. Fifties. All day he met them passing on the other side of the highway, an interesting phenomenon over there across the median strip. In their hundreds. Coveys, exaltations of motorcycles. " 'And hard they rode and black they looked.' Thank you," he said to his mother. He meant for reading him the old poem when he was little and giving him something to think with.

"You don't talk like a Mexican," the service station attendant said. He had acutely noted the Mexican brand on Rosinante.

"I was down there seven years," Williams said. "More. Seven years and more." He was trying to keep out of his voice all the things he wouldn't want to sound in a Wyoming service station. He was grateful to everyone who had refrained from putting a bumper sticker on his car. He even thanked hippolyta for not plastering him with SISTERHOOD IS POWERFUL. Alice Jo for BLACK IS BEAUTIFUL. Mexican customs and others for modestly resisting HAPPINESS IS BEING MEXICAN. He could imagine Pederson backing GUN CONTROL and anyone along the way sticking him with BEAT COWBOYS. He thanked individually. He forgave in general. Whatever they did to him, they could have done worse.

"What's with the motorcycles?" he said, trying above all not to pretend to come from some little place down the road.

"Rally in the Black Hills," Chuck said—at least he was wearing Chuck's jacket. "Big rally."

"Must be a thousand of them," Williams said.

"Thirty thousand, TV says," Chuck said. "They robbed me blind going in and now they rob me blind coming out. I'd close up until they're gone, but they'd steal the pumps."

"Jesus Christ," Williams said in his most agreeable way.

"Listen, mister," Chuck said, "around here we're Christian folks and we don't stand for that kind of talk. Just pay for your gas and get the fuck out of here." He jerked the nozzle out of the tank, sending a sheet of gasoline down the side of the car and over Williams's shoes. The pump read $8.32, not even half a tank. Williams wondered where he would find the next gas station. He gave Chuck a ten-dollar bill and didn't stay for change.

The motorcycles continued strong on into South Dakota until, strangely, he found himself quite alone in the heart of the Badlands, in the country of the moon, in a stage set for Death. It was all height and depth, monstrous shapes and desolation. He felt more alone than ever in darkest Mexico, so that the car with its hood up seemed at first a mirage, an optical joke at his expense. But he slowed as he approached it, although he was still ready to laugh at himself.

It was real enough, however—real as things are on the moon, in a dream of Death. But he stopped in spite of knowing he would probably regret it. The stage was set and he had his cue. Perhaps he had fallen asleep and driven off into some bottomless pit where he would never be found, and this was the beginning of his punishment. Hell is other people, Sartre claimed. And here was the other. He would be the Awful Roommate for Eternity. A vulture soaring in the gulf below Williams rose to the rim of the road and looked him in the eye and then sailed to the highest crag and sat, as if already smelling him.

This man, this stranded motorist, did not appear to be that Awful Roommate. He stood in front of his car surmising the engine, rapt like some lean Cortez in a business suit. "Trouble?" Williams said.

The stranger looked at him then and swallowed and swallowed again, retort after crushing retort, until he was left with the worst of all—silence. Williams knew he had said something foolish. "I guess so," he said. He wished it was a simple matter of offering the man a kid or an iguana or of repairing his engine so that it played nothing but punk rock. He stood beside the man and stared at Mystery. But it was company, by God. You couldn't knock it.

"Fuel," Williams said, "and fuel line. Radiator and hoses. Spark plugs and distributor. Alternator and generator—or are they the same thing? Vapor lock and battery." He ran through everything that had been tried on him in the old days in Mexico. He felt very wise and helpful.

He moved slowly around the front of the car, peering as if trying to get the right angle to see a fish in a shadowed pool. "Aha," he said. He had at last recognized something, even if it was only the handle of the dipstick.

"Aha?" the man said. He stood beside Williams and looked in. Williams pointed. The man leaned farther. Williams smiled and saw the familiar harness of a shoulder holster as the man's coat swung open.

Of course, it was a trap. The man leaned farther, reached. The frustrations of the entire odyssey swarmed upon Williams and he lashed out at the latest of his pursuers, whom he imprisoned by slamming the hood across his back and holding it. The man was at a complete disadvantage. He had no leverage anywhere. Now what? Williams said to himself. It was all very well to strike a blow for once, but he couldn't go on holding the hood down forever—or could he? Maybe he himself was the Awful Roommate. Not even Sartre had thought of that one.

But invention often saves a desperate man when his need

is great. He whipped off his belt. There must be something to tie. There were the man's feet, kicking and stamping, but Williams couldn't see what good that would do him. There was the hood ornament and there was the bumper guard, but the belt was too short for that. Perhaps he could tear up his shirt. He took the man's belt. The man kicked and bellowed. His pants fell down.

"Just be thankful I'm not the Buggering Bandit," Williams said. He joined the belts, made a loop around the hood ornament and the bumper, and buckled it tight. The man was thrashing and waving his legs like some half-swallowed Jonah.

Just then the two-way radio in the man's car came on. "Sergeant Peters," the radio said. "Sergeant Peters, come in. Have you got it fixed yet, Sergeant Peters?" Suddenly Williams felt he might have made a mistake. He tiptoed to his own car and rolled down the long grade before he started the engine. Possibly Sergeant Peters would think he was the victim of no mortal forces.

During the next day, Williams realized that the motorcycles were no longer picturesquely on the other side of the median strip but were flowing around him on both sides, tailgating, darting in front, and then slowing down. It was like being caught in a flock of sheep on the Yorkshire moors but not so jolly. Still, he kept expecting the shepherds and the dogs to round them all up and take them away.

But they were not taken away, nor did they go away. They traveled with him, holding him in the middle of their dense pack, and when they signaled a turn and swept him into a rest area, he saw that it was he who was being herded — a hundred dogs and one sheep. The angry red fireflies of their machines blinked out. The machines faded to silence. He could hear only the *tick tick* of his own turn signal. He flicked it off.

A thousand small birds sprang up from the grass near the rest area — prairie horned larks, long spurs, wheatears, and pipits, the birds of his childhood — and settled down again no farther off. He got out of the car carefully, no sudden moves, his hands ready to leap over his head, his body ready to spread against his car. One rider came toward him. The others hunkered beside their machines. Perhaps it was to be single combat, although that offered little comfort.

This man was not large. But he was compact. He was neither young nor old. He had no tattoos and wore no chains and no overplus of zippers. His leather was subdued and carefully tailored. He looked like a model calculated to set off an outrageous dress in *Cosmo*.

"What have we here?" he said as he approached. He was clearly looking at the Don.

Once again invention did not fail Williams, but it was the wrong invention. "Oh, that," he said. "It's a reliquary."

"A reliquary?" the man said. "Come now, Mr. Williams, this isn't Mexico. Reliquary won't do at all. Try again."

Williams made goldfish noises, although he was actually a bug, pinned and wriggling on a wall.

"Chair," the man said without unpinning Williams for a moment.

A large woman flung herself prone at his heels. He dusted the seat of her pants and plumped up her buttocks and sat down. "Chair for Mr. Williams." Another woman flung herself at Williams's heels. She was not quite so luxurious as the first but still very tempting.

"I'd rather stand, thank you," Williams said. He wasn't sure he could bend, or perhaps in spite of himself he had picked up an idea at hippolyta.

"Suit yourself," the man said. "Melville recommends it. I got the idea from him."

"Melville?" the goldfish was able to articulate.

"Herman, man. *Moby Dick*. Queequeg is his authority."

"Oh, Melville," Williams said, although Ishmael was familiar to him mostly as the seven-letter answer to 23 across:

Hagar's son. He had slept through the whole thing in college, except when the lecturer, himself a victim of narcolepsy, had tried to explain the dirty joke involved in unscrewing the doubloon that was the navel of the ship. The explanation hadn't seemed worth staying awake for. The joke was neither very dirty nor very funny. But later when he was reviewing everything in prison, he came to wonder if perhaps he had missed the point.

"Oh, yes," the man said. "We read. Just because you see us here, you mustn't think we are always like this. Far from it. At other times we are doctors, lawyers, TV executives, brokers—desperate men, that is, who need some way to support their chosen life style. You follow me?"

Williams's head traced an askew orbit somewhere between a nod and a shake.

"I thought you would," the man said. "Now, shall we try again? What have we here?"

"It's a suit of armor," Williams said. He was inspired to try the oldest of dodges, the truth.

"Yes, yes," the man said. "A suit of armor. Very good. Bought in Guanajuato in the shop of Juan Martinez. Anything else?"

"You seem to know a great deal," Williams said. Paralysis was masquerading as nonchalance.

"We don't infiltrate the CIA only for laughs," the man said. He laughed. "I mean, what have you got in the armor?"

"A sack," Williams said. He was just about at the end of the truth with nowhere to go.

"And in the sack?"

"Some skin, a few bones." He was ashamed that he hadn't been more careful. "What's left of a mummy."

"Oh, come now, Mr. Williams," the man said. He laughed again. "Surely you aren't trying to tell us you are the famous mummy thief of Guanajuato. Give us a little credit."

"I guess not," Williams said.

"Armor," the man said into Williams's navel. Four men

sprang to release the Don and lay him at their leader's feet. "Yes," he said. He squirmed a little. "Someone's been sitting on this chair," he said. "Replacement." He half stood. The woman rolled out from under him. She looked abashed. Tears ran down her face. Another woman slid into her place. The man sat down, squirmed, and grunted. "What's in the sack, I wonder?" he said. The new woman smiled.

Williams shrugged.

"We shall soon see," the man said. "Dr. Morgan, will you open the chest cavity?"

One of the men opened the door in the Don's chest. Williams wished they would find a bottle of good whiskey, but the report indicated a sack.

"A sack," the leader said. "Good for you, Williams. Dr. Morgan, the sackotomy—or is it sackectomy?" Morgan pulled out the sack and handed it over. "Ah, yes. Ah, yes."

"Just what I said," Williams said.

"Do you take us for fools, Williams? Do you still pretend this is really skin and bones? Clever. But not clever enough. Mortar and pestle," he said.

The woman who was the first chair looked hopeful. She produced a small mortar and pestle from her saddle bags. Tears still glistened on her cheeks.

The man dropped a bit of gray skin into the mortar. "Grind," he said. She ground. "Pipe," he said. She had the pipe in her jacket. "Fill," he said. She filled the pipe. He took it. "Light." He smoked. Closed his eyes. All around him his congregation was silent, motionless.

He opened his eyes and shook his head. "No," he said, "that's not it. Mr. Williams," he said, "would you care to elucidate?"

"I can't tell you what I don't know," Williams said.

"That's only your opinion of the moment," the man said. His smile would have changed any opinion Williams might have had, but as far as he knew he didn't have one. He began to wonder, however, if someone hadn't played another ghastly trick on him, a trick even worse than the car full of cocaine. Fool, his mother said, and he was once more back on firm ground.

"Grind," the man said. He dropped another shred of skin into the mortar and reached inside his jacket for a small gold spoon on a gold chain. He spooned the powder onto the cover of a paperback book, which Williams identified as *Zen and the Art of Motorcycle Maintenance*. The woman prepared the lines and handed over a gold quill. The man sniffed a line, sneezed, and sniffed another. "No," he said. A sigh went up from the host. "Mr. Williams," he said, "you begin to weary me with your constant evasions. Needle," he said. "Brew."

Williams felt he was being a very poor son indeed. Amen to that, his mother said. I'm doing my best, he said. He closed his ears to the reply but knew anyway that it was, A real man would &c &c &c. Unfortunately, during her life she had never bothered to define a real man or to point one out, so that Williams's notions of true virility were confused at best and his aspirations foggy.

"No," the man said when he had injected the brew into his arm. "No, that's not it either. So, Mr. Williams, we come to the moment of moral persuasion. Dr. Morgan, will you preside? And, Williams, it's nobody's fault but your own."

Amen, his mother said again.

Credo, Williams said, making the best peace he could.

Dr. Morgan unwrapped a small roll of surgical instruments. "Flaying?" he murmured to himself. "Or dissection? Flaying or dissection?"

"I always like a little flaying," the leader said.

"But I'm so good at dissection," Morgan said. "It's my specialty. From my first frog to my last cadaver, they always said, 'That Morgan—' "

At that moment, however, a police car passed with its lights flashing and its siren shrieking. "Perhaps," the leader said,

"the place is rather open to unfriendly observation. Mount."
He sprang up. A hundred motorcycles came on in full cry.
The same thousand birds sprang out of the grass and settled
back. A falcon flew among them, screaming terror and havoc
but striking none.

The leader made a sweeping gesture with his arm, and they
all streamed out of the rest area, carrying Williams along as
before. He couldn't decide if he was flotsam or jetsam or
maybe some worse detritus, and his mother refrained from
telling him.

They went on in this way until they came to a truck stop.
It was a twelve-story motel with a twenty-acre parking lot
set down at an exit of no obvious merit, but it was the place
the riders elected to stop for the night.

They stored him on the twelfth floor. "Think about it," the
leader said and left him to think about it. He thought about
dissection and flaying. His mother was his mother, of course,
but if she wasn't his mother, what was she? He thought of
the thumbscrew and the rack. The iron maiden and the Chinese
water torture. He thought of being staked on an anthill and
being torn apart by wild motorcycles. What was she? What
was she? He thought of strangulation and defenestration. He
thought of a butt of malmsey and boiling oil. Apparently she
was not hashish, cocaine, or heroin. She was too light for gold
and too scrambled for military secrets, although she might be
coded. He thought of disembowelment and the peine forte et
dure, extraction of teeth and fingernails, hanging by the thumbs,
the heels, the balls, burning, stabbing, shooting, mauling, and
being tickled to death with feathers.

It will be worse, his mother said complacently. There was
nothing left they could do to her.

He knew it was so. He sat at the window and failed to
think.

Out in the parking lot, huge trucks huddled in their hundreds.
The melancholy roar of refrigerators came up to him. Motor-

cycles patrolled the edges of the lot, wolves waiting their chance. A truck pulled into a space in the row nearest the motel, almost directly below him. The truck lights blinked. A woman came out of the motel, ran to the truck, and climbed into the cab. Interesting. He leaned out the window. Far more interesting than bamboo slivers under the fingernails.

Another truck pulled in. Lights blinked. Another woman climbed into the cab. A convertible with three women in the front seat drove slowly across in front of the first row of trucks: a blonde, a brunette, and a black woman. The car weaved among the trucks. Motorcycles weaved around it. It made the circuit again. And again. Finally, at the farthest edge of the parking lot another car appeared. It didn't drive in. It was simply there, waiting. There was a parley, driver to driver. If the cars had been horses, they could have flicked each other's flies with their tails. Both cars roared out of the lot. This was more interesting even than lighted bamboo slivers under the fingernails.

It was not more interesting, however, than a file of metallic green beetles crossing his window ledge from left to right. They were very determined beetles. They knew where they were going. They ran up his left arm, across his back, and down his right arm and kept going, although there was obviously no place for them to go — or to come from for that matter.

Another truck pulled in and blinked its lights. Curiously, no truck ever seemed to leave, but there was always a space in the front row just about there. This time, however, when the woman ran toward the truck, she was swept up by a motorcycle and carried off. The truck roared, flashed its lights. Other trucks answered. A dozen women, mistaking the signal, ran out of the motel. They were all captured by motorcycles. The uproar rattled all the windows in the motel.

The motorcycles paraded their trophies among the trucks. They circled the trucks, revving and weaving. Gradually, however, the trucks outside the circle formed a wall, nose to tail, a ring with the motorcycles inside. It was the ultimate western, the Indians circling the wagons and the wagons circling the Indians. The trucks tightened the circle like a noose. This was more interesting even than green beetles. It was so interesting, in fact, that he fell asleep.

He dreamed he was back in prison. They were all in the last courtyard of the old convent. Just beyond the wall, cars, motorcycles, trucks, buses roared past. Women's heels ground the pavement. It was the world at full cry. But they were safe, happy and laughing as they did their laundry at the nuns' old well. All around the well, the broad curb was sculpted into shallow depressions shaped and fluted like seashells. Over all was a tile roof supported on simple stone pillars. It was the perfect summer house for pretend tea parties. Birds sang in the bougainvillea. Hummingbirds buzzed past their ears like June bugs.

A man stood before each of the shells and did a hand wash, except that here and there a nun mingled with them. Other men and other nuns lay on the sunny pavement or sat in the shadow of the wall—the season was imprecise, although surely Edenic. Williams knew them all but could find no figure in which he could identify himself. Thieves and murderers—and worse, much worse—they sang at their work, told jokes, and rejoiced in the day. He was not surprised to recognize one of the nuns as the Witch of Coatlicue. He felt, really, that he should have known all along. The beads at her waist clattered with the vigor of her scrubbing.

Beside her, the hotel clerk from El Refugio shook his head and said, "Poor Williams, goddamn." There was a murmur of agreement. Some nodded and said "Alas." Some shook their heads and said "Qué lástima." But none stopped smiling and the singing went on.

It was still in his ears when he woke at the window and looked down into the deserted parking lot. There were no trucks. There were no motorcycles. Only his own car far out in the lot — he was glad he didn't have to sweep this lot. The Don seemed to be in his place. He hoped his mother was in hers. Trust me, she said. I do, he said. I do. There was no alternative.

His door was unlocked. He left the motel. He trudged to his car, expecting that every moment would end in bloodhounds and gunfire. But there was nothing. He looked into the Don's bosom. She was there. The bag was missing, but she was there, all of her as far as he could tell, all that hadn't been smoked or sniffed or brewed. This was more interesting than being smothered by the cushions of the softest of the motorcyclists' chairs. Chastened, he began to drive. There was no direction anymore except toward home. He even obeyed the speed limit.

XV

HE DROVE directly east, avoiding main routes out of habit and taking those roads everyone swears he will take next time when he isn't so rushed. He took state routes and county roads, single-lane cement slabs and well-kept gravel roads. He saw river towns abandoned by the river and country towns betrayed by the interstate, main streets destroyed by shopping malls, and a sleaze strip that went on before him, springing up again as he approached each raveling town. And at last he came into the heartland at the depth of August.

Sometimes he drove down canyons of corn stalks where the sky was straight up and even the air conditioner couldn't change the fact that the temperature stood at 98 degrees and the humidity at 98 percent. The rest of the time it was soybeans, soybeans all the way, except when his road soared over the interstate and he could see for miles across the ocean of green with here and there islands of farm buildings, houses, storage bins, tractor sheds, and their attendant trees, towering like messages over the landscape. Enisled, cut off by their own labors, men on other farms could see the trees and feel some hope. Children walking the beans and sobbing in the endless rows could feel less despair.

He was in the middle of nowhere as surely as he had ever been among the cactus and mesquite and rocks and the forsaken beds of dry rivers. Now only the sheriff's men stopped to speak to him, to ask him hard questions, to search his car, to rattle the Don's visor. They refused to believe that a car with Mexican registration could be free of marijuana. They even brought dogs to sniff out his cache. But the dogs only pissed on his wheels and found the marijuana growing in all the fence rows and ditches. The sheriff's men were never quite able to pin the local crop on him, but they moved him along anyway because he was clearly guilty of something.

No woman ever stepped out of a corn field to offer him a freshly cooked ear, a biscuit, or the smallest slice of the fatted calf. Sometimes he heard a voice among the corn, a woman singing because she was alone and hidden. He toyed with the latch of his hood but never popped it. Disappointment would have been too hard to bear here, for the truth was that wherever he was, he was home.

He circled and he hesitated. If there was one place they should be waiting for him, it was here. Still, he closed in. He came by Farmer City and Foosland and Flatland, by Shawnee and Pawnee and Kankakee, by Paris and Berlin and Madrid, by Danville and Georgetown and Arthur. He circled and he studied the signs, the high blue sky by day, the stars by night, and in the stillest moments the restless sound of the corn growing. He circled and he closed in, and at last he came to Alpha.

He smelled the town before he saw it, the smell of soybeans from the mill, the smell of something not quite right, something, in fact, just on the verge of going bad. But once he had zeroed in on the beans, he knew every house and every tree.

He knew the cold breath of the lawn sprinklers as he passed, and the taste of that water which was the norm by which he judged all the waters of the world. He didn't need the jolt of the railroad tracks to tell him where he was. He didn't need to follow the Business Center → signs to arrive at the four corners where the town's stores spread themselves as wide as they could but still took up less than half a comfortable country block.

He stopped and he looked about him. He was facing his lawyer's office, but that could wait. The building had been remodeled anyway, and the effect was striking, although it looked like the set for a movie no one could bring himself to make. The front had been opened out in glass and closed in in plants. Long, pale shelves of law books formed a backdrop for the deep green of the plants. The only thing lacking was the sense that this was where it all happened rather than in the same old shabby back office where the lawyer put his feet on the desk and swore at his clients. It was clearly all a front: the glass, the plants, the multitudes of the law. The entrance gave the show away, for the door was set at an angle and opened to face a brick wall as if the lawyer had learned something about the construction of strong points and bunkers. Perhaps he, too, had put his finger into the holes in Trotsky's wall or carefully traced a woodchuck's cautious burrow.

Across the street was the bank, also refurbished in glass as if it had nothing to hide and no money to protect. Williams didn't like the change, although he was comforted by a view of the back of old Mr. Wheatley's head still resting on the window ledge like a melon ripening. Next door would be his mother's shop, but where the shop had been was only a raw hole in the ground. Something was taking its course, and he didn't care to know what it was.

"I want to talk to you." The voice was massive and commanding. Williams turned. It figured. Home is where the end

is. "Where in hell have you been?" But it was only his mother's lawyer, striding across the street toward him. In his cow-
boy boots he was at least five foot two. He looked out from
under his Stetson like a very wet and angry elf sheltering
under the proverbial toadstool.

"I've been on my way," Williams said. He had never learned
not to answer rhetorical questions.

"Look at that," the lawyer said. He gestured toward the
hole in the ground. "I had to do it all myself."

Williams pictured him laboring at the hole with a child's
sand pail and shovel. "Sorry," he said.

"It was an offer I couldn't refuse," the lawyer said, "and
where the hell were you?" Williams shrugged. "They wanted
it for a country store in some crazy Disney World village and
took it apart stick by stick like they were moving some god-
damned castle. They even took out six feet of dirt all
around — sides and bottom — for au·then·ti·ci·ty, for Christ's
sake. And where were you when I needed you?"

Williams kept his thoughts to himself. Disney World be
damned. Underworld more like. But when he realized he knew
something the family lawyer didn't know, he wondered if this
was what it was to be grown up.

"Don't go away," the lawyer said. "I have to be in court,
but there's still a lot to be done about your mother." He
hurried off with the biggest little strides east of the Illinois
River. His car was the white Cadillac with the number plate
SUE-WIN.

The reference to his mother brought Williams back to a
sense of his first duty, so he drove around the block to the
old Wilson place. The house had been built in the 1880s by
the town's first banker. During Williams's childhood it had
been a wreck, the paint long past peeling, the fence rusted
and falling down, the lawn already waist-high in weeds and
reverting year by year toward the head-high growth of the
original prairie. Williams and his friends made an art of break-

ing into the house to look for the legendary hidden wealth of the Wilsons and for the secret passage leading to the vault of the bank. Later the house was reclaimed, and it entered the life of the town in the only way open to Victorian monsters. It became a funeral parlor, the Elysian Fields, although it was never called anything but Wilsons'.

He drove between the fieldstone pillars marked Entrance, and he stopped. He might be home but he wasn't home free. He wasn't even marginally closer to success than he had been at any point in his long journey, not even when all borders were closed and all roads were watched, not even when he had lost everything at Elko. They had been here before him. They had taken his mother's store apart splinter by splinter. They had even taken away the ground it stood on. They would be here again. They would be here now.

Cautiously he cast the Don loose from his moorings and plunged him into a vast forsythia bush at the edge of the drive. At least he would have a bargaining point, a hostage, although he was reasonably sure he wouldn't last beyond the first turn of the thumbscrew, the first drop of water on his unprotected head.

He drove on then. There were several cars already parked in the lot, but he parked as close to the door as he could. This time he remembered to back into his slot and leave the motor running. He was pleased to think he had learned something, particularly something from his time at hippolyta.

As he entered the cool, humming quiet of the house, he noticed the smell of death, which anywhere else would have been the smell of flowers, of life. He felt himself muted and hushed. There was no one in sight, although three visitor registers stood open on small tables in the hall. And now he heard faint organ music from another part of the house. To his right he could see into an office that was empty. The desk top was bare as if all the papers had been buried with the latest client, as if an open casket had proved too irresistible an opportunity for the disposal of trash, the weeding of files. He stood at a loss.

A door opened at the back of the office, and a woman came toward him. She wore a sober mortician's suit with a flowered blouse. He enjoyed the flowers. He enjoyed her organ music as she moved. "You're for the Murpheys?" she asked.

He shook his head. He even enjoyed the crumb at the corner of her mouth.

"The Cookes, then?"

He shook his head. She sensed the crumb and curled it in with the tip of her tongue. The secret intimacy of her tongue awed him.

She frowned. "The Abassis." Such a frown, but she could do no wrong.

He shook his head.

"Well, then?" she said.

"It's about my mother," he said.

"I see," she said. And she must have, for she turned and seated herself at the desk. She whipped a form from a drawer. "Name?" she said.

"Mine or hers?" he said humbly. She was even more beautiful when she was stern.

"Hers."

"Lura Williams," he said.

"Ell you are a," she said. It sounded like a velvet curse. "Yours?"

"Marc," he said.

"Em a are kay," she said, and it didn't even sound wrong.

"Date of death?" she said.

"December 22, 1978."

"Oh," she said. "A reburial. It will be closed casket, then."

"She's not in very good shape," he said. He thought of the bones, the scraps of leather, the hanks of hair he had entrusted to the bosom of the Don after hippolyta.

She made a check on the form. "Place of death?"

"Guanajuato, Guanajuato, Mexico," he said.

"What do you mean Guanajuato Guanajuato?" she said. The spelling didn't seem to bother her a bit.

"It's like New York, New York," he said.

"Oh," she said, delightfully at a loss. "When will we receive the remains?"

"Whenever," he said. "I've got her outside."

"Outside?"

"My car," he said. He didn't quite want to commit himself to *in* or *on* or *in the general vicinity.*

"Ashes, then," she said.

"No," he said.

"Well," she said, "I assume you have the necessary papers."

"Of course," he said.

"Mexican death certificate," she said, "release by Mexican funeral director who oversaw the exhumation, permit for international transport of the remains. The usual."

"Of course," he said. He wondered if she would take care of the Don while he flew to Mexico to have the documents properly forged. One of his cellmates used to swear by a photographer who had a shop in Tlaquepaque, near Guadalajara.

"You will want to visit our showroom and see what we have available," she said.

He let that pass and began to follow her up the stairs. He would have followed her up any grain elevator or water tower in the county.

"This," she said in an anteroom on the second floor as she put her hand on a small cement box, "this is a model of the vault. It's cement and very heavy, so we don't keep one on display. You have to have it anyway. That's the law." She opened and closed it as if this were a matter of no importance or interest, like an airline stewardess demonstrating the safety features of her plane.

Williams thought of a girl he knew in college who swore

that she used to have her slumber parties in her father's casket display room. The first sight of the room full of caskets went straight to his groin.

"As you can see," she said, "there are many types."

"And costs," he said to show that he was paying attention to what she said.

"Naturally," she said. "Some are luxurious. Some are plain. Some are simulated wood, and some are tastefully plain steel."

"I see," he said. "The choice is a serious matter," he said, groping for hesitation and delay and prolonged eye contact, the delicious lips moving, the sensual hands demonstrating, scarlet nails against white satin, smoothing the eternal bedding.

"One of the most serious," she said. "So let me first show you something rather special. It's brand new and might just fit your present circumstances." Williams wasn't at all sure what would fit his present circumstances, but he was resolved to spare no expense.

She led him to a casket he would rather not have seen even from a distance. It looked like a swan boat. The sides were mainly two large white wings. Wherever the wings didn't cover the metal, harps and horns and mystic circles were painted in gold.

"It's rather ornate," he said doubtfully. He was remembering the austerity of his mother's life, but he was also remembering the flash and dazzle of the huipil she had been wearing since then, and her headdress of many-colored ribbons.

"That's only the symbolism," she said. "This model has features."

"Oh," he said, "symbolism. Ah," he said, "features."

"This is the Resurrection Model." She paused for his admiration. "It is equipped with two-way radio in case of the Last Judgment or premature burial." She placed an object in his hand. "Note," she said, "the graceful, state-of-the-art design of the handset. Your loved one will be grateful that you have not left her to call God on inferior equipment."

"How true," Williams said, but he knew very well that his mother would need no intermediary, no mere mechanical contrivance, when it came time for her debate with God.

"This model also comes with the do-it-yourself option, a comfort for skeptics and the faint of heart. All you have to do is press a button." She must have pressed a button, for the lid of the casket began to rise slowly on four hydraulic lifts. "Feel the power," she said. "Guaranteed to lift a ton of earth and a thousand pounds of marble."

It was very impressive. Williams was impressed.

"Also air conditioning," she said, "so that there need be no discomfort while waiting out the long years of eternity." She ran her hand along the tips of the wings, and they sang out like wind chimes.

"Amazing," he said. He might have said more or perhaps not, but at that moment he heard a man's heavy footsteps in the downstairs hall. Doors banged and men called out to each other in classical Nahuatl, which he had long since learned to recognize as the language of doom. Some residual power in the witch's potion must have been activated by the very sound of the sacred language, and he knew he was trapped. Footsteps began on the stairs. The stairs groaned. Doom was very heavy.

"Quick," Williams said.

His guide stared at him. "This isn't how it was supposed to be," she said.

Without further comment, Williams backed her up to the Resurrection Model and tipped her in. He dove in after her, slammed the lid, and put his hand over her mouth in any order or all at once. He tried to keep intimacies to a minimum, but fortunately, even the generous Resurrection Model was cramped for two, and intimacies could not be avoided. They even had to arrange their arms around each other.

"I've been expecting something but not exactly this," she said into his mouth. Her breath was like a quick, light tongue. He decided it must be her ear he had covered with his hand.

The casket vibrated as someone walked about the room, fumbled for a moment with their lid, strummed on the wind chimes, and went away.

"Ever since those hoodlums showed up in town and began asking questions about you and your mother, I've been expecting something. Certainly since they tore down your mother's store and carted it away — for a Disney World, of all things."

Williams, of course, had been expecting it far longer, but he was strangely at ease. The old monks must have been right: there really was something about sleeping in a coffin that helped prepare you for death. "This is very snug," he said. In a sense he had achieved his goal. He had brought her to Alpha. He had brought her home. No matter what happened now, he had done that.

"Is it even better than a motel bed in Elko?" she said.

Williams despaired. She had to be one of his long-run murderers. They must think he had now led them to his mother's treasure and needed only a little persuasion. They had been watching him from that first moment in Guanajuato when the Indian tossed him the note that said *Don't go north*. They knew everything. They had probably sent the Kid and his landing barge to take him past the border. The bandit who stole and returned the Don must have been in their pay. Even the witch was no doubt preparing to cut out his secret with her little knife — no, that would have put her on the short-run side. And he had been afraid of Pederson's guns at the motel when all the while he should have been looking out for his peep holes in the apartment walls, ceiling, floor.

Disgust now overcame him. That man had sent Alice Jo to

him and had then watched through some hole. And had told this woman everything. Vile, really vile. He wanted to recoil from her, but he couldn't even take his arms from around her. He plastered his liver and lights to his backbone and made a very small bundle of his guts. His heart was small and backward. And his stomach was up by his head, which he was able to force back an inch or so into the quilted lining of the casket.

"You seem to know a great deal," he said. He was the North Pole itself.

She moved her top arm. Paper rustled like a brush fire. There was an odor he couldn't quite place, a very familiar odor, sweet and fruity, something cheap and dear. She was swelling against him, forcing him back, but there was nowhere to go.

"Look," he said, "really — "

"Look yourself," she said.

"It's too dark to look," he said.

"Flick your Bic," she said.

He managed to locate his lighter after a great deal of fumbling and groping and much misdirection of hands, which under other circumstances he would have enjoyed. By its light he saw that he was having a bad dream. Her head had turned into a balloon. He was having a nightmare. It was the witch all over. It was . . . Alice Jo. The balloon was bubble gum.

"Alice Jo?" he said.

She hugged him.

"You double-crossed me," he said. "You let him watch us in the motel — " But then he remembered he had himself invented all that. "Sorry," he said. He apologized with a hug. "But why haven't we smothered?" he said. "Are we dead?"

"No fear," she said. "Are you forgetting that the Resurrection Model comes with air conditioning?"

"You stole my car," he said, remembering grievances. "You

left me stranded out there with machine guns and bazookas the least of my worries. It could have been a fate worse than death."

"You only thought you had worries," Alice Jo said. "They weren't about to chase you past the gate, no matter what."

"Do you think we could get out of here?" he said.

"Not yet," she said.

"I had to walk to Elko," he said. "How about that for a worry? How about working at El Rancho Grande Motel?"

"It didn't do you any harm," Alice Jo said. "The whole point was to stash you away for a while where you wouldn't be noticed and to get that freaky car out of sight. Things were getting too hot. Pederson was about one step behind you no matter what I did."

"*You* did?" he said. "Who appointed you my keeper?" He was not at all pleased. He might have made a mess of everything, but he *was* here and he *had* done it himself.

"Nobody had to appoint me," she said. "As soon as I saw how many people were after you, I wanted a piece of the action. I didn't know what it was, but I wanted some." The two-way radio made a noise like elevator music.

"Is that God?" Williams said.

"Just as good," Alice Jo said. "It's Sheriff Cummings. He's got them rounded up. That's the signal."

"O.K.," Williams said. "Let's go." He was really angry. Things were bad enough when Alice Jo was trying to claim his mother, but she was going too far when she tried to claim his entire pilgrimage.

Alice Jo reached up to release the lid, but the catch was jammed. The hydraulic lift, guaranteed to lift a ton of earth and a thousand pounds of marble, groaned once and strangled. The phone was dead, and the air conditioner stopped in mid-whir.

"I guess that's it, Alice Jo," Williams said. "I tried—we tried." At the end, he could afford to be generous. "And here we are. Let's just hold on to each other." But Alice Jo shrank away from him. Her fingers scrabbled softly at the satin lining. She must, he thought, already be panicking for air. She writhed in his arms. The side of the casket swung out, and they rolled together to the floor.

"The Resurrection Model," Alice Jo said, still lying in his arms, "can double as a stage prop. Any competent magician can use it in the disappearing lady act."

"Oh," Williams said. He was almost too astonished to admire Alice Jo's legs as she struggled to get up, her lovely slip, her lace-trimmed underpants, true mates of those she had sacrificed to his disguise in Elko. "If I had seen your underpants to begin with," he said, "I'd have known you right away."

Alice Jo ignored him, standing on the Inalienable Female Mystery.

He was not ready to be ignored. "How come you're an undertaker all of a sudden, tell me that?" He was disengaging himself, struggling to his knees.

"Funeral director," Alice Jo said. There were obviously things that could not be ignored. He made a note of it. "I took a crash course," she said.

"I bet," Williams said.

"Really, it was my minor in college."

"Sure," he said, but he had heard enough. "Let's have it straight. Can you really do a burial?"

"By the power vested in me," Alice Jo said, "by the State of Illinois — you need any more? What did you have in mind?"

"You've got it all down on your form," Williams said.

"So you're really going through with it?" Alice Jo said. "And this is the end of Him? You had Him all the time, didn't you?"

"Jesus Christ," Williams said, "you aren't going to start that up again, are you?"

"You think I'm crazy?" Alice Jo said. "That was just something to keep us going, to pass the time."

"You could have fooled me," Williams said. In fact, she did fool him. He had never doubted for a moment that she really wanted the mummy, although he couldn't imagine why except for the usual reasons: it was full of dope and/or microfilm and/or diamonds and/or cash, it was a map disguised as a mummy, it was useful in medical research. The only thing that made any sense was that she didn't really want it at all.

"Well," Alice Jo said, "let's have Him into Reception and see what's to do. How about a child's casket? He'd got pretty small last I saw of Him."

"That's an interesting idea," Williams said.

"It would save you money," she said.

"A very interesting idea," he said. He thought he might like to bury her as a child. No one could take offense. Oh, yes, I can. She rose once more from the ashes of the campfire in Mexico. She wore her headdress of many colors and her huipil, and she could indeed object. The white patch on her nose left no doubt of it.

"I have to go get her," Williams said. "Just down at the end of the drive." He hurried down, released the Don from the thicket, and came back carrying him in his arms like a deposition. He lowered the Don gently to a gurney. This was the end of all that. Endless miles, interminable months, and now it was all over. He felt cheated. There should at least have been a "Well done" if not quite a "This is my beloved son."

There in the solemn room with the hush of the air conditioner, the rubber glove severity, the Don lay in something less than state. He was a sorry sight, his joints askew and wrenched, shot full of holes, piebald with paint chips of many colors. The happy face on his breast had good cause to smile upside down.

"Are we going to bury the whole thing or what?" Alice Jo said.

He hadn't thought of that. It would give his mother a sort of Viking funeral to be buried with her loyal retainer, the good Don. He regretted now that he hadn't thought of burying the car as well in some abandoned quarry or borrow pit, some old strip mine or cellar hole. Or he could have burned the car in a field, launched her flaming on her final voyage. Still, he was fond of the Don, would like to have him around, perhaps not on the roof of the car but at least in some discreet corner of the baronial hall.

"It might fit into a regular casket," she said. "But then again it might not. If we have to order a special number, that will be extra."

"Of course," he said, although he still wasn't at all sure what he would do.

"Well," Alice Jo said, "let's take a look at Him."

Reverently Williams undid the Don's helmet and removed the mask of the little old man. With all pious ceremony he unbuckled the breastplate and lifted it away. He then looked for the last time upon his mother — or he did not. The Don's bosom was empty. He seized the Don by the heels and rudely shook him like a rug over the edge of the gurney. A pinch of dust fell out and was instantly dispersed by the blast of the air conditioner.

"I don't know what to say," he said, which seemed to be all he did know how to say. He could hear himself stupidly repeating it. "I don't know what to say."

"I'm sorry, Bills," Alice Jo said. "I'm really sorry, but I guess that's the end of any funeral."

He nodded. He shook his head. He couldn't manage even the simplest sign.

"Let's put the old boy back together and get out of here," Alice Jo said. "They're still going to be looking for us."

He nodded. He got that one right and felt that he might be

on the way back. And as the Don began once more to take on human form, Williams had an idea. "Look," he said, "let's bury him." He saw at once that there was nothing else he could do that would so certify the humanity of the Don as to give him Christian burial. To make him stand in some corner, no matter how polished and admired, was to reduce him from the stature he had won in his travels.

"You've got to be kidding," Alice Jo said, but he couldn't tell if she was speaking as a friend or as a funeral director.

"It's the Don, Alice Jo," he said. "Don Q. He's been with us all the way. He has endured much. He has suffered loneliness and fatigue. He has been shot full of holes."

"You're crazy," Alice Jo said, this time clearly in the voice of a friend.

"She was there," Williams said. "You know she was there. She was always there, but she must have sieved out. She must be scattered over half the country. But she was there. The Don's insides must be impregnated with her dust. That's all there is to show."

"Ah," Alice Jo said. She seemed to be relenting on all fronts. "In that case—"

"We can say"—he was inspired—"we can say she was an insect and had an exoskeleton."

"That's very poetic," Alice Jo said. She smiled.

"It may even be true," he said. "All her life she was encased in armor."

"And in death," Alice Jo said, "they were not divided." Now she, too, was inspired, although it was the inspiration of a funeral director.

"Amen," Williams said. "But are you sure we can really do this?" Even piety toward his mother and loyalty toward the Don fell short of absolute conviction.

"Of course I'm sure," Alice Jo said. She drew herself up, every inch the funeral director. "And by the power vested in me by the State of Illinois," she said, "I now pronounce the

Don, also known as Don Q, also known as Lura Williams, a strong and perfect knight, worthy of all rites and ceremonies suitable to the funeraries of a soldier and a gentleman. Amen."

"Amen," Williams said. He felt a flush of pleasure, a blush of pain. "And now what? Where do we hide out?"

"That's easy," Alice Jo said. "We become Chinese and open a restaurant."

"荳腐湯?" he said.

"荳腐酸菜湯" she said.